PRIVY PORTRAIT

THE
SEAGULL
LIBRARY OF
FRENCH
LITERATURE

PRIVY PORTRAIT

Jean-Luc Benoziglio

TRANSLATED BY TESS LEWIS

LONDON NEW YORK CALCUTTA

This work is published with the support of
Institut français en Inde – Embassy of France in India

swiss arts council
prohelvetia

The original English edition of this publication was supported with a grant from Pro Helvetia, Swiss Arts Council.

Seagull Books, 2021

First published in French as *Cabinet Portrait* by Jean-Luc Benoziglio

First published in English translation by Seagull Books, 2014

ISBN 978 0 8574 2 842 4

British Library Cataloguing-in-Publication Data
A catalogue record for this book is available from the British Library

Typeset by Seagull Books, Calcutta, India.

Printed and bound by WordsWorth India, New Delhi, India

—But you didn't tell us what you do, said Buster to him.

—I'm a writer, he answered.

—Oh. What sort of thing do you do? Esther asked, dropping the weight of his hand, and looking down as though she expected to see it drop to the floor.

—Write.

—Yes, but . . . ah . . . fiction?

—My book has been translated into nineteen languages.

—I must know it, Esther said. —I must know of it.

—Doubt it, said the modest author. —Never been published.

—But you said . . .

—I've translated it myself. Nineteen languages. Only sixty-six more to go, not counting dialects. It's Celtic now. A lovely language, Celtic. It ought to go in Celtic.

—You mean be published?

—Yes, published in Celtic. Sooner or later I'll hit a language where they'll publish it. Then I can retire to the country. That's all I want, to retire to the country. Erse is next.

—It must be an awfully dirty book, said Buster.

Mr Crotcher gave him a look of firm academic hatred which no amount of love, in any expression, could hope to erase. —It is a novel about ant life, he said.

William Gaddis, *The Recognitions*

The door handle rattles—Jesus, someone's trying to get in. I jump off the seat. 'No point climbing up to the transom, body crabs here can jump three metres high.' I remember reading that once, but don't have time to wonder where.

Since the lock is wobbly and will give way if anyone pushes at all insistently, I stretch out my leg and plant the sole of my foot firmly against the door. Then I yell that it's busy. The handle keeps jiggling. I yell again that it's busy and add, 'There's someone in here!' Which is inane, because if there weren't anyone in here, who would have yelled that it's busy? Besides, if no one were here, the door would have been open, right? I'm not exactly the kind of person who leaves the door open *on purpose* while I'm at it. And while I am at it, why not walk up and down the hallway of some girls' school buck-naked under an overcoat?

In any case, whoever it was seems to have finally caught on. I hear some vague grumbling and steps shuffling down the hallway. Slippers and an old, moth-eaten housecoat. Probably one of the two Sbritzkys. The two of them have the exact same way of walking. If you can call it walking . . . A door slams in the distance. Phew. My leg was getting stiff. I shift the book slightly. The binding leaves a mark like a reddish scar on my bare thigh.

There were two of them. 'Two will be more than enough,' figured the dolt in the three-piece suit who came one morning to draw up an inventory. White collar and fake-leather briefcase.

Tacky. I almost didn't let him in. Almost told him I was already set with encyclopaedias, eyepatches, toothbrushes and insurance policies against this or that, including enucleation. So he declined all his credentials and qualifications ('*credentia et qualificatia, credentibus et qualificatibus, credentiorum et qualificatiorum*', etc.), and by the time I got over my surprise, he had already planted himself a few feet from my bookshelves, whipped out a pen and notepad and was eyeballing my books. 'I'm afraid this is going to be the big nut,' he said, 'at least six boxes.' I stupidly babbled that some of the books were light reading, some of them even, well, you know . . . He looked at me, amiable, businesslike, frowning slightly. 'An *aficionado*, hunh?' he said, 'Did you get that in a bullfight?' I shook my head and he didn't insist. 'What've you got in there?' Didn't wait for an answer and pushed open the door. I said I was sorry I didn't have time to make the bed and . . . The truth is I only make the bed on Sundays and no trained professionals are willing to go out and about on that day. Except, maybe, for priests. But I've never been sick enough for a priest to make a house call to say Mass. In fact, I've never been sick enough to go to Mass—*full stop*. Still, I'm wondering the whole time why anyone would ever apologize for an unmade bed. As if it were somehow dirty or shameful. For God's sake, sometimes people actually do sleep in bed, you know? With a bit of padding you can fool around on the kitchen table just as well. Besides, since when is fooling around dirty or shameful anyway?

As discreetly as possible, I pulled the covers over the condom sprawled in the middle of the sheets. He pretended not to notice anything. I thought it would be a good idea to explain it was a type of fingerstall, you see, I kind of sprained my . . . As distractedly as possible, he looked at me, friendly, businesslike: 'A fingerstall?' Shit—he really *hadn't* noticed anything. Anyway, it's her fault. Why can't she use a diaphragm like everyone else?

'And in the wardrobe?' he asked. I told him there was nothing special in there, just the usual things, suits, shirts, socks, underw . . . He'd already pulled opened both doors of the wardrobe. What the hell—make yourself at home. He turned round, smiling, friendly, businesslike, 'Don't mind me, right? I'm making myself at home, but, anyway, you're practically not at home here yourself any more . . .' Charming. But he was already diving back into the wardrobe, stroking the sleeves of my suit jackets with his pen, pushing my coats to the side. Piles of dirty laundry behind them. 'That's it?' I answered well, yeah, pretty much, that and what I had on me. He didn't look amused. It wasn't funny. 'Good,' he said and wrote something on his notepad, 'good, some odds and ends. Can I see the other rooms?' I told him only the kitchen and bathroom were left and I'd show them to him. But wouldn't he like a drop of red wine first? Startled, he looked at me, frowning, not friendly, not businesslike. 'Red wine? At this hour?' But from his disgusted look, I knew perfectly well he would have said the same thing no matter what time of day it was. Probably thought plonk was only good enough for the moving men. Me too.

So now we're in the kitchen. On the table, there's the bottle of red—plastic top, no label—and *the* glass I'd brought out. He threw them a quick look, walked round the table, opened the cabinets above the sink and became absorbed in contemplation of my moderately clean pots and pans. While his back is turned, I hide the bottle and glass in the pantry. Either you have tact or you don't. He's not exactly choking on it himself and I don't like his mocking tone when he asks what food cooked in pots like these tastes like. I don't answer. He shrugs and gets back to nosing around and writing in his notebook. Stops in front of the refrigerator. Considers it for a while. Shakes his head and goes, 'Tsst-tsst-tsst.' Wants to know if I'm taking it with me. I say yes, of course, naturally: I love ice-cold beer and, even more, spreading butter that's hard as a rock on my bread. This does not make him laugh. It isn't funny. It's even less amusing when he says that speaking of a nice, cold beer, he wouldn't say no to one right now. I don't have a single drop. 'I see, I see,' he says in a tone full of innuendo. 'If I asked you for one,' he adds, 'it's because your fridge seems to date from back before Louis XIV and I just happen to have a brother-in-law who could give you a good deal on . . .' I thank him and tell him I don't have any intention of getting a new one at the moment. 'Very well,' he says curtly, 'that's fine. If you think it's amusing to make my guys drag this huge, antediluvian monster round, you're the customer, right?' I point out that if I bought a new fridge from his brother-in-law, it would still be 'his guys' who'd be getting rid of the old one for me. 'Yeah, and?' he yells, 'You think they're wimps, or what?' Fine. We're about to leave the kitchen when he notices the larder. 'What's that there?' I tell him it's nothing, just the lard . . . But he's already opened the door. Obviously. The wine bottle and glass are right in front of his face. Pfff. Shuts the door rather brusquely. Leaves the kitchen.

There's only the bathroom left. I try to explain to him that there's nothing to see in there, that I have no intention of taking the bathtub with the shitty shower nozzle that sprays all over and that there's nothing in the cabinet except for a few towels that don't even soak up moisture any more and two or three fizzy tablets for hangovers. He interrupts me and gives me a lecture on customers who don't know anything about his business, who don't understand what a *mov-ing com-pa-ny* does, who forget to point out certain objects and then are surprised later when there aren't enough packing boxes or when they have to pay a supplement. You can't draw up an accurate estimate without a meticulous assessment of the site. Do I want an accurate estimate? I do.

After all, there's nothing wrong with hanging things up to dry over the bathtub. Everyone does it. And so what if a dozen socks marinating in soapy water give it a greyish colour and leave in the sink a ring of the kind of foam you see on the banks of our most beautiful rivers when, with the authorities' backing and the ecologists' curses, a factory is built upstream? The only thing missing is a shoal of fish, belly up.

His professional gaze sweeps the room, slides along the dangling underwear and skims over the polluted sink. The tension is extreme. I open my mouth to ask him to excuse the bit of a mess around the place, but he beats me to it and says, 'No need to apologize, I've seen others.' Apologize, me? Who does he think he is? It's still my home and I'm free to behave as I see fit and no one asked him, the pretentious little git. That is, someone did ask him to come here: I did. And I remember now that the only thing the moving company's goddamn receptionist wanted to know was what floor flat I lived on and into what floor flat I intended to move. About the rest of it—why I was leaving, whether it got me down and all that—she didn't give a shit.

It got me down.

'And this wardrobe, what's in here?' He's seriously starting to bug me, this guy. Without thinking I tell him there's a radio transmitter in the wardrobe that I use to send coded messages to London every night. Don't be too hard on me, friends, I lost my cool. Besides, he would have opened it anyway. I know his type, the arsehole. So, arrest me. Goodbye wife, goodbye children. Handcuffs on and move it out. *Ve haff vays of making you talk.*

He's got his hand on the key that opens the wardrobe. He says, 'A radio buff? Strange place to keep a transmitter.' The wardrobe is now wide open. No sign of a radio. He turns back towards me. *You know ze conseqvences of making fun of ze Cherman police*? I stammer that I was just kidding. He doesn't seem to have a sense of humour. It wasn't funny. Suddenly, as if to get back at me, the gentleman starts going through the wardrobe with a fine-tooth comb, from top to bottom. Perched on a stool, passing his hand over the top shelf, he exhumes an old comb missing almost all its teeth. Disgusted, he holds it out towards me, the edges of his cuffs black with dust. I make a huge show of surprise and swear that it's not mine. Liar. And he grumbles that maybe not, but that's no reason to fob it off onto the next renter. Chapter and verse about goddamn egotists and how much cleaner the world would be if people just swept their own doorsteps. Now he's going to give me a sermon on top of it all. I'm boiling mad and tell him he's absolutely right, that I agree with him completely. I'm about to toss the thing in the can when he scolds from up on the stool: Am I *absolutely determined* to leave the toilets clogged for the next renter? What the hell is it to him? I'm starting to wonder if maybe *he's* the next one. Lots of schemes like that in real estate. Lots of little old men and little old ladies are harassed until they give in and leave, so that some bastards—who adore their own little old mums and dads—can divide the flats up into seventeen studios. Yep. Or they pay off the concierge to get the inside scoop on who's thinking of leaving or of croaking. Or they publish fake ads with names like *Got 'nuff* or *Wut Ah Need* to take some poor suckers in. There are days when I wonder if there's anything more disgusting in this world we live in.

Except that, with this guy here, there can't be any scheme because I'm the one who called him, no one else did. Even though I did tell the goddamn receptionist that I lived in a coal mine two hundred and seventy-three metres below ground and that I was considering setting up house at the top of the Eiffel Tower. A five-hundred-and-seventy-three-metre difference in altitude—was this manageable, in her opinion, with a fridge on one's back? She didn't laugh. It wasn't funny. And besides, she didn't believe me for a second. Uh, is this a joke or what: she was quite aware that there are no refrigerators in a mine because coal keeps perfectly well at ambient temperatures. OK, OK.

Right, so when I get back from the kitchen, where I went to throw out the old comb, he's on all fours digging around on the floor of the wardrobe. Dirty snoop. Go ahead and dig, Fido, good boy, keep digging. Without turning round, he throws a sock behind him with his right paw. It lands at my feet. Well, look at that. I send it to join its polluted little cousins in the sink. Thirteen socks. As long as single socks come back into fashion soon . . .

From the wardrobe, I hear metallic sounds and his voice, a bit muffled, saying, 'What's this thing?' And all of a sudden he stands up and thrusts in my face a huge electric radiator whose heating unit looks a little like the acoustic horn of an old gramophone. There's no plug at the end of the cord, just two bare brass wires. How about that—I'd forgotten all about it. 'What is this thing?' he asks again and, before I have a chance to say anything, he adds, 'I'll tell you what it is. This is exactly the kind of thing I was talking about before, the kind of thing our customers don't think of pointing out to us or they tell themselves it isn't worth mentioning—"Just some measly little electric radiator. We don't want to bother these gentlemen with trifles like this. We'll just add it to the rest at the last minute." And the last minute comes, all the boxes are sealed, no room for anything else, not even a pin. It's all done. The guys have had a drink. The customer's looking for change to give them a tip—and by the way, I'd like to remind you that it's against regulations, expressly forbidden, to tip more than twenty-five per cent under any circumstances—it's all done, the guys are heading to the staircase, sagging under the last load, and all of a sudden the customer cries, "My electric radiator!" And the guys ask him what radiator he's talking about; there's no radiator on the inventory. The customer says maybe not, who cares, but they absolutely have to take it. "Take it in what?" the guys ask, "The boxes are full." So the customer says they can just carry it by hand. "Yeah, right," the guys say, "and if there's the tiniest little scratch or if it gets busted, you'll sue our arses, and we're fucked, because you'll win since we didn't follow the safety regulations. No way, José." So the customer begs them and wrings his hands, already freezing at the thought of next winter's cold snaps, fifteen below and all that. In short, it's a freaking circus. The guys have to call the office to order one more box and the lorry bringing it over gets caught in a traffic jam and all this time my guys' equipment is immobilized, doing nothing. The customer pays for it in the end, believe me . . .'

He was getting himself all worked up, ranting like a lunatic in my bathroom. I finally managed to interrupt him. I asked him if he seriously thought I wanted to drag this piece of junk round with me. He turned pale. He swallowed once, twice, three times. He murmured, 'Do you mean to tell me that you do not expect us to move this object?' I answered that of course I didn't, after all, the last time I plugged it in must have been at least in the era of Louis XIV. This didn't make him laugh. It wasn't funny. Even he didn't need to tell me that.

In the meantime, he calmed down. He even managed a strange smile when he said that he hoped I'd have fun trying to get rid of the radiator.

We returned to the main room. The rest was settled quickly. Having detailed his list, he'd lost all desire to discuss more details with me. His professional smile was barely forced. Mine became forced once he quoted the number. I told him I finally understood why people who live in fifty-room mansions—with full kitchen—never move. First they'd have to sell at least forty-nine of the rooms just to pay the moving costs, which wouldn't be that bad—it'd be economical, even—since they could move the one room that was left themselves and wouldn't even have to call a moving company. Did he follow me? His smile became tighter, more forced, stretched to the breaking point. He said, 'Yes, yes, I get it.' He seemed uncomfortable. He stood up and headed towards the door and, taking a last look at my bookshelves, said, 'That will be the big nut, but I think two of my guys can manage it.' We were on the landing. I asked him, by the way, if he hadn't seen the second one? He said, 'The second one? The second what?' Sock. He left so quickly, he almost missed the bottom step. I went back to my flat. In the hallway, I saw the trunk and I realized that, shit, I'd forgotten to tell him about it and the encyclopaedia volumes inside it.

As I was saying, there are two of them: one, built like a brick house, who seems to do all the work, and another, weedy like a stalk of asparagus, who doesn't do shit except for a few pirouettes while packing my porcelain in polyurethane foam.

'Sèvres, hunh?'

And he crushed out his cigarette butt in my little Greek oil lamp.

'Hmm?'

'I'm asking if your stuff there is Sèvres?'

'Maybe, I don't know. And could you please do me a favour and not use the . . .'

'Hey man, your flower pots—you swipe 'em or what?'

He lit a new cigarette and set the match down gently in the oil lamp. A brief flame, sizzling, and it all went out. When you see the kind of light it gives off, you understand why the Odyssey was written by daylight. Or why Homer went blind.

'Swipe? Well, no, I . . . It's just that I don't remember where . . . And I'd prefer, if you don't mind, that you use the ashtray over there by the sink.'

The ashtray is always the last thing you pack and the first thing you set out in a new flat. If you're a smoker, obviously.

Why would anyone who doesn't smoke bother schlepping an ashtray from one flat to the next?

'Yeah,' says Asparagus, 'that's what I always tell our customers. When you've got too much stuff, you end up not knowing what you own. Pretty symbolic of our times, don't you think? On the one hand, you've got people who have no idea of their wealth, and on the other, people who know destitution inside and out. At this lady's place, the other day, we found a full vermeil porcelain set in the back of a cupboard. With just what the teaspoons were worth, there'd be enough to fill the plates of I don't know how many hundreds of starving kids round the world. And Madame didn't even remember that she . . . This thing's not an ashtray?'

I tell him no. I explain what the thing is. He compares the real and the fake ashtrays for a long time. In his opinion, the fake looks much more real than the real one. But that's my business, isn't it, and he's not here to discuss his customer's taste. Still, given how long he's been going in and out of flats and how many he's seen, he could probably set himself up as an interior decorator. You can't even imagine how hideous and kitschy some of the places are, or the filth, Mister, tons of filth, even in places where they're loaded and have fifteen flunkeys running around. As soon as you move the furniture . . .

Wiping his forehead, Brick House appears in the doorway. He tells Asparagus he'd be better off getting to work than being a pain in the customer's arse with his fuckwit lefty theories. Asparagus grumbles something about alienation and starts wrapping up my Egyptian statuette. 'Sixth dynasty, hunh?' I don't answer.

I'd had to get up very early. It was still night-time. Like executions, moves take place at dawn. 'Public opinion is not yet ready to accept the abolition of moving house. But as soon as the current wave of the fidgets that has overcome our social body has subsided, we . . .' Hypocritical arseholes. The red lampshade filled the room with a warm, welcoming light I'd never paid attention to until now. I almost called them to cancel the move. 'It's nicest at home.' Schmaltzy music, eyes brimming with tears, fake fellow feeling—it's all for shit. You'd think you were watching an ad for I don't know what fucking brand of instant coffee. In any case, it was too late, their lorry had probably already left. I wondered if that happened sometimes, at the last minute, when they're standing there, on the doorstep, solid, competent, sleeves rolled up, and the customer cracks, becomes hysterical, dissolves into tears and refuses to let them in? Then it takes a couple of them to hold the customer down, tie him up and lock him in a room somewhere. In any case, by the time I'd swallowed a cup of I don't know which fucking brand of instant coffee, they were here. That is, their lorry was—that's what I heard first. A rumbling out on the street, the sound of brakes, a motor idling. And then, right after, one horn, two horns, three horns. Raving maniacs. It doesn't matter how early you are, there are always some other guys who are already late. Well, they're going to have to get up pretty early to impress my movers with their horn concert. The only thing their racket could do is to wake up half the neighbourhood. I felt vaguely guilty. My nose pressed to the window, I tried to see what was going on in the street below. But the gauze curtains were in my way. So, eureka!, I climbed onto a chair, pulled off the rods and threw it all on the floor, rods, curtains, everything. Moving does have its little advantages. I should have pissed in the sink last night. I've held myself back for years now. I'm not talking about in hotels—that's so common I wonder if some folks end up washing themselves in the bowl of the crapper? Be that as it may, I have a better view now. The lorry's flat roof. It's completely blocking the street. Leaning out of the open car door—there must be a specific level of exasperation at which just rolling down the window is not enough—Brick House exchanges a few words with the driver stopped behind him. 'Well, shit, I'm working.' 'Yeah? What about me? You think I'm out here freezing my balls off at seven in the morning for the fun of it?' You know the sort of thing. This goes on for a while, then the lorry drives up to a zebra crossing twenty metres further on and parks in the middle of it. Behind it, the line of cars, a little longer now, is still waiting. But the problem is that zebra crossings are just wide enough for a normal car to park in—you wonder what our city fathers were thinking—but notorious for being too small for a lorry to fit comfortably. So they leave their contraption at a slant in the middle of the street and, ignoring the honking, now twice as loud, they go after the cars parked on either side of the zebra crossing. Pushing and pulling, they finally widen the space, get back into their lorry and, not without some difficulty, finally manage to park. The line of cars files by, engines roaring, first gear, second gear, and then stops short twenty metres further on, second, first, idling behind a delivery van parked in the middle of the street, doors wide open.

When they rang my doorbell, they seemed nervous. And my eyepatch didn't reassure them. It always has an effect the first time.

'You're not going to get hysterical, I hope?' Asparagus said to me as a greeting.

'Hysterical? . . . Why on earth do you think I'd get hysterical?'

'Oh, I don't know,' he answered. 'Seems to be a mania among some of our customers at the moment.'

They had come in. Not exactly feeling at home, not like complete professionals, but not the way normal people normally enter the home of some normal person either. Maybe it was because I didn't welcome them with the customary ritual, 'How nice of you to have come.' Yeah, right. 'Please come in and take off . . .' And take everything off the floor, while you're at it. 'Now, really, you didn't need to . . . They're lovely. My wife will be delighted. Stérile, dear, bring a vase. The Sbritzkys were nice enough to bring . . .' I don't have a wife any more. And the only vase I have is in my nightstand. Childhood memories. One night, I remember, we filled it with whisky and . . . Memories of adolescence. Six roses of the liver. Memories of death.

They'd come in and were shuffling around the living room. Brick House notices the curtain rods on the floor and, to be nice, to say something, he asks what happened to them. I say it was the storm. 'It was?' he says. Why do they always stare at me like that? 'But,' he adds, a little embarrassed, 'there wasn't any storm last night?' I answer that he's one lucky guy who doesn't seem to need sleeping pills at night. He smiles, nonplussed. Why do they always look at me like that? 'Pardon me for asking,' he says, 'it's not really my business, but your eye, there, was it like that from birth?' And I say I don't remember, I was too young. Get it? No, obviously, they don't get it or only partly. In any case, he turns abruptly to his companion and says, 'Let's go, Asparagus. Let's get to work.'

Since they walked in, Asparagus has been standing in front of my bookshelves, mouth open. When his colleague calls him, he jumps and turns to face me. 'Well, shit,' he says. I don't answer. What's there to say? 'That's one shitload, I'm telling you,' he adds. 'Did you read them all?' Modestly, I answer yes. Who does Asparagus think I am, one of those arseholes who buys books by the metre? On the very top shelf, out of everyone's reach—except, maybe, some basketball players, but there aren't any in my family—there are two and a quarter metres of books whose pages I haven't even *cut*. But it was a great deal, on the quay, it covered a hole, and it always impresses the arseholes. '*The Black Beast*—is it good?' Asparagus enquires once he's close enough to the books to make out a couple of the titles. I tell him it was pap but someone had dedicated it to me, so . . . 'You know some writers?' There's admiration in his voice. If only he knew, the poor guy.

'OK.' Brick House was getting impatient. 'Are we gonna get started or what?' Asparagus answers sweetly that obviously, if it's a question of getting cultivated, you can just forget him. 'This is not the time to get cultivated,' the other one says. 'Yeah? And when is that time? At night, maybe, when you're rotting your brain with the shit on the television? Or when you're reading your damn racing forms?' They aren't going to start fighting now, are they?

Twenty-three volumes, plus the index and the atlas—at one volume a day, it worked out just about right, because the move was supposed to happen a month later. If you didn't count Sundays, when the buses didn't run, it actually worked out perfectly. And since the condition *sine qua non* of my taking the room—'You want me to rent it to someone else, maybe? There are ten others in queue behind you who would like that.'—had been that I pay each month's rent in advance, I already had somewhere to store them. Everything was perfect. The trunk I could deal with later. And the radiator.

Twenty-five days in a row, I took the same bus at the same time, one volume of the encyclopaedia under my arm. In my arms. Jammed between my hip and my arm. Slipping down and caught with my knee. Slipping down and not caught at all, despite a sudden grab with my right hand. (Volume XI, *4to, brown half-calf, decorated corners, stained, with slight water-damage, wear on corners, slight wrinkling*. Of course, on that day it had to be pouring.) The damn books are heavy. Inconvenient. Despite everything, the first few days didn't go too badly. I even decided that if you got an early start and took the bus on off hours, you could do the whole move yourself this way. Except for the wardrobe. It would make you too obvious to dodge the fare. And I don't want any bus yelling abuse, you know? The real abuse is how much they charge for one miserable ticket just so we can crawl along at four kilometres an hour. And so if someone were to skip this usurious fare to transport a few possessions, what would be the harm?

It started to go wrong around Volume VIII. My nose pressed to the window, I was watching Japanese tourists file by when some guy wanted to sit next to me. The nerve. When the seat next to me was free, I always put my encyclopaedia down on it. It squished my gut if I didn't. I asked him if he couldn't he see that it was *oc-cu-pied*. The seat reserved for the blind was free. He didn't care for that at all. Told me that if I didn't free up the seat immediately, he was going to refer the matter to the conductor and *pronto*. Oooh. Me, if someone threatens to refer matters to anyone whomsoever, I just crumble. So I clumsily grab hold of the book and put it on my lap. Which it crushes. Then I turn to the window sullenly. That's when I hear him say, 'Please excuse me for insisting, Father, but you have to admit that you were taking up a lot of space just for yourself.' Father? Father??? I turn to look at him, astounded. Way too old to be my son. He could even be my father. Besides, haven't I got enough trouble already these days, without some bastard showing up and carrying on about paternity between bus stops? Blasted Stérile, hadn't I told her there was nothing better for sterility than an IUD? Well, I regain my composure and, my voice still a bit uncertain, I ask him why he called me Father. He tells me that for several days now, he's noticed me on the bus with my Bible under my arm. I say it's not a Bible, and besides, do I look like a priest? He goes, 'Oh, you know . . .' One point for him: it is less often true that the habit makes the monk, and maybe that's why more and more Benedictine brothers are bootlegging Bénédictine. Even so, even so: My black shoes? My black trousers? My black sweater? My black vest and barely visible white collar? 'It's just that with priests these days,' he says, 'you can't be too sure.' Yeah, maybe. 'Still,' he starts in again, 'if it's not a Bible, what is it?' I say it's nothing, just a book. 'And that huge thing, you drag it around with you every day?' I say yes. 'Kind of a bother, isn't it?' I tell him, shit, it might bother me, but for Chrissake not as much as he does.

The conversation stopped there but for the next two weeks, every day on the bus I could feel him looking at me. A suspicious and perplexed look. I didn't sit down because I didn't want to risk finding myself stuck next to him. Somehow, he always managed to find a place from which he could watch me at his leisure. Irritating after a while. I tried diving in to my encyclopaedia to put up a front. After a lot of effort, and not without having planted my elbow three times in my neighbours' faces, I managed to open it. Its weight, together with the bus' lurching, almost made me tumble forward. I dropped my book on the foot of a woman, who let loose an ear-splitting scream, and steadied myself as best I could by grabbing the scarf of the man in front of me, half strangling him. In short, there was a commotion. I picked up my book, excused myself to everyone around me and shrank into a corner. But the Eye was still on me. There was even one day, it must have been around Volume XV, when the bus was almost empty and I saw my guy go up to the bus driver and, ignoring the sign asking him, personally, not to talk to the operator of the vehicle, start lecturing the driver, frequently casting his Eye in my direction. From where I was sitting, I could see the driver rise up in his seat, trying to catch sight of me in the rear-view mirror. I looked away. They couldn't do anything to me, after all. I wasn't breaking any rules. That must have been what the driver explained to him, because the Eye finally gave up, shrugged and returned to his seat, head down, sheepish. And I'm sure it was pure coincidence that the driver asked to check my ticket at the final stop that very day. It was pure coincidence, too, that on that day, I happened to have the right ticket.

Two weeks of this circus. And the atlas, alas. Heavier and even more troublesome than its colleagues. But what's the point of knowing everything about Baluchistan if you have no idea where Baluchistan is?

There was a departure point and a terminus, and it was the last day. The Eye, scowling even more than usual and watching with even more suspicion. That's when I had the idea of giving him his money's worth. And, for the twenty-sixth and last time, I got onto my usual bus.

Hands conspicuously in my pockets. To my great satisfaction, I saw the Eye do a double take, rub his eyes and twist his neck to get a better look. But no—I wasn't carrying a thing. I smiled at him, let him stew for a bit and, with complete nonchalance, took out the book I had hidden between my wrist and my watchstrap. It was one of those minuscule books in which some maniacal printer had managed to fit, in an extraordinary and pointless tour de force, the complete *Pensées* of Pascal, La Rochefoucauld or Nesuhi Ertegun. Postage-stamp format. (Let's not exaggerate: the format of a *small* postage stamp.) I held it delicately between my thumb and index finger, lifted it to my eyes and pretended to be absorbed in reading it. I saw the Eye freeze, blanch, ready to crack. He even seemed to be trembling. Mouth open, he stood there, staring at me for ten or twenty seconds, then turned away and feverishly attacked the stop signal button, launching himself out of the bus before it came to a complete stop. Strange—it wasn't his usual stop.

Coming back into the living room, Brick House muttered that I shouldn't pay too much attention to what Asparagus rambled on about. 'You see, he studied for a few years, sociology or something like that, and he's always trying to impress the customers.'

I'm not paying any attention. Something is missing in the room and I can't figure out what. Spot the difference. Oh right, I've got it. My big leather chair. I turn to Brick House and ask him what happened to the leather chair that was sitting right there just a second ago, which he doesn't deny. You can still see the impressions in the carpet left by the four feet. He seems surprised by my tone of voice and answers that, well, yeah, he took it down, the chair. It's in the lorry. 'Why? Weren't we supposed to?' Good Lord, that's right. I'm moving. I nod my head and say, yes, yes, of course, you were supposed to. 'By the way,' he adds, 'if I've understood correctly, not everything is going into your new flat. Part of it is going into storage, right?' And I answered that yes, the new room's not very big. I was only keeping the bed, the table, the chair, a few of the dishes and the bookshelves. And the fridge, of course, because I love trying to spread butter that's as hard as a rock on my bread. He didn't laugh. He said, 'The room?' I said, 'Mmhhmmmh.' He said, '*The* room?' and I said, 'Yeah, of course, the room!' He looked round. My studio was pretty roomy. He said that most people, when they left someplace, it was to move into something bigger. Oh really? 'You'll say it's none of my business,' he added, 'but what happened to you? A setback?' I told him it was none of his business. Besides, I had already told him that until then there had been two or three of us but now I was more or less alone, you see? My explanation hadn't seemed to convince him. Me neither.

I hadn't tried to figure out why the very first arsehole had had that strange smile when he told me to have fun getting rid of the radiator. Two or three days before the move, I put it in the trunk and, with difficulty, took it all down to the courtyard and left it next to the dustbins. At night, when I got home, there was a small sign posted at the bottom of the staircase:

WOULD THE TENANT WHO LOST A TRUNK CONTAINING A RADIATOR
PLEASE RECLAIM IT FROM THE CONCIERGE IN THE LODGE.

I knocked several times at the concierge's window. But the television was blaring so loud she couldn't hear me. So I went in and tapped her on the shoulder. Six cats jumped out of their skins and scattered throughout the front lodge. Grumbling all the while, she deigned to lower the sound slightly. Ever since she figured out I was leaving before it was time to hand out Christmas tips, she'd been sulking. 'Whaddya want?' I said I'd come about the trunk. 'Oh, it's you,' she said. 'I'm not surprised. There you go, it's over there.' She pointed her thumb towards a corner of the lodge and turned the sound back up, loud. Goddamn singer with a voice like nails on a blackboard. What could I do? I took the trunk and, with difficulty, hauled it back up to my flat.

Later, when everyone was asleep, I took it back down. It wasn't easy. This time I put it outside, right on the pavement. Phew.

She knocked on my door early the next morning. At first I thought she might be bringing me a letter from Stérile. But no. 'So what is it with you always losing this trunk?' she asked. 'Couldn't you be a bit more careful? Yer lucky those darkie garbage men are a little more honest than their crooked friends. Really had to pass them some dough.' She put out her hand. I gave her some dough. Probably five francs net profit for her. 'It's in the hallway,' she said, a bit mollified. 'Go get it. It's in the way.'

I went to get it. It wasn't easy. I hauled it back up to my flat. Around midnight, and it wasn't easy, I carried it back down. Intending to leave it somewhere far from my place. I hadn't gone five hundred metres when a cop car trapped me on the pavement. Flashing lights and the whole shebang. A bit blinded, I saw one cop get out and press his gun into my belly button. I guessed there was another cop in the car, his piece pointed right between my eyes.

'Where do you think you're going, like that?' the first cop asked.

I made a vague gesture. It's hard when you're holding a trunk with a radiator in it. The cop took a step back. His colleague cocked his rifle. Ssschlak. Crazy just how relaxed I felt.

'Put it down on the ground,' the cop said. 'And anyway, what is that thing?'

'It's a trunk,' I said, 'with a radiator in it.'

'Yeah, looks like it wasn't much of a harvest tonight. Stand there, face the car with your hands in the air.'

'The memo,' his buddy said.

'What?'

'The memo. We aren't allowed to be rude to these dirty wogs any more.'

'He's white.'

'OK then,' the cop says.

Fine, so they check my papers and we talk things over. By the time the sun is ready to come up, they're pretty much convinced of my good faith.

'OK,' one of the cops says to his partner, 'you interested in a trunk with a radiator? 'Cause if we swiped it from this gentleman, this gentleman wouldn't go complaining, isn't that right?'

'Not at all,' I say, filled with hope.

'I don't want that shit,' says the other cop.

'Awright, if that's the way it is,' the first one turns to me again, 'go home and take your junk with you, and make it fast. Don't let us catch you out here again, walking around with junk in your trunk, or we're gonna cram you in the slammer.'

They howl with laughter, bent double. I could easily disarm them and, with one salvo, bend them into thirds and fourths.

I went home. I climbed my three flights of stairs. It wasn't easy. I needed to sleep. The movers would show up in a few hours. I put my trunk back where it was before. We'll see.

Brick House has crammed himself into the cage of the lift, buckling under the weight of the box he's carrying. I close the front door behind him. I've always hated it when the door's left open, even only for a minute. Gives me the feeling that the entire building is going to rush into my flat. And anyway, it gives me a way to explain why, to my surprise, no one ever does intrude on me here. Visions of a Fourierist phalanstery, with people camping on top of each other and open house twenty-four hours a day. 'Come in, friends, come in. If there's room for eight, there's room for twelve. We'll just put out some sleeping bags. Would you like some milk for your little one?' Gales of laughter, complicity, warmth. God, that'd be great! God, I'd hate it!

Hushed whispering in the hallway. Here we go again. If it was her, earlier, I bet she bitched to her john: 'Sbritzky, that individual is at it again, monopolizing the . . .' The door handle rattles again and there's knocking on the door at the same time. And not a light knock with an index-finger knuckle. With a fist. I yell that it's busy. 'Are you sick or what?' asks Sbritzky's voice. 'You've been in here a good quarter of an hour . . .' I don't answer. 'I'd like to remind you that the loo on this floor is for everyone, so get on with it.' I still don't answer. The steps retreat down the hall. Phew. Today, at random, I'd opened Volume III. Letter C. Colon cancer.

Brick House is back and wants to know who's the arsehole who keeps shutting the fucking door. Asparagus yells from the kitchen that he, at least, hasn't moved an inch. I can feel the weight of Commissioner Brick's eyes on me and stammer that it must be a draught: with the door standing open like that, you know? 'Yeah,' Brick says, 'right . . .' He looks round, hesitates, then goes to the bookshelves and pulls out a thin book. *The Death of Ibid*. 'Is this thing valuable?' And I answer umh, sort of. I didn't even remember I had it. 'Well, in that case . . .' he says and jams it under the door. 'Now it won't move,' he grumbles. He stacks a few chairs and disappears with them into the stairway.

Standing in the middle of the room with the door wide open, I feel naked, vulnerable. Drumroll: 'Step right up, Ladies and Gentlemen, the show is about to begin!' And it worked. I could have bet on it. A timid little cough and there she is with her umbrella and her fox-fur stole.

'Excuse me,' she says, 'but the door was wide open, so I didn't ring the bell.'

Her smile is warm, friendly, solicitous. I don't know what to say. I don't say anything.

'I'm your next-door neighbour,' she adds.

As if I didn't know, after all the time I've spent trying to avoid her.

'You're probably the new tenant,' she continues. 'I'm very happy to meet you. Just imagine, the last one was a real ghost, one strange customer. I never saw his face, not even once. But you seem a very pleasant sort and if there's anything I can do to help you with your move . . .'

At this juncture, Brick House walks in wiping his forehead with a chequered handkerchief. He glances at my neighbour and asks, 'OK, boss, what should we take now?'

The neighbour starts, presses her lips together, then says that this sort of prank from a person like me doesn't surprise her at all. She straightens her fox tail and leaves with dignity.

'Did you do something to the old biddy?' Brick House wants to know.

I say I did nothing, nothing, nothing, NOTHING.

Asparagus sticks his little ferret face through the kitchen doorway.

'Something wrong?'

Exasperated, I sigh that no, everything's fine.

'I was just wondering if maybe you weren't starting to get hysterical?'

He almost seems disappointed he didn't find me on the ground, chewing on the rug.

'The rugs,' I tell Brick House.

'What, the rugs?'

'You asked me what to take down next, didn't you? Well take the goddamn rugs, for Chrissake, before I start chewing on them.'

He stares at me briefly, then shrugs.

'You're the boss, after all.'

He's still looking at me and seems to be waiting for something else. What?

'For you to move,' he says. 'How am I supposed to roll up the rug if you're standing there right in the middle?'

I don't know where to go. What to do. I wander around like I'm in a strange flat. With the bed gone, the bedroom looks enormous. You could easily fit a pool table. But it's hard to sleep on a pool table. Except in a morgue. My two wrinkled balls on an ice-cold pool table and, instead of a cue, the doc's scalpel. Tssst.

I hear Asparagus calling me from the kitchen. What does he want now? I cross the living room again, noticing the large, light-coloured square on the carpeting where the rug had been.

The best way to keep a carpet clean is to cover it completely with rugs. But then what's the point of the carpeting? Some days nothing is more irritating than my own logic.

'Look what I found completely by chance in the pantry,' Asparagus exclaims, brandishing the bottle of red.

I'd forgotten all about it.

'And?'

'What, and?' he says. 'I don't suppose you intend to move it too, do you? These things are fragile. Besides, it's got a plastic cap instead of a cork . . .'

'Exactly. I'm going to leave it for the next tenant.'

Asparagus makes a face and says that with this rotgut, the new tenant will certainly think I was taking the piss out of him. I don't answer. Time passes.

'Do you know what we call "the movers' breakfast?"' he asks me. 'Cheap plonk.'

'What a charming custom,' I say.

'Yeah. Unfortunately it's disappearing.'

I tell him that it's certainly a shame. And he says, 'Isn't it?'

'Go ahead,' I tell him. 'Help yourself.'

'Help myself? Help myself to what?'

The son of a bitch *sincerely* seems puzzled.

'To *what*, do you think? To some wine, of course.'

'Oh? To some wine? You're very kind, but such rotgut, so early in the morning, I don't know if I . . . Well, fine, if you insist.'

He lifts the bottle to his lips. One gulp, two, three, four. He suddenly stops, wipes his mouth on his sleeve and tells me that he hopes I don't think he invented the whole story with the movers' breakfast just so that . . . And I answer, no, no, of course not.

'That's good,' he says, holding the bottle out towards me. 'Your turn.'

Ugh. But if you don't take a drink when you've got the blues, then when? I take a swig, two, three. I put the bottle down. Asparagus reaches out to grab it when Brick House reappears.

'You almost done?' he asks. 'I need your help with the big table and . . .'

He notices the bottle and, turning, says to me, 'You know what they call the movers' breakfast?'

Five minutes later, the bottle is empty. We debate for a while who is going to carry it down. They should, of course, but they'd rather not. The estimate doesn't list any bottles, empty or full, and what if there were an accident, if they broke it, for example, and someone in the building fell on it and cut themselves . . . I sigh and say I'll take it down myself.

'Good, we're not done yet,' Brick says, 'the table's next. Get going Asparagus.'

For those who know how to pray, this would be the time. I don't know how. I cross my fingers behind my back and, powerless, I watch the show.

The table's width just fits through the doorway, a few millimetres to spare on either side. Good. But the back half is still sticking into my flat when the front of it hits the bars on the cage of the lift. No way round it. I knew it.

'Aw,' Brick House yells from the hallway, 'let's take it back in and try a different way.'

Which they do. They turn the table on its side, legs to the right. The width just barely fits through. Compared to their first try, they've managed to win a few more centimetres. The table is three-quarters out the door. But they have to stop there. It's stuck on every side. Asparagus is fed up and leans against the table. The doorframe creaks. No way round it. I knew it.

'Stop, for Chrissake,' Brick yells. 'It won't go through like that. Let's take it back in and try a different way.'

'A different way' means still on its side, but with the legs to the left this time. You are bright bulbs, gentlemen. And don't forget the egg of Columbus. I've closed my eyes. I don't hear any more banging or creaking. Then Brick's voice yelling that, shit, we're almost through this time, just a hair to go, go on, one more try and—

'Shit! Stop, stop, stop! We're going to trash everything. It was almost through but it's not going to work. Let's take it back in.'

The table sits in the middle of the living room. They glare at it, frowning, as if it were the table's fault.

'The window?' Asparagus suggests.

'Don't be an idiot,' the other says. 'It's way too small.'

'If we stand it on end? We haven't tried it standing on . . .'

'Same thing. It would be too tall. Aw shit, shit, shit. We're going to have to take the goddamn thing apart and that's a pain in the arse because it seems really solid and I don't know anything about taking furniture apart.

'The neighbour,' I say.

'What about the neighbour?'

'Maybe, and it's just a suggestion, I'm not a mover, but maybe if she opens her front door, which is just to the left there on the landing, you could slide the front legs into her hallway. That might get you the extra room you need to fit the back end through?'

Brick scratches his head.

'Not so stupid, after all,' he says. 'Besides we don't have anything to lose in trying. But you know, I'm thinking . . .'

I don't like the way he's looking at me.

'You couldn't have said anything sooner?'

I swear that I only just thought of it now.

'Yeah. And how did the movers get it in here in the first place?'

'Shit, I don't know,' I lie. 'I wasn't here at the time.'

'Sure,' he says, 'if you say so. Are you going?'

'Going where?'

'To ring the doorbell, of course. You don't think the door's going to open by itself, do you?'

'Why me? You're the movers.'

'Movers, yeah,' he says, 'but not diplomats, or kamikazes. I've seen her, the biddy next door.'

'But she can't stand me . . .'

'Buddy, that's your problem. You've got to move people to move people.'

The last time I heard laughter like that, it was the two cops. I wonder if there's anything in the world I hate more than puns.

After he calmed down a bit, I said that maybe I could telephone the neighbour.

'Telephone,' he says, '*te-le-phone*—when all you have to do is stretch out your arm and push on her doorbell? Here . . .'

I want to yell, no, no, no! Too late. He rings twice, good God, and each time long, very long. Then he sprints back to my flat, brushing past me on the landing. I can't turn back—massive, solid, sleeves rolled up, leaning against the doorframe, he bars my retreat.

It's a three-storey jump into the abyss.

a) Discomfort following defecation.

There's the sound of steps, shuffling, hushed, in the neighbour's hallway. Then a voice from behind the door asking who it is. Behind me, I hear A and B snorting with laughter. I swallow and say that it's me, Ma'am, your neighbour. There's a pause, then the sound of the lock, then the door opens a crack. But the chain is still fastened. Kilometres of chain are still fastened. 'Don't leave yourself vulnerable to burglary. Be on your guard. A real plumber may actually be an impersonator. Would you swear on the Bible that this inspector really is one? But be careful, don't go too far—he is under oath, too, it will be your word against his.'

'What is it?' she asks again.

I mumble my little story.

'Your table legs in *my* hallway?'

'Yes, that's it,' I say. 'It will only take a second, no more than that.'

'I see. So the one and only time in three years that you knock on my door is when you need something from me, hmmm?'

I wanted to ask why else I would have ever knocked on her door. You remember, my friends, surely you remember when, ear glued to the wall, we followed, step by step, the amorous frolicking of that old lady next door? In any case, she certainly seemed old at the time. She must have been about the same age as we are now. She had a limp. Seems it turns some people on.

I stammer that, well, the thing is . . .

'Tell her to hurry up. We haven't got all day,' Brick House whispers in a stentorian voice.

I explain that these gentlemen are in a bit of a hurry. They have other obligations they need to see to, don't you know, and if she would be so extremely kind as to . . .

Open up, you old witch, or I'll kick your goddamn door in myself.

'Aren't you all polite all of a sudden?' she says. 'Fine, I'll open. But just one second. I need to get dressed.'

'What for?' Asparagus whispers. 'She can open it as she is, stark naked.'

I motion to him to be quiet. The moron is going to ruin everything. Fortunately, she didn't hear him.

A minute goes by, two, three.

'What the hell is she doing, for Chrissake?' Brick house grumbles. 'What can she possibly . . . ?'

The sound of chains. Cerberus is coming out. Cerberus has come out. She's wearing a pale green dressing gown over some sort of pink thing with lace. Pretty much the same colours on her face except for her eyebrows which she has drawn over with a thick black line.

A and B just stand there, gaping.

'If these gentlemen wouldn't mind getting started,' she mews without looking at me, 'I was going to take my bath and . . .'

These gentlemen come back to earth and get started. For a second, we're left alone on the landing.

'What happened to your eye?' she asks quickly, still not looking at me.

I look at her without answering.

'Listen, now that you're about to leave for good,' she says insistently, 'you certainly could . . .'

Asparagus gets me off the hot seat when he appears on the landing, backing towards us, holding the table legs and yelling, 'Watch your backs! Coming through!' I can only imagine in what kind of greasy spoon Asparagus must have studied his sociology.

In the empty room on the sixth floor, the stack of encyclopaedias grew taller by one volume a day. I had, of course, no end of trouble convincing my new concierge that I wasn't some salesman, eager to stick his foot in his peaceful neighbours' doors, but a peaceful tenant just like them. Well, almost.

'And that book, under your arm, what is it then?' she asks suspiciously.

'It's a kind of fat dictionary,' I say. 'But instead of having one book with all the letters of the alphabet, in these, there's just one letter per volume, pretty much. Twenty-five volumes total.'

There's no one better at explaining simple things to simple people than me.

'If I've understood your gibberish properly,' she said, 'then what you've got there is just an encyclopaedia.'

'If you like,' I answered, annoyed.

'I see,' she says. 'My son sells them. So don't go poaching on his territory in this building, right? In any case, your set's worthless compared to his. I bet Cabbot and Ostello aren't even in yours?'

I didn't dare admit I had no idea who they were. I said I'd check. Pfff.

Panting, A and B have crammed themselves into the stairway, this one pushing, that one pulling, this one lifting, that one lowering, this one cursing, that one swearing. It worked with the table. I knew it. Cerberus has blessed them with a last charming smile and returned to the pits of hell.

'You know, I think she had the hots for us,' Asparagus snickered.

'She had the hots for *you*,' Brick House answered quickly, like a good sport.

Except for the bookcase, the last boxes, the radiator and the trunk, the flat is now almost empty. It may seem paradoxical but without curtains, the windows seem an even darker screen between me and the outside world. Windows in an asylum, in an army barrack, in an old people's home. However, if you look closely, it's hardly surprising. The windows are filthy. I open them wide. I won't ever be too cold or too hot in here again. But it's filthy outside too. 'It was here, for five long years, that Bovary lived, suffered and loved.' Tssst. I wander from one room to the next, with no goal. The rooms are almost empty, virginal. Speaking of virgins, wasn't it right here that I took little whatshername's cherry? I can't remember her name or how I managed it either. And all that's left are four holes in the carpet where the bed used to be, four holes of crushed, blackened threads. Maybe this is what the entire flat has become—*home sweet home* is the scene of an accident, a crime, a life in which the holes in the carpet would replace the chalk drawings on the pavement that delineate the placement of the bodies. One more word and I'll be roaring with laughter.

Slight headache. Probably the cheap red wine. Which reminds me that on one of my bookshelves, behind the works of an ancient philosopher, I'd hidden a bottle of old cognac. Corporate gift from a girl to thank me for my corporeal services. You about done with my bottom, Don Juan? I dumped her, but quick. She's one of those women whose sole preoccupation is whether it will be windy after they've dropped three hundred at the hairdresser's. In short, I was keeping the cognac to celebrate something but like the other one said, 'You've got to drink before celebrating, lest you die before drinking.'

I still had the bottle in my hand and sticky lips when A and B walked in.

'At least you're not bored while others are working.'

Reproaches, now? What does he expect me to do then, apologize?

'The hemlock of the departing,' I say apologetically.

If you're going to make elitist jokes, you have to expect to be the only one able to understand and appreciate them.

'That's right,' Asparagus says, 'and to whom do you still owe the rooster?'

I look at him blankly. I have no idea what he's talking about. Is he taking the piss or what?

'If I'm in the way, I can leave,' Brick says sullenly.

I smooth things over by offering them both a drink. They each take a swig and hand the bottle back to me. I hand it back to them. They hand it back to me. As a result, when we finally tackle the bookshelves, the horizon line inside the bottle has dropped almost ten centimetres.

'What a crying shame to drink nectar like this from the bottle,' A remarks, obviously delighted.

At the same time and methodically, from top to bottom, left to right, B has begun emptying the shelves and stacking the books in boxes. Now and then he stops to read a title and look at me, whistling between his teeth. I shrug and say, 'Yeah, well . . .' I'm feeling uncomfortable. The truth is I feel like an idiot. A little drunk, too. I hear myself telling Brick House that I probably won't keep it.

'Keep what?'

'That book,' I say, 'the last title you read out.'

Brick didn't have any objections. I was the boss. But what were we going to do with the book? I say that I don't know—throw it away, probably.

'Throw it away!' Asparagus cries, 'Throw away a *book*?'

He looks horrified.

'Maybe you want it?'

'Are you kidding or what? You think I have time to waste reading shit like that? I'm sorry, I mean . . .'

The first thing I did in my new room was to measure the longest wall to see if my bookshelves would fit. They did, but just barely. I lucked out. Then I made sure that the taps on the sink behind the folding screen worked properly. The *cold*-water tap worked perfectly. But perhaps one shouldn't ask for too much on one and the same day?

I tell Asparagus that I understand exactly what he means. That I don't entirely disagree. That all these books are shit. That is not what I wanted to say. Cognac.

'If they're shit,' Brick House says with a burst of laughter, 'then you have a good supply of toilet paper ready, hunh?'

Half joking, half outraged, I point out that, however moribund it might be, he could show a bit more respect for Gutenberg's galaxy.

'For Gutenb . . . what?'

Aridly and pedantically, A explains that Gutenberg's the guy who was there before television was invented.

'Like a kind of Cabbot, then?'

Good God, here we go again. I swear to myself that I'm going to look the name up in my encyclopaedia.

'Whatever it is,' B continues, suddenly professional again, 'if you're going to start tossing every second book, then we'll end up with boxes left over. Can't have that. The office computer will melt down.'

'Maybe we could use one of them for the radiator,' I suggest timidly.

'The radiator? What radiator? There was no radiator listed on the estimate.'

I don't insist. How about another round? Yes, yes, I insist.

'Speaking of boxes,' Asparagus says, handing me the bottle, 'we'll be pretty well-boxed ourselves at this rate.'

I laugh. Not as hard as he does, but I laugh. Warm and fuzzy atmosphere. Three pals, all brothers. Come on—life's not so bad and tomorrow's another day. Brick, whose face is starting to turn red, gets Asparagus' joke after a short lag and starts howling with laughter. I look at him fondly. He's a good guy.

Suddenly I'm cold. I get up to close the window, swaying ever so slightly. A notices and, hiccuping, says that at least now I won't be bumping into the furniture. Badda boom! And they're off again.

'Especially since it's got to be even harder with only one . . .' A starts and suddenly interrupts himself.

I turn and stare at him. Apoplectic brute.

'Only one what?'

'Nothing, nothing,' he mumbles. 'So, should we get back to work?'

They get back to work, embarrassed, in silence. I regret being so sensitive. I broke the spell. After all, whether they want to be or not, they are my last visitors. A house-cooling party. At the end of the rope, the stinking corpse of days past hung limply. Tssst. I don't know what to do. I hate sitting around when someone is working in the flat. That's why I never got the plumber in. He would be knocking on the door and I wouldn't answer. Then the plumber would leave and I'd call and complain. 'But he came to your home,' they'd answer, 'and you weren't there.' And I'd tell them that, quite to the contrary, I was here the whole time and that's exactly the problem—he came when I was home. 'And how is he supposed to get in if you're not home?' they'd yell into my ear. Yeesh. I was starting to understand why so many guys get married.

In short, to keep myself busy and so I wouldn't seem to be keeping an eye on them, I went back to the window to peer out of the splotchy panes at the sizzling drizzle spitting from the sky. Tssst. You like my onomatopoeia? This is probably the last time I'll be watching what's going on down in the street. Very moving, certainly, but that doesn't make the show on the street any more interesting. Now as always, some dogs are trying to squat over the few empty spaces left between the cars. Now as always, frantic pedestrians are trying to avoid the dogs without stepping in their mess. Even if they cheer you up at first, it's an endless battle to get rid of them later.

Behind me, I hear the two of them whispering and snickering.

'Well now,' says A, 'how about that . . .'

Eighteenth-century etchings. I go back towards them.

'Not back, right?'

Asparagus nods yes energetically. His eyes are shining.

'Hey, wait, wait,' he cries when Brick starts turning the page. 'Wait! I couldn't see. That one there, is it a guy or a . . . ? How about tha-a-a-t! Did you see where she's got her mouth, the one who . . . And the other one, behind her on all fours licking her girlfriend while she's getting it from the guy who at the same time—no shit!—is licking the arse of the one squatting on the dresser and stroking her own . . . oooh . . . Excuse me, could I please use your bathroom?'

A little disconcerted by the suddenness of his question, I tell him, of course, naturally. He scurries off.

'Please excuse him,' Brick says, apparently embarrassed, 'but he's young, you see, and . . .'

I'm ready to retort that I've seen plenty of older people needing to rush off to the toilet, when all of a sudden I think I get what he's trying to say.

'Oh,' I say, embarrassed myself now, 'do you think he . . . that he . . . ?'

'Well, I mean . . .'

I nod, for once not unhappy to be old.

In silent agreement, we avoid looking at Asparagus when he comes back.

'OK,' he says aggressively, 'let's put the damn book away.'

He grabs it so that the book opens. A page flutters out.

'What is this?' he asks, picking it up. 'It looks like a kid's drawing.'

Oh! Oh, good Lord! It *is* a kid's drawing. Surrounded by yellow stars, a little, dark blue man straddles an orange sliver of moon.

Asparagus studies it for a moment, slips it back into the book and says that say what you will, he thinks it's disgusting to put a child's drawing in a book like this.

No one answers. They get back to work in silence. A few minutes later, it's all done. The last book fits exactly into the last free corner of the last box.

'Bravo,' I say. 'You are masters.'

'Question of habit,' Brick replies modestly. 'It comes with practice.'

'But if I understand correctly, it would be best that I not have a single book left over.'

'Yes,' he says with the utmost seriousness, 'it would be best that you not.'

I shudder, thinking of my encyclopaedia. I avoided one hell of a catastrophe by a hair's breadth.

'And what about this, then?' I ask, pulling my mini-book out of my pocket. You would need at least two hundred of these to fill a pocket.

Brick looks at the book, looks at me, looks at the book again and says, 'You're a real joker, aren't you?'

'You think?' I ask, delighted.

'No.'

Oh well. Two hundred and fifty thousand centuries ago, someone must have cursed one of my ancestors and condemned him and all his posterity to being, henceforth, the only ones who ever laugh at their own jokes. I can see him clearly, my pain-in-the-neck loud-mouth cut-up ancestor, dressed in animal skins and already bursting with laughter, rushing into the chief's cave without even knocking or wiping his feet to ask the head of the tribe, point-blank, if he knows what a chameleon is. The chief, already on his guard, says no. And the ancestor guffaws and says, rolling on the ground, 'It's a dromedary with two humps.' And the chief, beside himself with rage, hair on end, eyes shooting daggers, and foaming at the mouth, points a trembling finger at the poor old man and howls, 'Cursèd, cursèd be you and all your . . .'

With a 'hup', Asparagus loads one of the boxes on his shoulder. Gosh! I never would have thought he could do it.

'Don't drink it all yourselves, right?' he says, pointing his chin towards the bottle. 'I wouldn't mind another drop when I come back up.'

'What a lush,' Brick grumbles as he grabs the bottle by the neck. 'May I?' He may. He throws one back and goes out in turn, a box on his back.

More and more alone in a flat that's more and more empty. That drawing earlier. Lord, how time flies. Light years before the IUD, Stephanie. Blond hair and sucking on her felt-tip markers, either end, indiscriminately. Lips spotted with colour, pointillist. Enough.

Another sip—after all, you don't move every day. But first I wipe the mouth of the bottle with my hand. I would never dare do that in front of my drinking buddies. 'What's with that, man? You think I've got the clap or what?' When you answer, yes, you always seem to be nosing around someone else's business, especially when you hardly know the guy.

Time seems to be speeding up. Resurfacing from I don't know where, Asparagus looks at the cognac reproachfully. 'Hep' a good swig, 'hup' another box, exit Asparagus. A space—I stand motionless, staring at the wall, trying vaguely to remember which painting hung there yesterday, this morning, where there's a white space now. It's funny: you see things for years, people too, and all it takes is a mover's hairy hand or an undertaker's and, pouf!, everything vanishes, memory, recollections . . . In a haze, I see B waving. I hear him say, 'Just one for the road,' and a second later it's A who's loading up the last boxes. I think I smile at him. I think I'm tired. They've been working and I just . . . ouch . . .

Time passes.

'Would you mind not sitting right there? You're blocking the way.'

Why am I sitting on the floor? Startled, I struggle to my feet. I seem to have had another . . . fit of . . . And yet, it's been a long time since . . . A and B are both back, massive, solid, sleeves rolled up. They can take a lot, those guys.

'Just two sections of the bookshelves left,' says Brick, 'and we're done.'

Out of sheer habit, I walk round the spot where my table used to be and go to the bathroom to freshen up. To think there was a time when, returning to my flat, staggering a bit and not too clear-headed, I'd felt reassured to see my furniture always in the same place, massive, solid, feet on the ground, immovable. Immovable, yeah, right.

When I come out, my two mules have just walked in. A is holding something in his right ha . . . Oh no! Not again . . .

'It's a custom,' he says, 'We have a tradition with the customers we like. You know, the way stonemasons plant a sapling when they finish a job.'

What can I say? After all, there aren't all that many people who like me. I thank them awkwardly and watch him uncork the bottle. Bordeaux, if you please, with a real cork and everything. I feel more than a little ashamed.

'Should we sit?' Brick asks.

And there we are, all three of sitting round a sealed box on which Asparagus has placed the bottle.

'It just occurred to me,' Asparagus says, 'how about we play Second to Last?'

'Play what?' asks Brick.

Only much later do I understand how perfectly they had their spiel down.

'You know,' says A, 'you've played it before: the second to last to drink pays for the bottle.'

Oh yes, B suddenly remembers. A lot of fun, this game. They explain it to me: the bottle is passed from one person to the next. Each person can drink as much or as little as he wants. You just have to watch out for the person drinking right after you. If he finishes it in one go, then you're second to last and you have to shell out for the bottle. Did I get it?

I got it. Juvenile. Let's play, my friends, let's play.

We play. The first turn is a sort of observation round. Each one takes a swallow. The same goes for the second and third turns. The tension builds. No one says a word. The bottle lands up with me, about half full. And if I finished it? I can just picture Asparagus' face, the bastard, when he realizes that he's second to last. But, no, that's insane, no one drinks a half litre of wine straight. Fine, I pass it to Brick after barely wetting my lips to leave as much as possible for him. Shrewd tactics for a beginner. He looks at me, smiles, throws his head back, brings the bottle to his lips, his Adam's apple rising and falling, and glub, and glub, and glub, and glub . . . Hang on! He's not going to . . . he takes a breath and glub, and glub. And glub.

Shi-it.

Asparagus laughs and tells me that, obviously, the game *really* gets fun when there are at least a dozen bottles. Because if it's always the same one who wants to be the wise guy . . .

I force myself to smile and ask how much I owe them. They tell me with perfect unanimity. Christ, their cork wasn't just any cork, it was solid gold.

'You can add it to the tip you're not allowed to give us,' Armoire lets me know and adds that they've got to split. They're not done yet. They still have to unload.

We're in the hallway and I go for broke. I tell them about the trunk. And the radiator.

'Oh, that. In the corner,' B says. 'I noticed it before but since it wasn't listed on the inventory, I figured you'd made other arrangements.'

I tell them I hadn't. I ask them if, by chance, they might be interested in it. I'd like to get rid of it, you see and . . .

'The old trunk, if absolutely necessary,' Asparagus says. 'I could store my records. But there is one condition . . .'

'Yes,' I say, resigned. 'Yes, I'll take it down myself. And you,' I say to Brick, 'you're not tempted by a radiator?'

'Depends,' he answers. 'First, how much?'

I protest, 'There's no question of payment. Really!'

'But there is,' he says. 'But there is.'

Nice guy.

Hesitating, I say, 'I don't know . . . Twenty francs?'

He shakes his head vigorously. 'Not enough.'

Brutal, but honest. Scrupulous.

'But it's old,' I say, 'and I'm not sure it works all that well any more . . .'

'That doesn't make any difference.'

After all, if he insists.

'Thirty?'

'Fifty,' he says. 'At the very least.'

I'm a bit embarrassed. I'm sure it's not worth fifty. But for once in my life I could be making a deal . . .

'OK,' I say. 'For fifty.'

'You can add it to the tip you're not allowed to give us, along with the price of the wine. You see, the transportation alone to the dump, the petrol, wear on the tyres, all that . . .'

Oh? Of course. Get a grip, you boneheads, with your shitty theories about humour.

We go downstairs, them whistling, hands in their pockets, me, struggling with the trunk and radiator. This seems to amuse them. Not me.

'Good,' Brick says, 'first we'll drop off whatever goes into storage and in about an hour, we'll meet you at your new digs. OK?'

Fine. And come to think of it, I forgot to ask if, by chance, they had found a sock anywhere.

A sock . . . ? No . . . They hadn't looked at me that strangely for a while.

. . . due to the similarity in early symptoms (light haemorrhaging, intestinal discomfort) colon cancer is often confused with haemorrhoids. Eighty per cent of cases are treatable through surgical procedures with a complete cure rate of fifty per cent.

Candelabrum: *a decorative motif in architecture derived from the pedestal or candlestick, used to hold a lamp or a candle.*

Candia (Iraklion): *See Heraklion.*

Farewell studio, farewell years of my life, farewell Stérile and Stephanie, farewell my one-night-stands with their skirts lying crumpled on the floor, farewell smell of coffee on a Sunday morning, farewell solitary birthdays, nights of insomnia, hands balled into fists and stomach tied in knots, farewell telephone that's stopped ringing and now sits, alone, in the centre of the bedroom like a snail at the end of his long, twisting trail of slime, farewell my ray of morning sun, faithful and fleeting, farewell sound of the doorbell ringing back when I could tell, from a particular trembling tone, that it was you, farewell useless old sink, constantly stopped up and constantly unstopped with a knitting needle, farewell wasted days, hours fled, minutes like moths, farewell wood fires I never built because it's too much trouble to find wood in the city and these days the Christmas trees are all made of plastic, farewell, good Lord, how time flies, farewell to the flood of black-bordered death notices I received here and which could have fed the fires of hell if they hadn't all been Catholics, farewell burglars, two-bit crooks, my brothers, trespassers and, between us, looking back: Was it really necessary to pour the jar of rose hip jam all over my sheets? Farewell dirty yellow walls whose every crack and stain has its own story, tomorrow will bring a new coat of paint that will allow other lives to start fresh. Farewell, which people was it, which religion, the gentle naïfs who always kept some sacred book of spells hidden in their homes to call divine blessings down upon them? . . . I wonder if in Auschwitz they also . . . Tssst. Which reminds me that, earlier, Brick House asked me where I was from, with a name like that? I asked him what did he think? And that I was just as French as he was. Well, almost, because, in fact, I was Swiss. I lived there for about twenty years and for the last fifteen I've been living in Paris, you see, where I . . . He interrupted me, grumbling that, whatever, it was still a funny kind of name.

If you say so.

Standing alone in the middle of the empty living room, throat dry and a little tight, I play the last dissonant chord in my little sonata and turn off all the taps I'd opened because they were the only things that worked any more. Then I pick up the tube of lipstick Stérile had forgotten, put it in my pocket and leave without looking back.

Farewell, God bless and up yours.

Outside, I hailed a cruising taxi and gave the address to the driver who turned round and asked me if I could explain where that was because he was new on the job, don't you know, and it was his first day . . . I *always* end up with a new one on his first day. I told him it wasn't complicated: not far from a city hall, behind a small park, and . . . 'Kind of like it is right here?' he asked. Shit! I'm such an idiot: I'd given him my old address of the block of flats we were sitting right in front of. I gave him the new address and reflected on the fact that the one thing in this world that is harder to do than to get rid of your old habits is to get rid of your old habits.

At some point, Asparagus asked me what the hell I did in life. I told him that for a long time I had sought to understand the world around me. I was grateful to him for not saying that that wasn't a job. He just nodded and said, 'And now?' Now, I was unemployed.

I didn't think it necessary to tell him about my years of study, my diplomas or my many little jobs. As if, by the way, I had had any 'big' jobs. Not to be confused with those jobs for which you have to be big, which are generally the smallest, being a cop, for example. 'Go on, you say that now but when something isn't working, you sure are glad they're there.'

At first, my height was one of the few assets I had for my last job. And being able to read, of course, which meant that I could decipher the job listing. It is, no doubt, to get rid of illiterates from the start that employment opportunities are advertised in writing. Imagine their faces if the physician they'd just recruited after a barrage of extremely complicated tests were to sign his employment contract with a crude X.

I had prudently abstained from admitting to them that money and everything associated with it had always inspired an instinctive revulsion in me. On the one hand, this sort of confession might have reassured them that I wasn't the kind of person to dip into the cash register, but, on the other hand, it might have worried them that I wouldn't be ready to defend it with the necessary conviction the day others went after it. That's why, when the guy interviewing me asked what my 'relationship with money' was, I said it was normal, nothing more. He took advantage of the moment to state my eventual salary. I swallowed my tongue. 'And you call that normal?' he remarked. I coughed up my tongue, which was half choking me, and stammered that it wasn't really much. He smiled. 'I appreciate your reaction,' he said, 'my lengthy experience has taught me to watch out for anyone who claims to have a normal relationship with money.' He repeated the word contemptuously, 'Normal . . . Armchair idealists, usually. Lefties.' Still stammering, I said I was glad to have reacted properly for his little test and enquired after the *actual* amount of my salary. 'All you ever think about is money, you and your kind,' he said in a different tone. 'I told you the amount of your salary, just now. Do you see a reason why it would have changed in the last minute?' None. He stared at me for a while, impassively, and then suddenly leapt to his feet behind his desk and yelled, 'Hands in the air!' Good Lord, I was so terrified I couldn't move, but sat there stupidly, gaping at him as he pointed his finger at me. Was he joking or what? All I can say is that he didn't seem to be. I gathered my wits and was ready to obey him when he sat back down and muttered, 'Fine, on that front things are fine. You don't seem to be too impressionable.' I wanted to say, 'Me? Impressionable?' with a debonair wave of my hand for emphasis. But, on second thought, I skipped the emphasis. He might have been surprised at how much it was trembling.

The interview started again. That is to say that he went back to looking me straight in the eye and frowning. Psychologically very sophisticated, all this. 'Will your nerves withstand this test?' To reassure myself, I reminded myself that I had read Freud's complete works, whereas this guy probably didn't even know who Freud was. It's crazy how much thoughts like these can help. It's like picturing your examiner naked in his bathroom—advice given to me by some moron sitting for his degree for the ninth time. 'If you don't want to be intimidated by him, all you have to do is picture him buck-naked brushing his teeth in his . . .' Radical, it's true. Fifteen years later, the entire faculty of L**** University is still wondering why it was that that pale, weaselly little cretin was shaking with laughter throughout his entire oral examination on Roman law.

'Hey,' he says, 'I'm talking to you.'

I jump. I apologize. I'm all ears.

'I was asking if you spoke German.'

I don't get what he's after.

'German? No. Your ad didn't say it was necessary.'

'I *know* what the ad said.'

Here we go. I've irritated him by answering a different question. 'You must inform them,' said Sigmund, 'of the approximate duration and cost of the treatment. And afterwards, for the love of God, *keep your big mouths shut*.'

'The fact is that we might acquire some guard dogs soon—to reinforce security, you understand?'

Do I understand? . . . I don't get it all. But I nod with such conviction that, had he read only the jacket copy on one of the Master's books, he would have found my reaction suspicious.

Silence.

'Following our regulations,' he says, 'we run a brief background check and . . .'

Cat and mouse, that's what he's been playing. I get up and thank him for his time anyway, sorry for the imposition and all.

He must not have expected me to play that pawn. Obviously surprised, he asks me to sit back down. Oh really? I'm not going to get a lecture on being a good citizen on top of it all, am I?

'And the results were all acceptable,' he continues, 'for these times, that is.'

'For these times . . . ?'

'Not too long ago,' he spits out, 'they'd have thrown you in the clink for less. But I don't make the laws.'

Silence. I ponder these strong words. He is tapping his left palm with a ruler.

'One last question before I make my decision,' he says. 'If you were on a desert island and could only have one companion, which one would you choose, Marx or Jesus?'

Nuts, this guy is nuts. And his goddamn bank, seventy-two-point-four per cent denominational. I'd better watch my step.

'Don't hesitate,' he says with a nasty, saccharine smile, 'Speak to me as you would to your father or, better yet, to someone very close to you who has your complete confidence.'

Right. Slowly, choosing my words very carefully, I tell him that his background check surely revealed that for several years, and in a manner that could honestly be called fanatic, I had militated . . .

He interrupts me. 'Why do you think I brought prison up just now? Because you stole five francs from your grandmother?'

Gosh! He even knows about *that*.

'. . . Militated, as I say, without paying much attention to the finer nuances in the ranks of . . . I was young. I believed. I was sure I was right, convinced that those who weren't with me were against me, that the world was divided in two: the bastards and the rest . . . And I shouted my beliefs at them all. I shouted down all those who didn't agree. I scorned them, ridiculed them and occasionally beat them up. I admit it . . . But believe me, I've changed my ways now that I've met Him. Today I'm more mature. I now appreciate that everything is relative, and this new conviction, believe me, I'm ready to defend it with my fists, ready to impose it on all those goddamn imbeciles who persist in fighting for the erroneous theories that I myself mistakenly defended for so long. Those bastards will have to be made to understand, even if it means shaking them up a bit to root out the Error from their hardened hearts . . . And who better to do this, tell me, than I? Who better than the converted wolf to turn these wolves into lambs? Who would be a more effective mouthpiece? Please tell me what is, for the mass media, more tedious, more banal, more boring than an individual who clings, obstinately and in bad faith, to the same belief his entire life? Whereas I, illuminated by my encounter with Him upon Whom I spat only yesterday, believe me, I will be raw meat for . . .'

Silence. Did I hit the mark? He looked at me strangely.

Silence.

He leans back in his chair.

Silence.

He examines his fingernails.

'You are not easy to read,' he finally says. 'But we've got to get on with things. Choose a number between one and six.'

I don't understand. I say, 'Three.' He takes a die out of his drawer and tosses it onto the table. The die rolls. Three.

'At least you're lucky.'

If you say so.

'OK. You're hired. On a trial basis. Three months. Do you have any experience with firearms?'

Very proud of myself, I answer that I served ten months military service without ever wounding anyone. Skilful, aren't I?

'No handguns, then,' he says. 'Why the hell would we give you a gun if you can't even manage to hit anyone?'

I see.

And that's how I ended up pushing buttons at the bank of Thingy & Co. It sounds easy when you put it like that but . . . Fine, let's not put on airs. It was easy—child's play.

Outside someone rang. The bell above my head went 'Bzzz.' Startled awake, it was my duty to examine the applicant through the glass door and decide if he had an ugly enough mug to be a real businessman up to doing business with Thingy & Co. Let me point out that this was, in fact, my interpretation of the task incumbent upon me, a task that my employers had not defined in precisely those terms. According to them, all I had to do was refuse entry to anyone who was obviously suspicious-looking. 'And I'm not even talking about those who show up at the door with a submachine gun,' the assistant manager said, laughing, and I asked him why not.

'Why not what?'

'Why aren't you even talking about those who show up at the door with a submachine gun?'

He stopped laughing, opened and closed his mouth, then shrugged. Why was he looking at me like that? Why were they *all* looking at me like that? The colleague who ran up to me on the first morning, before I'd even taken off my coat, and said in a devastated tone, 'Have you seen? The dollar?' I looked all around. 'Which dollar?' In any case, I didn't give a shit. For me the dollar was just some kind of screwed up bass clef. But that doesn't go over well in a bank, to be honest. Good to know.

In short, the assistant manager explained in detail that it was a question of tact and discernment: groups of several men are suspect; protruding bumps under overcoats are suspect; long thin packages carried by hand are suspect; anyone whose face I haven't seen before is suspect (but he only said that for form's sake since I was new); anyone trying hard not to be noticed is suspect . . .

'And you aren't even talking about anyone with stockings over their heads?'

'That's right, I . . . Are you making fun of me?'

'Not at all,' I said, 'By the way, have you seen, the dollar?'

I was just trying to win him over, but I blew it. He started yelling about why the hell I was talking to him about the dollar right now, that that wasn't the question, that . . . he stopped short and asked, 'What about the dollar? What's going on with the dollar in your opinion?'

I pretended to be hurt by his reaction and said nonchalantly that there wasn't anything going on with the dollar, nothing at all . . . He finished my introductory training, but seemed rushed and worried. He quickly returned to his office, asking my colleague on the way, 'Have you seen, the dollar?' My colleague blanched and stood up as the boss slammed the door behind him.

Ten minutes later the entire bank was buzzing with people anxiously asking each other if they'd seen, the dollar?

I wasn't too unhappy with myself.

For a first day.

But let's get back to my job, which consisted of pushing a green button to open the door for those who looked worthy to enter the holy of holies of the golden calf, of consulting my superiors in questionable cases, and, as a very last resort—'kind of like a train whistle,' the assistant manager told me—of smashing my index finger down on the terrible red button that controlled the automatic closing mechanism on the heavy steel curtains and rang alarms on the bedside tables of all the local police chiefs. 'Was everything clear?' Clear as day, Mr Assistant Manager, sir. 'Let's go through it all one more time, shall we?' Docile, stupefied, the scrawny little chicken put his dried-up starfish of a foot on the button that released twelve grains of corn.

My first customer was the assistant manager himself. A test. Like the general who, despite his exhaustion and the late hour, goes to the trouble of making one last round through the camp to check that the guards are at their posts. He had put on some sort of balaclava and only his eyes were visible. He had gotten a hold of some long thin box and, after slipping out through the small back door, had come up to the main door and rung the bell. I reacted immediately and pushed the green button. I have to admit that his secretary Katia who, for some strange reason, had taken a liking to me had in the meantime whispered something about him in my ear. He seemed stunned to see the door opening in front of him. He hesitated a moment then rushed inside brandishing his package like a lunatic and yelling things we couldn't make out through the balaclava. I leapt up and yelled, 'Happy birthday, sir!' He stopped short, dumbfounded. I pictured his big mouth opened in an O under his stupid-arse mask. That's when Katia came out of his office carrying a cake covered with lit candles. 'Happy Birthday, sir.' What could he do?

Little things like these create bonds and that very night I went to bed with Katia. She found my studio very pleasant and told me that behind my constant snickering, she had immediately seen evidence of latent despair . . . Stark naked, I walked round the bed, took the tube of lipstick Stérile had forgotten out of the bedside table drawer and, smearing it all over my forehead, nose and cheeks, I told her not to waste any time thinking about it and as for the studio, I'd be moving out soon. Then I turned to face her, 'Whyyyeee?' She didn't find this in the least bit funny. She predicted I wouldn't last very long at Thingy & Co. She had no idea how right she was.

There was also the incident with the little old lady, one freezing November morning. I don't know why I didn't trust her. Maybe it was her big black bag with some vegetables sticking out. Is it not true that in films, weapons are usually concealed under several layers of cauliflower and turnips? 'What you got in your bag there, hayseed?' asks the cruel swordsman at the city gates. 'Cauliflower and turnips, Mr Soldier, sir, at your service,' the wily peasant answers. 'That's fine. Get a move on, you yokel, and take this in remembrance of me.' A kick in the arse. Be patient, peasant, the hour of revenge is at hand . . . Tssst. Besides, despite the way she'd begun hammering her umbrella on the front window after the third time she had rung the bell in vain, she still seemed so frail, the little old lady, so harmless that I couldn't help but think that this was the perfect disguise for any huge brute of a bank robber who wanted to appear harmless and frail. In short, the conditions for the second case were, in my mind, self-evident. I was therefore obligated to refer the situation to my superiors, leaving the alleged little old lady with her so-called vegetables to cool her heels in the icy North wind.

Katia wasn't in her office, so I had to knock directly on the assistant manager's door. Nothing. I knocked again and, when there was no response, I pushed open the padded door. The assistant manager was on the telephone. When he saw me, he motioned for me to come in and sit down. I sat in the hot seat and if I'm alive today to tell the tale it's only because the electric current to the chair I was sitting on had been cut off.

'Yeah,' he was saying into the receiver, 'yeah, I know . . . Speaking of which, have you seen, the price of gold? One hundred thousand this morning . . . What? . . . Of course, but at that level, who could have ever predicted it? Fine. I've got to go. Let's have lunch one of these days?'

He hung up, a long furrow between his eyes.

'Have you seen, the price of gold?'

'Disgusting,' I said.

Too late, but for form's sake, I counted to ten.

'What do you mean, "Disgusting"?'

'What I mean is that I've always found it ignoble, ugly, and stinking to high heaven that on the pretext that some distant country is having troubles, if it's not already drenched in blood, thousands of snivelling cowards here only are only worried about one thing: how they can speculate on anything and everything. Over there they're eviscerating each other, dying of hunger, the torturers are outdoing each other, entire towns are in flames—and what's on fire here? The stock market.'

'Well,' he said, 'well . . . When I considered the excellent tips you gave me on the dollar the other day, I thought of giving you a portfolio to manage . . . Who was it again, who hired you?

I reminded him.

'He's getting long in the tooth, the Old Man,' he murmured, lost in thought. 'Good, what was it you wanted?'

What I wan . . . Oh yes, that's right—the little old lady. She must have been freezing her balls off out there. Well, if she isn't *actually* a little old lady, that is. I explain my dilemma to the assistant manager.

'And that's why you're in here bothering me? . . .' he begins. Then, 'a little old *what*?'

I explain again from the top, the little old lady, the black shopping bag, the umbrella, the . . .

'Good God,' he bellows, 'Old Lady Bildanver . . .'

To summarize: she was an important client, Madame Bildanver, a shareholder and all that. The rest of the morning was spent trying to placate her and making her coffee to break the ice. Her suspicious-looking moustache was still bristling.

'What do you mean, "a suspicious-looking moustache"? What do you mean, "a suspicious-looking moustache"?' the assistant manager kept yelling once she had finally left the bank. 'Madame Bildanver has a little peach fuzz, at the most, on her upper lip. You're lucky your probationary period is three months long, because otherwise I'd fire your arse this very minute.'

And so my days at Thingy & Co. bank flowed by peacefully. With time, they grew somewhat used to me and my watchfulness relaxed slightly. In truth, I was so completely absorbed in a fascinating study the assistant director had loaned me—*How to Increase Bank Security*—that I hardly paid any attention to whomever was ringing the bell. Furious at being interrupted while reading a gripping crime novel—*The Central Bank Break-in*—that I was holding hidden inside the very interesting study so amiably lent to me by the assistant manager, I automatically pressed the green button and returned to my reading without even raising my head.

'You'd better be careful,' Katia said to me that night. 'I don't give a shit about the bank. They can clean it out from top to bottom for all I care. But I don't want anything to happen to you, my favourite zombie. You know, I am starting to like you and . . . *Would you please leave that tube of lipstick alone.*'

Yes—I pushed the red button. Just once. It was a week before the accident and two weeks before my probationary period was up. Something was telling me it would not be extended. I sometimes have premonitions like that. I wonder where they come from. I was gloomily watching the snow falling outside when I noticed a tramp walk up to one of the dustbins on the pavement right in front of Thingy & Co. and start rummaging around inside. The moron—what did he think he was going to find in a bank's dustbins? Some old cheque stubs, maybe, and all he could hope for from them is to find out what the rates of alimony support are from one end of the country to the next or how much dough some damn client wasted so that he could eat in some damn four-star restaurant.

And then suddenly, almost in slow motion, he collapsed between two dustbins. Splat, just like that, his face in the snow. He wasn't moving. I could see the soles of his shoes, worn through. He only had one sock. I pushed the red button.

'Don't shoot, I surrender,' the assistant manager yelled as he ran out of his office, hands in the air. 'The keys to the safe are . . .'

When he saw that everything was normal, he endeavoured to prove, ranting and raving at the top of his voice, that I was not.

'If you saw some guy lying on the pavement, dying of hunger, you wouldn't sound the alarm?' I asked, when I was finally able to get a word in.

'Of course not.'

All right then.

Murderer.

As for the cops, who flooded onto the scene as if they'd come to shut down a demonstration by North Africans, they proved rather understanding in the end.

'Certainly,' the ranking officer said to me, 'you were too cautious. But you were right to be so. One can *never* be too cautious. That said, if you do it again, and disturb us for nothing even just once more, you understand, you'll find out what the consequences are in the nick.'

And so my days at Thingy & Co. bank flowed by peacefully. I had learnt, on first arriving at the bank each morning, to ask in a calamitous tone, 'Have you seen, the dollar?' Or 'the Swiss franc,' or 'the German mark,' or 'the British pound,' or 'the price of gold.' At random and arbitrarily. It always worked. My only flop was when I asked one morning, 'Have you seen, the Italian lira?' The lira? No one knew what it was.

Then came Black Friday. I remember it was Friday because the day before was a Thursday and because I was looking forward to an entire weekend of waving my fist at the television since everything it showed seemed utterly inane to me. In short, on Thursday evening, I'd had my first real argument with Katia. 'Is it really not possible to talk to you about anything but the weather?' she had asked. 'Is it really not possible to talk to you about *us*, among other things, without you immediately smearing lipstick all over your face?' Again, in short, that Friday evening my buzzer went 'Bzzz' as usual and, as usual, I pushed the green button without looking up. I was too caught up in my crime novel to notice the particular kind of silence that spread through the bank until I noticed the barrel of a rifle pointing at my nose. I merely pushed it away with my hand, still not looking up, and said in irritation, 'Not a second time, sir, not a second time.'

I took it in the face, the gun. Or rather, the bullet. With such force that I thought my skull had cracked. I vaguely remember another round of gunfire, then nothing.

Later, in the hospital, when I opened my eyes, I realized one was missing.

All right then.

One was still enough to see that Katia was gone.

All right then.

'Damages? Damages? If I thought that they were going pay damages to some guy who was only on probation, well, here's a thumb in your eye . . . Oh, sorry.'

The nurse was not amused by the red lipstick all over my bandages. It looked like blood.

Sanbenito: *A rough penitential garment, often decorated with a red St Andrew's cross, that those condemned as heretics by the Holy Inquisition were forced to wear on certain days or their entire lives depending on the severity of the sentence.* Really?

Still shaken by what I'd been through, I sit down as best I can on three or four volumes of my encyclopaedia. What the hell are A and B doing, for Chrissake? And, obviously, there's no ashtray.

People are nuts. Out of their minds.

So just now, as I walked into my new building, I saw some cretin trying to shove two planks twice as tall as he was into the lift. Twice as tall as the lift, in other words. I point this out. Nicely. He looks me up and down and asks if it's any of my business. I can tell he's holding himself back from commenting on my eye.

Very well, my prince, you can figure it out on your own. But since it's going to be a while, I decide to take the stairs. In passing, I notice that someone has nicked the pommel at the base of the banister. As usual. Why the hell do they steal those things? All that's left is the yellow stem that the ball sat on. Like a skeletal finger pointing towards the upper floors. Brrr.

I follow the pointer and start climbing, lost in thought, imagining a kid sliding down astride the banister, going faster and faster until he impales himself on the metal stem, tearing his stomach open from bottom to top. Serves you right, snot-nose brat, that'll teach you to steal the pommels to play boules.

I'm so distracted that when I get to the fifth floor, I think I'm on the sixth. It's hardly surprising. The two floors are exactly symmetrical: same doors, same hallways. So I go to what I think is my room and put my key in the lock. Naturally, it doesn't work. I keep trying, without catching on. That's when

I hear, from inside the room, a sharp detonation and some plaster falls off the wall behind me. Good God, four inches from my head there's a hole this big.

'Are you dead?' calls a voice from inside.

I stammer no, but almost.

'That'll teach you,' says the voice. 'What do you think, that I'm going to let you break in to my place just like that, without defending myself? And if by some miracle the cops do catch you, you get to spend three weeks in prison with television and everything, then they can't release you fast enough so that you can start all over again. And now piss off before I shoot again.'

Those idiots who claim there's nothing more valuable than human life must not have owned any gold pieces or colour televisions or tea services inherited from Aunt Henrietta.

Someone knocks on the door. I jump up and yell, 'One more step and I'll shoot!'

Brick House's worried face appears.

'What the hell is wrong with you?'

And I tell him that nothing's wrong, nothing at all. I was just joking. And I tell them about my adventure.

'If we put a bullet in the brains of nut jobs like that,' Asparagus says, 'humanity would be no worse off. Speaking of nut jobs, there's some guy blocking the lift, trying to fit in two wooden planks that are two times too long.'

'Yes, I know,' I say. 'So what?'

'So we can't do anything until he's done.'

I point out that the lift is so small that hardly anything they have to bring up to my place would fit into it anyway.'

'And you think we're going to let ourselves get stuck dragging this stuff up the stairs when there's a lift,' Asparagus says.

I agree that yes, quite right, all the while thinking that something in what he's saying doesn't add up.

Turning in a circle, Asparagus makes the round of the property.

'We've seen bigger,' he says soberly. 'What's with the books on the floor?'

'My encyclopaedia,' I say. 'I moved it all on my own.'

Modest, but not unhappy with myself.

'It's not hard with the lift,' the other one grumbles. 'What are you worried about? That we'll get it dirty with our big old paws?'

Sensitive chap. So I have to tell him the whole story.

'Yeah,' he says, 'if you had taken it down yourself and given us a little something, we would have taken care of your encyclopaedia. In any case, it's done.'

'How about we play Second to Last while we're waiting . . . ?' Asparagus begins.

I say no, out of the question. And why don't they go take care of my things?

'What if the guy with the planks isn't done?'

'Push him around a little. You're movers, not choirboys.'

'Me, hunh?' says Brick, 'If you want to start off badly with your neighbours on the very first day, it's not my problem.'

'Given how things stand . . .'

It's true that the cowboy lives right under me. I'd better not make any noise after official hours. 'Would you like to dance, Duchess? Just one last dance before you head back to your fortress,' and boom! A bullet in the foot. I don't care. I hate dancing.

A thundering torrent rushes down the large pipe on my left. The Great Flusher upstairs is at it again. His television must be broken or it's time for commercials again. Good thing for commercials, otherwise I bet cases of constipation and enuresis would reach epidemic levels.

Leaning forward, trousers bunched round my ankles, my butt cheeks on the very edge of the seat, I try to find the volume for 'I', so that I can get depressed reading all about *Iraklion*. I imagine it's a beautiful island, Crete. If I were on it, I'd be lying there naked in the wind and the sun and would say to Watsernamia, my beautiful wahine with the strange name, that I almost felt I loved her. She would be naked as well, in the wind and the sun, a tang of salt on her skin, and we would return to our house carrying the seashells, pumice stones and starfish we'd gathered. Our house would be white and covered with creeping vines here and there. Inside, on a rustic table facing the enormous bay window, I would find three letters leaning against the bottle of ouzo. The first would contain a cheque for three thousand francs in payment for the inane story I'd have written practically in my sleep for a glossy magazine the month before. The second would certify, with X-rays as proof, that I have thirty more years to live and can smoke as many filterless cigarettes as I want. As for the third, some anonymous scrap of filth reminds me that war can rage in this country as well as in others and that on some days the water here teems with so many jellyfish, octopuses and squid, you're stranded on the beach, baking in the violent gusts of scorching wind. 'Whence the shadow that suddenly veils your steely blue gaze?' my wahine, Watsernamia, would ask. Clenching my jaws I would answer, 'Nothing, my love, nothing. Just the green-eyed monster.'

Where on earth could it be, the 'I' volume? After all, I'd arranged them carefully at first, alphabetically and everything. Three piles of eight, more or less. Who's been messing with my things?

An avalanche of fists against the door. This time the Sbritzkys have come by two. Like commandos. And they give me an ultimatum: either I come out *im-me-di-a-te-ly* or they're going to get the concierge, the firemen and the cops if they have to. Do I understand? I understand. I yell that I'm coming out. I readjust myself. I flush for form's sake.

'You should go see a doctor. It's not normal,' the woman spits out angrily when I pass them.

I don't answer and, while they rage at each other over who gets to go 'in there' first, I return to my room. Their television blares out the merits of a hyperactive anti-cavity toothpaste. As usual, the neighbour on my right is moaning non-stop.

I first met old man Sbritzky when A and B went back down to their lorry. I was stacking my encyclopaedias in one corner of the room when he pushed open the door. Without knocking, of course.

'I'm the neighbour. What kind of arsehole are you moving in here?'

OK, fine—I'm not decked out like the Prince of Wales, but still . . .

I try my best to smile and explain that I'm not the one doing the moving, but the one being moved. *Moved.*

'Is that right?' he asks, not in the least embarrassed, giving me the once over, head to toe. 'Is that right? Well, I hope we get along.'

I stammer that I do too.

'We're not difficult, the wife and me.'

I stammer that I don't think I am either . . .

'Besides, the wife and I are old enough to know that there's nothing like kids or dogs or some other animal to poison relations between neighbours.'

I reassure him. *Stephanie and her stuffed elephant.*

'Whatever. You're white, that's what counts.'

I stammer that yes, as a matter of fact, I . . .

Old bastard.

'By the way,' he continues, 'the concierge told me your name the other day. What kind of name is that?'

I mumble my little story.

'Really?' he says. 'Swiss? I wouldn't have thought . . . You understand, I don't have anything against yids . . . Jews, but they don't belong in this building, see?'

Yeah, I saw. My eye.

'And . . . and your eye—were you born that way or did you have an accident?'

Luckily there suddenly is violent knocking on the wall, so I don't have to answer.

'The wifey,' he says, 'She's calling me because our show is starting. You watch the noon serial?'

I'm not done mumbling that no, not really, not the one at noon, not the . . . In fact, I no longer have a television and . . .

He interrupts me. He's not at all interested in my mumbling. I don't blame him. But who made me start mumbling? The world is divided into two groups: arseholes and mumblers.

'Don't hesitate to bother us if there's anything you need,' he says. 'Anything *important*, that is, because my wife and I hate being disturbed.

He's got his hand on the doorknob. He's finally going to leave. He turns back, once more. He points his chin towards the wall that separates me from the other studio flat, the one to my right.

'As for that one,' he says, 'don't worry too much about her. You'll end up getting used to it.'

Finally, he's gone. I have no idea what he meant with his wink.

What the hell are they doing, my two mules? I'm anxious to have a few familiar things around me here. This room looks so cold and bare. Luckily I don't have a phone because if I did, I'm sure I'd call just about anyone. *Stérile*. 'It's the way it is, you know,' she said, 'we all have moments in our shitty lives when the egoism of the happy couple starts to leak and we remember those we left behind. That is precisely the time, if you want my advice, to take a sharp pair of scissors and cut your telephone wire into as many pieces as necessary.' And me, the idiot, on the other end of the line, I kept saying, 'What? What do you mean? What? What? What?' But I knew exactly what she meant. So I let it go and hung up.

The door flies open and Brick House appears, sagging under a box of books.

'Would you mind leaving the damn door open, for Chrissake?'

He puts down the box, wipes his forehead and tells me there's a snag.

'A snag?'

'Yeah. The top part of your bookshelves.'

'What about it?'

'It doesn't fit.'

'It doesn't fit where?'

'It doesn't fit, that's all, anywhere. There's no way we can bring it up for you. The lift is too low, too narrow.

I say that it's not possible. Just not possible. There has to be a way. I'm attached to my bookshelves. More than I am to all the rest.

'There might be one way,' he says. 'But I don't know if . . .'

'What? Bring it in through the window?'

He laughs—have I looked at the window?

Crestfallen, I lower my head. I have to admit that the window is small, that I hadn't noticed just how small.

'About all that would fit is that little book you've got.'

He's exaggerating.

'And your solution?' I ask.

'The guy with the planks,' he says.

Big old drunk of a sphinx, your arsehole riddles are starting to get on my nerves, to get under my feet. What has four legs in the morning, two at noon . . . ? Tssst.

'So what about the guy with the planks?'

'He says that if he saws off the top of your bookshelves, he's sure it can fit in the lift . . . And that works for him because there's no way he can get his own to fit.'

Silence.

'I wouldn't mind a drink,' I say.

'You don't really know what it is you want, do you?' Asparagus chimes in as he enters carrying two chairs.

I admit it. What I don't admit is that it wouldn't take much for me to burst into tears. To weep and weep for no reason.

'I think there's a bottle left in the lorry,' A says. 'And if you have some cash, I could buy another at the cafe. The more bottles there are, the more fun it is to play Second to Last.'

'Sure,' says B. 'But first, we finish the job.'

'Yippeee!' A yells, rushing out the door.

'What an overgrown kid,' Brick House smiles, shaking his head. 'OK, boss, what do we do with your bookshelves?'

'There aren't thirty-six solutions. If you really can't get it up here, then you have to take it to storage.'

'Yep. We'll have to charge you a supplement, then. Because it's not in the contract.'

To think that two or three of my Jewish ancestors were liquidated on the pretext that their business gene was overdeveloped.

'Listen for a minute,' I say, rubbing my hands together and scratching my nose which is hardly of Bourbon proportions—all the while stealing the money right out of his pocket, draining his kid's blood and poisoning his wells—'Listen, it's not *my* fault if your guy who came to do the inventory didn't pay attention to how many socks I had or whether or not my bookshelves would fit in the stairway . . .'

I'm always proud of myself when I have the guts to start yelling in business transactions. It makes me feel normal. Aryan.

Brick shrugs and says if I'm not happy I can just sue the office.

'Let's drop it. I'll pay what I have to.'

I'm sorry to bother you, Herr Obersturmbannführer, but I've lost the way. The road to Dachau is this way, isn't it?

The pipes are still gurgling. And the smell, shit . . . You've got to do what you've got to do. And that way, at least I know I'll be left in peace for a while. Theoretically, there's only Old Lady Sbritzky left on this floor and she has just returned to her happy home after relieving herself. Copiously, if you go by the black spots covering the bottom of the bowl. I sit down and take the volume on the top of the pile. The 'S' again. How did that happen? That's not how it should be. The 'S' doesn't go there. I'd like to know who . . . ? On the other hand, there's no rule saying that I have educate myself in alphabetical order. So here we go with S. I open it randomly. *Sephardi*. That vaguely reminds me of something. Let's see.

Sephardi: *Descendants of Jews who lived on the Iberian Peninsula during the Middle Ages. After their expulsion from Spain (1492), they settled in France, Holland, Great Britain, Italy, Turkey, Palestine and Northern Africa. Wherever they settled, they maintained their own customs, religion and 'Ladino' language, a sort of mediaeval Spanish with numerous Hebrew terms.* Really? *Following the Conquest of Constantinople, Turkey wanted to attract Iberian Jews and, after 1492, the Sephardi streamed in by the tens of thousands. 'Ye call Ferdinand a wise ruler,' the Sultan Bayezid is said to have exclaimed, 'he who has impoverished his own country and enriched ours?' There is an anecdote relevant to this topic.* Great! I love anecdotes. *A Jew in Turkey was trying to convince a friend who had stayed in Spain to join him in Edirne.* Where is that? I'll have to look it up. *He promises to lend his friend five thousand florins upon his arrival and, in advance, sends him five hundred which the friend could consider his own if the lender did not keep his promise to provide him with the balance. Seduced by the offer, our Spanish Jew soon arrives in Edirne. Whereupon the first Jew not only refused to lend him the remaining four thousand five hundred florins, but demanded that the five hundred advanced be reimbursed. They go to consult a wise rabbi who condemns the new arrival and requires him to pay back the five-hundred-florin advance because the first had acted in order to rescue the second from the hell of Christian Spain.* And wham!

And wham on the door as well. Then Sbritzky's belligerent voice wanting to know if I'll be much longer. The old witch, I'm sure she's doing it on purpose to annoy me. She left less than five minutes ago. She can't already be . . .

'Should I bring your books up anyway?' Brick asks.

'Yes,' I say. 'I'll find room for them wherever I can.'

'With all these here, it's not going to be easy,' he says, pointing at the stack of encyclopaedias.

Do not ask him if it's any of his business. Do not ask him if it's any of his business. Do not ask him . . .

'Is it any of your business?' I ask without thinking.

'Fine. I was only saying . . .'

Silence. He's about to leave.

'I apologize,' I say. 'I'm a bit stressed and . . .'

'It doesn't matter,' he says, turning back at the doorstep. 'You know, compared to some customers, you're relatively normal . . .'

That's reassuring. Very reassuring.

'Oh really? What kinds of things do they do?'

'My colleague can tell you better than I can, if you're interested. He writes everything down. He claims that with the current craze for memoirs, there's no reason people won't be after him.'

'His,' I say.

'What?'

'Nothing,' I say.

He shrugs and goes out the door. I light a . . . Damn! The ashtray! I rush outside and lean over the banister.

'Could you bring up the box with the ashtrays?'

'What?' he calls from the floor below.

I repeat my question, louder. He yells back, not without common sense, that he has no way of guessing which box that is. I admit, yelling, that his reasoning is sound and it's too bad. At that moment, my neighbour to the left suddenly appears on the landing, not looking very happy, and says—yells?—something I can't hear over the roars from his television coming through the open door. I point at my ears, shaking my head. 'Turn down the sound some, for Chrissake, Sbritz,' he bellows from his doorstep. Apparently full of goodwill, the cops and robbers in the television series put a quiet end to their blunderbusses. Phew. Sbritzky turns back towards me and asks me, at the top of his voice, if maybe I'm finished yelling like a banshee on the landing. He can't hear a goddamn thing at home, shit. He stomps back into his den and slams the door behind him. I do the same. Now, really.

'Now, really. You must be kidding.' Brick yells. 'Did you vow to make me crazy or what? You think it's easy to twist round with twenty kilos on your back and push the goddamn handle down with your elbow?'

He can't even keep from flying off his own handle. Tssst.

I promise to be more careful.

'Whatever you say,' he mutters, 'we're almost done.'

'That's good,' I say, going to close the door.

'For Chrissake! I said *almost*.'

'That's good,' I say, going to open the door.

'Thank you,' I hear from a winded box under which I can make out Asparagus' head. 'Where d'you want it? It's getting crowded in here . . .'

'Put it on the bed for now. We'll see later.'

'Well, I wish you a good night's sleep,' he says, laughing hysterically. Then to Brick, 'OK, all we have left is the table. That's about it.' Once again, to me, 'You got the money for the second bottle?'

I don't want to drink any more, but I don't dare tell him. Let's go on a tangent.

'What makes you so sure I'm the one who's going to lose?'

He's laughing, the son of a bitch. Laughing himself sick. My tangent didn't work out.

'What makes me . . . ? What makes me . . . ? You're right, boss. I'll gladly advance you the money, as long as you have enough to pay me back later . . .'

Two floors down, I can still hear him laughing. You'll see, wisearse, you will see what you will see. I am resolved.

I already feel sick.

Now the moment has come. Each of us is sitting, as best he can, on three or four volumes of the encyclopaedia in a circle round an upside-down box on which there are two bottles. Brick has just said that they'd better not take too long because the office might start asking questions. The office knows they aren't exactly moving Versailles on this job . . . He took a look around and said that even if part of my bookshelves is missing, I hadn't done too badly.

If he says so. There are books everywhere, in stacks along the walls, under the table, under the bed, on the chairs . . .

'If it weren't for your encyclopaedias . . .' he adds, looking at me out of the corner of his eye.

It is true that they're in the way. We've moved them at least ten times from one side of the room to the other as A and B brought in pieces of furniture or boxes. As though on purpose, the encyclopaedias were always exactly in the wrong spot. 'Couldn't you move those books so I can put this box down?' Brick grumbled, staggering under the weight in his arms. 'Say,' Asparagus giggled, 'if you'd like me to put your table up against the wall, you'll have to move your encyclo-pedestrians.' And the two of them, in chorus, 'We're going to end up breaking our necks if you keep leaving these piles in the way.' I squatted down and pushed. I knelt down and pulled. I bent down and . . .

It was our fifteen minutes of cultural exercise.

'I can see why you don't need your television any more, what with the racket she's making next door.' Asparagus says, uncorking the bottle. 'You'll save on the bill, too. And I'll tell you something: nine-tenths of the movies and documentaries are so—how can I put it?—so explanatory, so long-winded that you hardly need the pictures.'

'Yeah,' I say, 'and it's not every day we get lucky and a major film director dies so that we can finally watch an interesting retrospective.'

'Are we drinking or chatting?' asks Brick, apparently irritated by our aesthetic reflections.

Now I'm up against the wall. You can tell the drunks when they're up against the litre.

Why would they change their tactics, since it worked so well with me? *In my place*? Two exploratory rounds and the bottle falls to me, half full.

The first two gulps go down reasonably well. Then the mouth of the bottle starts knocking against my teeth. Two streams, nose to nose, equally strong. Which one will flow into the other? Through my eye, hazy with tears, I can see Asparagus snickering. One more gulp, two . . . It feels like it's going up my nose. Nausea. I lower the bottle and take a deep breath. Hiccup.

'Give it here,' Brick says, holding out his hand.

'Wait.'

I bring the bottle back up to my lips. I can feel the pressure of the liquid against my closed mouth. The kiss of death. What I am doing, no animal ever . . . I open my lips and my cheeks balloon. Either I swallow or I . . . I swallow. Earth, tannin, barrel, cork. And that red-hot rod boring into my forehead. Come on, just three more swallows and I'm done. Three more mouthfuls, gentlemen, and I admit to everything. *Yes—I rested on the Sabbath*! But take this funnel from me. I can't take it any more. My stomach is ready to burst. Swallow, cretin. For God's sake, swallow.

I swallow. And I turn to Asparagus. I would like to say a word about my triumph, but I'm worried that if I open my mouth, I . . .

'Yeah,' he says in complete bad faith, 'it's not very clever to force yourself to drink just so you can win. You should see your face . . .'

I manage a smile, not a brilliant smile but a smile all the same.

'Are you contesting my victory?'

'Oh, victory . . . Victory. . . There's still the second bottle . . .'

I look at it cross-eyed. With just one eye, it takes some doing. I see double. With just one eye, that's miraculous. The volcano in my stomach has calmed down some. The last lava flow dwindles into the sea. And then I get the giggles.

'What is so funny?' asks Brick, who is already attacking the other bottle's cork.

'Nothing,' I say, 'I was just thinking . . .'

Four o'clock in the morning. I'm almost certain no one will disturb me at this hour. And yet, the pull chain is still swaying. Strange. A draught? 'The man who only had a toilet pull chain left to hang on to.' It's hard to laugh on your own at four in the morning.

I sit down without dropping my trousers—this late, I doubt I'll need an alibi.

Let's see: What was it I wanted to look up the other day? Ah yes, that city, what was it again? **Edirne.** It's just amazing, this encyclopaedia. All the knowledge in the world. So many things I don't know. So many facts I don't give a shit about . . . Tssst.

I'm cold.

Naturally, the 'E' is in the wrong place. Between the 'S' and the 'T'. If I get my hands on the bastard who gets his jollies from . . .

Edirne. Edirne . . . **Eden** . . . **Edinburgh** . . . Ah, here we are! **Edirne (Adrianople):** *Capital of the Edirne Province in Turkish Thrace. Situated near the Greek border on the banks of the Tunca River where it meets the Maritsa, almost two hundred and thirty-five kilometres from Istanbul.*

The modern history of this city (population fifty thousand) was eventful. The city was part of Turkey from 1362 to 26 March 1913 (except for two periods of Russian occupation in 1829 and 1878). Edirne became part of Bulgaria from March to July 1913, then reverted to Turkey until August 1920. From that date until November of the same year, the town fell under Greek jurisdiction before the Treaty of Lausanne . . . hmmm, another godforsaken place that reminds me of something . . . *definitively* (?) *returned it to Turkey.*

Well now. Maybe there was a soccer field behind Selim II's mosque. One of those good old fields with just enough rope between the spectators and the players and a tiny wooden gallery to shelter the tiny prominent citizens. I can picture it as clearly as if I were there—the local cripple at the gate, almost invisible in his hut, with his two fascinating rolls of blue and red tickets. I can smell it as if I were there—the heavy, pungent smell of ointment from the locker rooms . . .

EDIRNE CITY STADIUM

21 October 1877

TURKEY VS RUSSIA. The crowd: 'Go Turkey, Go Turkey, Go!' A joker: 'Go Russia!' Trampled.

10 March 1878

RUSSIA VS TURKEY. The crowd: 'Go Russia, Go Russia, Go!' A yokel: 'Go Turkey!' Lynched.

15 July 1900

TURKEY VS BULGARIA. The crowd: 'Go Turkey, Go Turkey, Go!' A visionary: 'Go Bulgaria!' Shot.

8 April 1913

BULGARIA VS TURKEY. The crowd: 'Go Bulgaria, Go Bulgaria, Go!' A scatterbrain: 'Go Turkey!' Stoned.

29 May 1919

TURKEY VS GREECE. The crowd: 'Go Turkey, Go Turkey, Go!' A dreamer: 'Go Greece!' Dismembered.

1 August 1920

GREECE VS TURKEY. The crowd: 'Go Greece, Go Greece, Go!' An amnesiac: 'Go Turkey!' Beheaded.

19 November 1920

TURKEY VS GREECE. The crowd: 'Go Turkey, Go Turkey, Go!' A nostalgic: 'Go Greece!' Drawn and quartered.

It's enough to make you schizophrenic, for God's sake, having to change jerseys constantly. Or you could just put on a white one and become a shrink.

Cold.

There's a knock on the door.

'Not now,' I say, startled. 'You know what time it is?'

'Yeah, and?' says Sbritzky's voice, 'There are set times for pissing now? That's rich . . .'

It's all I can do to turn my head and face Asparagus without using both hands. Heavy, so heavy. And yet, the commands for it to move are coming from my head. They don't have to go far. Not as far as commands for my toes. Picture Asparagus' face if, slowly, oh so slowly, I turn my toes towards him. I snort stupidly.

'No one would accuse you of being a modest winner,' he says. 'But wait 'til the second bottle before you start showing off.'

'Pfff,' I say, 'enough said. But first, before the becond sottle, the second bottle, I wanted to ask something. Your buddy told me that the people you move sometimes act strangely. Could you tell me stories . . .'

'Why do you want to know?'

'Just because. I'm curious.'

'You're not going to use it in a book or anything like that?'

I burst out laughing.

'You see *me* writing a book?'

It's his turn to laugh.

'No, I really don't.'

'There you go,' I say.

'Should I tell him the one about the bathtub?' A asks B.

Who shrugs. Unless it was some gesture with his wrist to uncork the bottle. Or both at the same time.

'If it makes you happy,' he says, 'but don't forget we don't have all day, right?'

'So there's this . . .' Asparagus begins.

And wham! It hits me again. My pelvis goes shooting forward and my right leg juts out straight completely on its own. I have to place my right hand on the floor to keep from falling off my encyclopaedias. My left hand is balled into a fist. If I had a mirror, I suppose I'd see a contorted grimace of pain. And a little fog. As long as there's fog, there's hope.

'Are you OK?'

'I'm fine. I'm fine . . . It's nothing. It happens to me once in a while. Like a stabbing pain or a red-hot iron in the . . . in my . . . Well, I mean, in my posterior.'

'In your arsehole, you mean?'

I nod. The shockwave slowly dissipates.

'You should see a doctor, you know,' Asparagus says.

I shake my head. Everything starts spinning. A black veil. 'Ground control to Tango Ziglio? Hello Tango Ziglio? Hello? Come in Tango Ziglio.'

'I'm OK,' I say, still grimacing, finally landing on my stomach. 'I'm doing well, in fact. So your story—are you going to tell it?'

'You're sure that . . . ?'

'I'm in perfect shape, I'm telling you. A nice little room, freshly repainted, a good bottle, agreeable companions, what more could I ask for?

'Minimum wage at two thousand seven hundred francs,' Asparagus answers without missing a beat.

'Leftist,' Brick says as he sniffs at the bottle.

I nip their argument in the bud. 'So what about your story?'

Then I wipe my hands on my trousers. Disgusting, that nipped bud.

'Right. One day we're moving a certain Mr Something-or-Other. I won't tell you his real name. First of all, I've forgotten it and second of all, we have our professional secrets, our Aesculapian oath. In any case, it wasn't a very interesting moving job because the customer had insisted on packing everything himself. He was taking food right out of our mouths, this guy. We were only there to carry his things—pack animals in other words, Negroes as my friend would put it, who thinks anyone with even a slightly tan complexion is good only for sweeping the streets or raping our women.'

I raise my hand to prevent an eventual quarrel. Brick House, however, is too busy memorizing the label on the wine bottle and doesn't react.

'On the appointed day, we ring his doorbell. No answer. We ring again. Still nothing. So we make sure we've got the day and the customer right because, between you and me, the office sometimes gives us the wrong address. Not very often, but it happens. Or the wrong floor. That reminds me. One day the office told us the fourth floor instead of the fifth. Disciplined as we are, we go to the fourth and ring the bell. 'Gentlemen?' says the guy. Then we tell him we've come for the move. He gives a big sigh and tells us to come in and do our work, and adds that he didn't know the marshal's ashes had been repatriated . . . The thing is, we later found out his name was Rosenthal . . . Hey, Brick! I said Rosenthal. Ro-sen . . .'

'Dirty Jew,' Brick says automatically, without raising his head.

'You see how ingrained it is? . . . In any case, it was the right day and the right customer. So we go down to the concierge on the chance she knows what's up. We go down to her place and she's floored. 'What do you mean, not home, Mr Something? What do you mean not home? Of course he's at home, because he's moving out this morning . . .' We tell her we doubt that he's moving today because, you see, that's what we're here for. She starts exclaiming, 'How silly of me, and won't you have a drink, sirs?' We don't say no and knock one back quickly. Then we go back upstairs with the concierge and her master key. We ring again, still nothing. The chatterbox says no mistake, this isn't normal, we've got to go in, she'll take it all on herself. 'And the back of my hand, you'll take that too?' my partner here very cleverly thinks it necessary to add. I tell her he's joking, that he's always got a wisecrack, that he has a *terrible* sense of humour. She plays along, more or less, after all he's three times her size. In any case, we enter the silent, darkened room, but it's just light enough for me to see that the flat is completely prepared for the move, the boxes sealed and stacked, rugs rolled up, not a nail on the wall or a pin on the floor, perfect, I'm telling you, immaculate, not a speck of dust and . . .

'Aren't you thirsty?' Brick interrupts.

'Just a minute, damn it, I'm finishing . . . At that point, the concierge pushes open the bathroom door and lets loose a scream that is still ringing in my ears. She staggers backwards and falls into the big guy's arms.'

'I'm not fat,' says Brick.

'Well, as you've probably guessed, the guy had slit his wrists in the bathtub—not a pretty picture. The concierge told us then that he'd been looking for work for months without luck and maybe at the last minute he couldn't take the thought of emigrating to cheaper digs with lots of immigrants and hoi polloi . . . Funny, hunh?

He really does seem to find it amusing.

'If you say so,' I say. 'I was expecting something a bit more . . . well, picturesque.'

'You think my story wasn't picturesque? Maybe I could also tell you the one about the divorced couple where the woman was leaving the flat and they were insulting each other right in front of me—I've never heard anything like it—over the slightest thing she wanted to take with her, the least little spoon, the tiniest bauble. Wham, she'd throw something in the box and bam, he'd pull it out again. Wham, she'd throw it back in and bam, he'd pull it back out. She called him every name in the book, wanted me to be her witness, me, trembling little sod behind them. Had I ever seen a bastard like that, such a piece of shit? And him: a dirty slut like her, you met many? Good Lord, I didn't know where to hide. The more I tried to calm them down, reminding them there was once a time when they held hands and exchanged tender glances over the *same* wedding gifts, the more they . . .'

'You know what time it is?' asks Brick, who slams the bottle down so hard on the box a bit of wine spills out and drips down the neck.

At least that's a bit more gone. At least that's a little bit less I'll have to drink.

'OK, old man,' Asparagus says. 'Let's play, drink and take off.'

He's got the bottle in his hand. He looks at me, sizes me up, assesses me. Am I up to repeating my exploit? He apparently decides I'm not because, despite their earlier defeat, he doesn't change his initial tactic of swallowing just one mouthful on the first round. Brick does exactly the same. And I get the bottle just about three-quarters full.

Suspense.

Brick House stares at me with a frown. Looks like I've finally managed to worry him a bit. It's not exactly a huge consolation, but it's better than nothing. I'd like to draw this moment out. Facing the best gunman in the West, I hit the target on my first shot entirely by chance. Didn't even know which end of the 6.35 calibre was which. But now the hour of revenge is at hand and Buffalo Bill is staring at me with a frown.

'You going or what?'

Pretty arrogant tone.

I bring the bottle to my lips. The odour, good God, the odour alone, is . . . You'd think I was getting ready to drink fresh paint off the walls . . . A good, thick paint, nice and oily with greyish fingerprints here and there. I hiccup. A spasm spreads from the depths of my gut. I hand the bottle abruptly to Asparagus, excuse myself, and lunge at the sink behind the screen. The sink is dotted with cigarette butts, tails in the air and shreds of tobacco clinging to them. I just have time to catch a glimpse of my ugly mug and bloodshot eyes in the mirror, then I lower my head and I let loose and let loose.

If there were a dog around, I'd bet my last shirt that it was never as sick as I was.

'We decided to finish the bottle,' says Asparagus when I come out from behind the screen. 'We figured that you . . . What's the red stuff all over your face?'

'Nothing. Nothing.'

They look at each other. They stand up. They look embarrassed. Why?

'I was saying, we decided to finish the bottle ourselves. We figured you wouldn't . . . that is . . . Now we'll draw up the bill and we'll go. We're already pretty late.'

Since they're the ones who finished the bottle, under no circumstances can I be the second to last. Irrefutable reasoning. *Un-der no cir-cum-stances.*

Bent over the table, Brick scribbles on a scrap of paper.

'So, in addition to the move,' he tells us, 'we . . .'

He stops, pen in the air. The Sbritzkys' television has momentarily gone quiet and from the other flat, the one on the right, we can hear very clearly long moans alternating with groans and hiccups.

'Shit,' Asparagus says, 'is she getting laid or dying?'

Brick shrugs.

'This is some place,' he says. Then, 'So in addition to the move, strictly speaking, you owe us two bottles . . . What?'

'Nothing,' I say. 'I didn't say anything.'

'Two bottles, plus the cost of taking the radiator to the dump, plus the tip you're not allowed to give us of at least twenty per cent. Which comes to . . .'

'You know, she really seems to be in there by herself,' Asparagus interrupts, his filthy ear glued to the wall. 'I don't hear anyone else. Do you think she might be . . .'

'The toilets are on the landing, at the end of the hallway,' I say affably.

He gives me a dirty look.

'Did anyone ask you where the crapper is?'

I stammer that no, no one did. You do someone a favour, and . . .

In short, I write a cheque and hand it to Brick. He's facing me on the other side of the table. I take a few notes from my pocket, bend down and hand them to him. Under the table.

Once again, I'm the only one who thinks I'm funny.

'OK, boss,' says A, who has returned to the middle of the room, and trips over a stack of encyclopaedias, 'OK. The office hopes that you're happy with us and that you won't hesitate to call if ever you move again.' Then to B, 'First time I've managed to say that bullshit without screwing up.'

Leaving.

My buddies are leaving.

And I'll be left here alone.

Alone.

'Listen,' I say, 'listen, I've probably got some whisky around here somewhere. You're not just going to leave . . . After all, you're my first guests in the new palace and . . .'

Drank enough already. Drunk enough. Don't like scotch.

Oh well.

Door opens onto dark landing. We shake hands and all that. Brick wades into the hallway.

'Trust me, you should take a look in the mirror,' Asparagus says quickly. 'You've got red stuff all over your face.'

The door closes.

Me and me for the first time in a tête-à-tête in my new home.

At the Sbritzkys', an expert explains to the dear television audience how to get rid of their varicose veins. I'm wondering if the other neighbour's moaning is preferable.

My attempt to throw myself down on the bed, head spinning, seeing double, did not do me much good. I'd forgotten the two or three volumes of the encyclopaedia half-hidden under the covers.

Jews (wedding ceremony): *Jewish weddings are celebrated with lavish, extended festivities, even in less wealthy households. The ceremony displays a wise balance between gravity and joy, sorrow and rejoicing, symbolizing both union and separation. In her paternal home, the future bride mourns the end of her childhood, clings to her mother's apron strings, proclaims her fear, her dislike even, of the 'strangers' who are her future groom and his parents. Sincere or feigned, the ceremony plays upon the leitmotiv, rhymed, sung and orchestrated, of 'Weep, oh bride, weep!'*

Yeah, right—weep, oh my Stérile.

Our harmony lasted long enough for Stérile and me to hear the 'yes' said without conviction that everyone pronounces before an indifferent functionary who, we learn later, is in a hurry to finalize his own divorce in a neighbouring office.

Then we gradually sank into our mutual deafness, troubled only now and then by a few echoes of 'Shut up!'

There is nothing funny about it.

As is the custom, the door to the marriage bureau was left open so that at any time, right up to the last second, anyone at all could burst in and raise objections to the proceedings, objections which both of us were willing to consider with the utmost goodwill. But no one spoiled the festivities. Instead of rendering this kind of small service, it would seem that in these circumstances, friendship requires that one stuff one's face at the princess' expense and deliver, in an advanced state of inebriation, tearful and inane wishes for happiness. Not to mention the fight over the garter belt, the smell of cigars or the refined commentary, once night has fallen, that accompanies the departure of the bride and groom.

Around midnight, reasonably drunk but not so far gone that I could not rely on my senses, I discovered that Stérile was not a virgin. No one takes into consideration, when sleeping with his future wife before the wedding, the shock such a revelation can bring on one's wedding night.

'I assume you're joking, 'Stérile had said before turning her back to me and falling asleep, 'because with you, you never can tell . . .'

I, too, supposed I was joking and that I had never *seriously* intended to hang a blood-spotted sheet from the balcony so that no one, *urbi et orbi*, would be unaware. And I enjoyed the thought of how the five hundred thousand faithful gathered in St Peter's Square would react if one glorious Easter morning, instead of the long-awaited apparition, a zealous cardinal were to hang such a trophy from the pontifical balcony.

Even though this wasn't funny, I shook so much that the bedsprings started squeaking and Stérile moaned in her sleep. If the neighbours were listening at the wall, they'd have assumed the two of us were not exactly bored. My honour, at least, was safe.

I, too, would have liked to sleep. It helps pass the time. But since I couldn't, I started thinking about our next trip.

As much out of respect for a tradition we found ridiculous as to celebrate such a lugubrious event, we had agreed that, in the guise of a honeymoon trip, we would get off on each other and take off—by air—to that town in Turkey, the cradle of my family, and then would kvetch and catch a flight to Israel where I thought an uncle of mine, about whom I knew nothing—not even his name, and his honourable wife Felicity had ended up after yet another move and where, full fathom five, their days flowed by. Or maybe in the back of a launderette. I knew nothing about them. Nothing. They were my closest relatives on that side of the family and I knew nothing about them. Nothing. Only once in his life—apart from the group photo that I only discovered well after his death—did my father unbutton his white coat in order to take from his vest pocket a photograph of a small girl about my age, in her Sunday best in honour of some ritual festivity. Not in honour of Sunday per se, in any case, because for them as for me, though for different reasons, that day is a day like any other. Confusion. 'It's your cousin,' my father had said. *Shalom*, cousin. Special *Slalom*. Ah. Ah. Ah. Tssst . . . I looked at the picture for a long time. Too long, probably. Because once I'd got up the courage to ask the man in the white coat what this cousin's first name was, he had already rebuttoned it up to his neck.

Farewell, cousin.

'I could visit the mosque of whichever Selim it was,' Stérile had said, 'and while I'm there, you could hunt down your past . . .'

You could never tell whether she was joking.

Still, I didn't really turn down her suggestion. I was getting old, dammit. For all those years in Switzerland and the first few years in Paris—up until my marriage, in fact—youth, my youth, had seemed a vast territory to exploit, and mysterious enough as well, exciting enough, that I didn't waste a single minute contemplating the various cemeteries, crematoria and other mass graves in which an unknown number of my ancestors were rotting in general indifference. 'Mr Undertaker, while I don't doubt your good intentions, I respectfully request that you stop sending me a report at the beginning of each year on the occupant of grave number one eighty-seven.'

Mhhmm.

And who knows if the fact that, after so many centuries of tribulations, voluntary or not, the man in the white coat had chosen to settle in the most homebound country there is and to assume its religion, its nationality and the running of a very honourable, if a little screwy, institution—the right to asylum and to be the director of one—who knows, then, if this fact did not play a big part in my indifference towards my family history? I had a well-placed role model, after all. And if, finally, after endless upheavals, indescribable massacres, visas by the truck load, dozens of residency permits revocable at will, mass deportations, dubious certificates of statelessness and years of more-than-irregular status in a certain number of more or less hostile countries, if, finally, thanks to him, I received in my crib, on a platter as it were, the Swiss passport that is the envy of the world, should I be more Catholic than the Pope and badger him with questions about a past that he patently did not want to discuss with me?

Forgive me for being so long-winded.

Then he died.

Without apologizing for being short-winded.

That's life.

Through the intermediary of a lawyer who had bent over backwards to get their address, I wrote my first and last letter to Uncle Thingy and Aunt Felicity. They had inherited an old slipper—the second of the pair was nowhere to be found, a narghile, a curved dagger, a box of Turkish delight that was no longer very fresh and a set of encyclopaedias in twenty-five volumes. I was keeping all of the above at their disposal or that of their descendants'. There was no answer.

(I still have it! If they read me! Cousins! Blessed be the Literature that brings our relatives back to us! Hilarious.)

Through their wobbly stumps of teeth and a shower of spittle, wise men sometimes claim that when a man dies, a library burns. That may be. But as for me, I inherited a superb library of which not a single superb book answered the least little question I would have wanted to ask the deceased. I burnt every last one of them and covered my head with the ashes. Old custom, isn't it? I do know, however, that there was much whispering to the effect that, before coming to the funeral, I could at least have washed my hair.

Time passed. I emigrated, got married, lost illusions and hair by the fistful, and soon felt so old, so ugly, so dusty, that I imagined the child that I had, it seems, once been coming to trace with his pink index finger in the grime on my back window or on my bonnet the words 'Wash me' or 'Filthy arsehole' or 'Dirty old pig' . . . It didn't help to keep telling myself that the fantastic privilege of old age is being able to act young when it's too late. This powerful, sibylline thought was poor consolation and did little to dislodge the leaden ball of anxiety that made my stomach clench certain nights before I fell asleep.

Which is saying something.

Which is also to say that the closer the moment approached when no one would be left to close my eyes, the stronger grew my desire to know, before it was too late, that exotic patch of ground where the man in the white coat was born and to learn a bit more about him from whatever family wreckage might still be floating around between Adrianople and Tel Aviv. Or at least about myself.

A plan endlessly cherished and endlessly aborted until the day Stérile, looking for a place that was sticky and sweet enough to properly accommodate a honeymoon, put her finger on the map: Didn't your family come from somewhere around here?

Somewhere around there, that's true.

She persisted, asking if it wasn't an excellent idea to kill two birds with one stone and combine our honeymoon trip with a return to my origins? The groom's get-up with the pilgrim's garb, that would be funny, wouldn't it?

No.

For all sorts of reasons, I'd have preferred we go to her part of the world, somewhere in the suburbs. But the prospect of a half-hour trek in an overcrowded bus did not exactly appeal to her. Seizing the travel guide that was always lying around our bathroom between the spare toilet paper and the deodorant, she started to list all the monuments, museums and mosques she could visit while I was ringing my forefathers' doorbell.

Weary of battle, I surrendered.

And, two days before our departure, down in Uncle Thingy's hometown, one of those good old classic wars broke out, the main effect of which was to close all the airports to strangers and permanently close the eyes of several thousand native inhabitants. Make sure you dress warmly before you go out, Aunt Felicity.

Stérile declared that this really was bad luck; the one time she got married, war could damn well have broken out somewhere else.

Several months later, after the bomb craters in the runway had been filled in and the big silver birds could once again deposit their quota of pasty tourists and red-faced businessmen sweating with excitement at the thought of selling to both sides the weapons that would enable them without fail to win the next war, she and I were so far beyond any honeymoon, there was no longer any question of travelling. With each passing day it became ever more obvious that one of us was not cut out for marriage. Each of us, of course, was convinced that the other was the problem.

As if that made any difference.

The brotherhood of lawyers all over the world came together to inform me that my nameless uncle was done for. From what I understood, an explosive from God knows where fell right on him as he stood in queue with a jug in each hand waiting his turn for water at the one tap that still worked in his devastated neighbourhood.

Biblical.

Still, unlike the explosive, I had missed him by a hair.

At the risk of spending all my money on official documents, I commissioned the lawyer to enquire into Aunt Felicity's fate. 'Or Felicia. Or Felice. Figure it out.'

The answer, for once, did not take long. She had given up the ghost almost five years before. After the other war her health, don't you know, was not what it used to be. 'At least she didn't have to live through the most recent war,' the lawyer kindly pointed out.

My cousin, my cousin, now you're an orphan.

At this juncture, Stephanie was born.

Life went on.

The first time I saw her, what struck me most were her eyes. When she bothered to open them, she stared at me as if she were never going to see me again.

On that score, she was mistaken. Visitation rights, for God's sake, weren't invented for pigs.

But I'm putting the cart before the horse.

After the man in the white coat disappeared, the disappearance of Uncle Thingy made me, as far as I know, the last male representative of the family to the west of the Bosphorus.

That such a cosmopolitan lineage—full of sound and fury, blood, sweat and tears—should be represented from now on by a furtive, cretinous little homebody like me, was certainly laughable. And I laughed as I sat with my behind perched on the ice-cold throne and put a crown of twisted toilet paper upon my half-bald head. David, you should have been present to imbue this coronation with immortality. Or Goliath—I'm not so rebellious as that. Advice to treasure hunters and other archaeologists: the crown of Luc IV, chief of the Ziglio clan, should be floating in the sewers somewhere between here and the sea.

But my vague desire to conduct myself like a responsible patriarch clashed with Stérile's utter incomprehension. When, for example, I proposed right away that we engage Stephanie to be married to the pharmacist's son who was also about six months old and seemed to promise a brilliant future, she tapped her finger on her temple and asked me what godforsaken barbarian country I thought I lived in.

Other countries, other customs.

And so it went. In this vein, even though Stephanie was undeniably a girl, her mother and I judged it best to argue occasionally about whether we would have had her circumcised had she been a boy. What gave the argument a certain piquancy was that Stérile, Christian and Aryan since the beginning of days, was in favour of circumcision for hygienic reasons, whereas I, descendant from a herd of Jews, was against it. Out of prudence.

'What if it all were to start up again?' I would say, 'Then it would be best to give our children as many chances to remain undetected as possible.'

It was a harmless enough remark, yet it never failed to drive Stérile around the bend. And out of our flat. When she came back, her eyes a bit too bright and having left me in charge of changing, feeding and rocking Stephanie to sleep, Stérile would fall into my arms and hug me close, sobbing that I was insane, that it would never start up again, never, nev-er, but even if, by some extraordinary chance, the persecutions of years past did resume, weren't we fortunate to live in a country that would not allow a single hair of its citizens to be harmed? Pensively, I'd answer that I wasn't sure of it, no, not at all sure.

'Imagine,' I'd say, 'imagine a random government of lunatics—you can find them round the world—threatening to shut down the oil pipelines or to set off some cute little atomic bomb if the local Jews weren't expelled within thirty-six hours. What do you think would happen?

She looked at me for a second, mouth open, then shook her head violently and, deploring the fact that the man in the white coat wasn't here any more to allocate one of those nice padded rooms to me at no cost, went to burp our daughter. Maybe to knock back a final glass as well, so they could burp in unison.

Please excuse me.

Other times, she would light into me, claws out, and demand that I stop once and for all my ridiculous routine about the enormous gap between two borders, two cultures, two worlds. It didn't matter how often I told her that, with regard to time and space, it would, after all, have taken very little indeed for me to open my eyes under far less clement skies and, things being what they were at the time, I'd have run the risk of closing them earlier than necessary—in my opinion—only slightly reddened by the gas. No matter how I tried to explain that this newly acquired nationality, acquired almost by chance and in passing, could not magically erase thousands of years of history with a single seal, a single stamp, a single certificate, no matter how official-looking the parchment, she was not persuaded. She thought my approach was nothing but masochism and tearfulness.

'You'd be better off looking after the living,' she'd say, 'after Stephanie and me, among others—we're *your* family, too, aren't we?—instead of chewing over this dying past, about which, by the way, you know next to nothing.'

She was exaggerating, as usual. I was far from obsessed with my family history at the time. Let's just say I found it intriguing. I would have liked to know, for example, how an oriental Jew—the son, I was pretty sure, of an exotic grocer—could have become a respectable Swiss psychiatrist.

'You're *pretty sure*,' Stérile would ape me while swallowing her peanuts. 'You expect me to believe that you're not even sure what your *grandfather's profession* was?'

I wasn't quite sure, as a matter of fact. But try to convince a young woman whose own grandfather, a suburban bicycle salesman, had given her a new bicycle every Christmas . . .

'After all,' she'd explode, 'it's not believable. You want to tell me that not once did your father ever mention his father or mother in front of you? You want to tell me that you don't know their first names either?'

Yes, that was exactly what I was telling her. Even though 'mama' was his last word, as he was dying. A little late, you'd agree, for me to try and find out more. And a little early to worm information out of him.

And Stérile would say that if this was meant to pass as humour—black or otherwise—it just wasn't funny.

She was righter than she knew. I had an enormous lump in my throat.

But enough. I don't like to hear myself talk about Stérile.

As an aside, I realize today that my daughter will have spent just enough time with me to remember my first name and that I did mention the existence of her grandfather in her presence, once.

Maybe because he was dead.

Or because children are condemned, inexorably, to repeat their parents' mistakes.

Ever since he settled in Switzerland, the relentlessness with which the man in the white coat—*sanbenito*?—pretended to have been born without a belly button could make you think his was in the shape of a star. A yellow one. Ha ha ha.

And who knows? Maybe he decided to dive into the minds of others in order to keep his own empty?

What difference does it make, anyway?

And since none of this is bound to interest the masses, let's give them a break with an anecdote. Supposedly funny. It goes like this.

As generous and hospitable as it is, Switzerland did not offer shelter and citizenship to just anyone. Among other proofs demanded of the applicant—proof, for example, that he was not on the fast track to becoming a sponger—he was required to undergo an examination meant to show how interested he was in the history of a country that no longer had one. And can you guess on what subject our young man in the white coat was examined, around 1937, by two grave experts in wing collars, swollen with self-importance? This young man, keep in mind, was the descendant of several tribes that, over the course of the centuries, had paid their tribute to wars, pogroms and deportations. That subject was the itsy-bitsy civil and religious war that ravaged and bloodied a tiny corner of Switzerland in the middle of the nineteenth century. And caused several dozen deaths.

Sometimes this story makes me laugh so hard, I cry.

Sometimes it doesn't.

It depends.

It's not easy being anyone's son. But being the son of someone who, throughout his sole, unique and brief existence, changed not only his wife (OK, you'll tell me . . .) but also his nationality, his religion and his first name—the Semitic whiff of the old one was a bit too strong—could reasonably, at least I found it ever more reasonable as my hairline receded, lead the ugly little gentile duckling who succeeded him to ask a few questions pertaining to his identity. And when, amid tens of thousands of screaming compatriots, I was bawling the national anthem at the top of my lungs just before the referee signalled the kick-off, my voice would occasionally seize up at certain passages of the song.

Not just with laughter.

What the hell was I doing there?

Is it at all surprising if, hopping over the black hole that the life of the man in the white coat had been for me and over the black hole his grave was for me now, I was sometimes seized by the desire to cross generations and seas and, led by some great-great nephew who would feel both embarrassed and suspicious, to stumble onto the usually horrendous concrete building that would have inevitably risen on the site of our (?) ancestral home?

Would it be a problem to add some warm water—this bath is ice cold.

'Go, already. Just go and be done with it so that we don't have to talk about it any more,' Stérile snapped. 'Anyway, a few weeks apart won't hurt . . .'

Things weren't exactly idyllic between the two of us.

I was almost decided. But at the last minute, an issue always came up, major or minor, that forced me to change plans.

'Any pretext is good enough for you, isn't it?' Stérile said, white-faced.

What I liked about her was that she panicked at the thought I might leave her, even for a second.

And I retorted, pompous, livid, unhappy, that an unexpected increase in my workload was not a pretext.

Yes, indeed—because at the time I still had a normal occupation, my interest in which was inversely proportional to the remuneration.

And I was earning money by the shovelful.

One night, as we were celebrating the conclusion of some contract in the back of a bar, one of my colleagues, whose confidence was probably inspired by the scraps of my life story I'd been telling him, confided to me out of the blue, darting furtive glances all around, that he was an observant Jew. Without actually hiding it, he preferred that the main office not know. Certainly I understood why? Without giving me time to answer, he added that if I wanted to rejoin my 'spiritual family' he was ready to make things as smooth as possible. Knew plenty of people in the Jewish community and . . .

Slightly tipsy, I forgot to count the seven arms of my menorah before answering and told him that his family was, no doubt, very spiritual but he wasn't, with his lousy proselytizing.

He did not find this clever. In his view, I was too defensive, too aggressive, to not be . . .

'Besides, I was born Christian,' I reminded him, and called to the waiter. 'Two more!'

He dismissed my objection with a brusque gesture. His glass shattered on the floor. We were rarin' to go, the two of us.

'Bullshit!' he yelled, 'Bullshit! Just a scrap of paper, a soap-opera baptism, pure opportunism. The history of our People is overflowing with these repudiations. Because you're Sephardic we can talk on a personal level, OK? You know perfectly well who the *Marranos* were and that deep down . . .

Deep inside the bar, every head had turned to look at us. Getting on my nerves, this colleague.

'For God's sake,' I whispered furiously enough to strike water from a stone, 'try to understand that I'm not interested in the religious side of the issue. I don't give a shit about religion. Besides, for all I know, my ancestor back there could well have been a communist or a freemason or an atheist or an Islamic convert or a sun worshipper, what difference does it make? Does it change anything?'

'Precisely,' he said. 'It doesn't change a thing. 'Whether you like it or not he was and he remained a Jew. Like you.'

'Only part,' I said.

'Now really,' he began, 'why do you always have to renounce, play down . . . What do you mean by "only part"?'

'What I mean is, my mother isn't one.'

He choked on his drink.

'Your mother's not Jewish?'

'Nope.'

'But then,' he spluttered, 'if your mother isn't, then you . . . Then you, sir, are not one of us *at all*! Do you know what Solomon said?'

I wasn't even sure *who* Solomon was . . .

' "There are three things which are too wonderful for me, yea, four which I know not. The way of an eagle in the air; the way of a serpent upon a rock; the way of a ship on the sea; and the way of a man with a maid." So why the hell are you bothering me with the state of your soul and trying to get me to discuss it?'

Me? I? The nerve.

He had gotten up and left, shoving a few tables out of his way. We never spoke again, but when the company was restructured and the head office had to throw out a few valiant co-workers, I learned he hadn't exactly supported my cause . . . Dirty Jew.

That just slipped out.

Sometimes I wonder, if all the decks of cards in the world were stacked one on top of the other I would ever get a winning hand. Sniff. 'Hark, good citizens, to the tragic story of the wandering Jew, who not only wasn't a Jew but whose wanderings and years of childhood wonder, clinical, aseptic, were bound by the four flowery walls of sweet Helvetia.'

Very funny.

First thing the next day, I went straight to the travel agency, determined that this time . . .

'You're certain, completely certain, absolutely sure?' I asked the agent.

Since she was already telling me.

'Fine,' I said, 'all right, but you know what happens . . . I mean . . . sometimes you confirm that, yes, there is room and then at the last minute you . . . Or you put people on a waiting list and . . .'

'Listen,' she said mildly aggravated, 'do you, in fact, want to leave on the eleventh?'

'Absolutely.'

'On the nine-fifteen flight?'

'Of course,' I said, 'I've told you three times.'

She swallowed.

Glub.

'That's not very attractive,' I said.

'What?'

'The way you go . . . glub, right in front of your customers.'

'Listen,' she said.

'No need to discuss it,' I said magnanimously. 'Everyone has their little flaws. Let's get back to my ticket, if you don't mind.'

She nodded.

'Should I reserve a seat for you or not?'

'Naturally. Why do you think I bothered coming here? For the pleasure of your company? But I do want to confirm that we're talking about the nine-fifteen flight on the eleventh?'

'Yes,' she said. 'Yes, yes, yes, yes, yes.'

'Because it's the only one I can take and . . .'

'Yes.'

'Well then,' I said with a huge sigh, 'if there's a seat available, let's book it. That's why I'm here, isn't it, and this would surely be the first time that a customer got angry with you because he *actually found* a reservation on a flight that he wants to take.'

'The very first time, that's true,' she said in a very small voice.

Then she started to issue my ticket.

'And what about strikes?'

She raised her head and said, 'Excuse me?'

'Strikes,' I repeated. 'Maybe, on the eleventh there will be a strike that will paralyze traffic city-wide and then goodbye, trip . . .'

'I thought of that, don't you know,' she said. 'But the only strikes scheduled for this month will be on the fourth, ninth, seventeenth, twenty-first and thirtieth.

Off by two days, shit.

'I suppose it's too late to change my departure date?'

She put down her pen, folded her hands and looked at me. All a bit too calmly for my taste.

'We are at the customer's service,' she said.

'You should swallow your spit every once in a while,' I said. 'It's flowing all around inside your mouth.'

She did and asked me on which *new* date would I like to leave?

I pretended to hesitate.

'The ninth, possibly . . . Or the seventeenth.'

'The ninth or the . . . But those are strike days . . .'

'I know,' I said, 'I know perfectly well.'

She suddenly became so pale that I quickly reversed course and told her we didn't need to discuss it further, let's go with the eleventh, over and out.

She grunted and handed me the ticket. I grunted in turn and got out my chequebook. Then I opened my mouth.

'Please don't say another word, I beg you,' she said imploringly.

I swear.

I had only wanted to mention, for a joke, that the only course left was diverting the flight once we were in the air.

But maybe that wouldn't have been funny.

For the entire stretch home on an overcrowded bus, I left the ticket visibly sticking out of my pocket. No one wanted it. How did those goddamn immigrant Turks get home, anyway? Did they walk?

Yoohoo, Cousin! Here I am. It wasn't easy, by the way. The taxi got lost at least twenty times and it's so hot here . . . Don't just stand there, Cousin, on your doorstep, looking at me distrustfully. I clash a bit with the decor, it's true, but I'm your cousin, Cousin. The man in the white coat and your poor father were brothers, cousin all dressed in black. *Understand*? *Your father and mine were* . . . Yep. It smells funny in your home, Cousin, of oil and peppers. *No comprende*? *I make little drawing* for God's sake, cousin, so that you finally get it? Could you maybe get this tribe of neighbours out from under my feet and back in their huts? Let's try again, calmly, with my passport as evidence. Look, cute little cousin, look my family name is identical to yours, well, except for a few letters, maybe, because over the centuries our name went through some changes, too, you see? And after all, shit, I'm not even sure about *my name*. But that doesn't really matter, cousin, since you obviously can't read our writing. Assuming you know how to read at all? Maybe you can, you'll have to tell me everything. Our grandparents, maybe you knew them? Did they sacrifice everything so that the man in the white coat could finish his studies and were they left without a single kopek for their other son, your esteemed father? But I'm chattering, my lovely cousin, I'm nattering and you keep shaking your lovely Madonna's head in terror. Me, I, *ego*, am, are, *sono*, your cousin, Cousin, your cou-sin, Uncle Ben's son, right?? And a risotto, Otto, for table three! Tsst. I didn't travel thousands of kilometres just to . . . But a tiny gleam of recognition lights up my dear cousin's eye. '*Uncle Ben*?' she echoes. That's it, beautiful, that's it, *Uncle* Ben, the Swiss one, you've got it: *Switz-er-land*, the one who was . . . Shit, how the hell do you *mime* a psychiatrist? And if I mime one of his patients, I could frighten the little kitten . . . But the tiny gleam has spread to my cousin's other eye, illuminating her entire face. '*Uncle* Ben?' she says again, pointing at me, '*Doctor*? *Switzerland*?' She doesn't think I'm him, does she? But no, she must know he's dead. Who knows, maybe she inherited some no longer very fresh Turkish delight as well? We've been passing the box back and forth in the family for so long now . . . That's it, little cousin, you've got it: *Uncle* Ben . . . and me. I trace a contorted genealogical tree in the air, which starting somewhere above my head peters out around my belly button. A little sketchy, but she still seems to have followed it. '*Uncle* Ben . . .' she begins crossing one wrist over the other. It's either death or handcuffs. I'll go with the first—better death than dishonour. I nod sadly, saying ah yes, ah yes. Then she points at herself with her thumb and says, 'Baba, Mama.' And once again, she crosses her wrists. I know, my cousin, I know. Let's hope my reaction fits the circumstances. I try to see inside over her shoulder. Maybe we could get off this goddamn landing and away from these goddamn neighbours who keep staring at me like I'm some strange animal? Cousin seems to follow my gaze, steps back, and motions for me to come in. Inside, I try to picture her again as best I can. Why not sitting across from me on a funny pouffe, with a low table covered with sweets between us and in my glass some kind of horrible port wine, thick and sweet? Nevertheless, it's cool and the semi-darkness that fills the room gives it a sort of intimacy. Cousin smiles shyly. I return her smile. I suppose she's wondering what has brought me here, what good wind, what developments? Unless she thinks she has inherited a new box of Turkish delight. Or that I'm a lawyer, come straight from Switzerland to tell her that her distant cousin from that country drove straight into a tree at a hundred and fifty kilometres an hour and has left her everything he owns. Hang on a minute—I feel just fine, damn it, even though that blasted port wine . . . Cousin has gotten up and is handing me a photograph. 'Baba,' she says, 'Mama.' You'd think we were playing dolls. With cadavers. I take the photograph gingerly between thumb and index finger. A couple with two children. Classified ad: Couple with two children seeks coffin of good standing with a view of . . . Tssst. Hello, Uncle. Hello, Aunt. I'm sorry to have arrived so late. I didn't picture you like this. Especially not you, Uncle. You get ideas, sometimes . . . He doesn't look at all like the man in the white coat. If I had seen you in the street, Uncle, I wouldn't have recognized you. Maybe that's why our paths never crossed. But keep in mind, Uncle, if it makes you feel any better: I could have seen the man in the white coat out on the street and not recognized . . . Come now, one doesn't joke about these things or about the dead. And who, sweet cousin, is that young man next to you in the photograph, as proud as one of the Three Kings and looking ready to go out and conquer the world? Another cousin, no doubt. So this trip won't have been useless, after all, if I can add a twig to my family tree. I put my finger on the young man and turn my head questioningly towards my cousin who is leaning over me. That is not on, understand? 'Nissim,' she says, 'Nissim.' Greetings, Cousin Nissim. My arms at my sides, forearms pointing towards her, palms up, fingers spread wide, chin raised, eyebrows drawn together in a frown, I try to imitate someone asking *where* someone is. Weird situation. But the little one isn't stupid. She seems to get it and says a word I don't understand. *No understand you.* '*Chermany*,' she chirps then. And to chirp *that* takes some doing. So some flesh of my flesh is flipping burgers or making sandwiches in some Munich bar. Funny, life. Cousin has sat back down, facing me, still smiling. She crosses her legs and her stockings rustle. She's not bad, my cousin. You done with that? 'A dangerous imbecile scaled the walls to violate a close relative.' Tssst. I've come, Cousin, to . . . I wanted to ask if your father had ever spoken to you of the man in the white coat. And our grandparents, Cousin, if they were still alive when you were born, what did they look like? Don't hesitate, my dove, don't hesitate to go into all the details, even if they seem trivial or irrelevant or God knows what. I don't know anything about them, you see, *nothing*, and my own existence is my sole evidence of their existence. We don't have to go back to the Great Flood—we don't have that much time—if you could tell me, I'd enjoy hearing—no, that's not the right word—if you could tell me, for example, what the man did who was the grandfather of your father and of the man in the white coat? Are you following me, my little cousin? What I mean is, what the hell did he do to make a living, in exile around 1880? It's not that long ago. I mean, was he a pirate or, I don't know, a banker or pistachio merchant or shepherd or did he make olive oil or . . . ? My cousin looks at me, half amused, half worried. She doesn't understand a single word in this flood of speech. She keeps spreading her arms in a gesture of desolate impotence. Raising my voice a bit, I say shit, it's true, I'm an arsehole and all that, and the next time I want to know if my grandfather died of hay fever or was crushed under a pile of carelessly stacked crates of dried fish, I'll organize an international conference with simultaneous translation and the works. This time, I really did scare her. She scooted backwards on her pouffe and stared at me without trying to hide her fear. Take off your veil, whatever-you're-called, Cousin. I recognized you. You're getting on my nerves, Cousin. Let's quit now before I break one of your worthless glasses of undrinkable port. I get up. She gets up. She doesn't get it. From start to finish, she won't have understood a single thing about my visit. I won't either. I flew thousands of kilometres for nothing. You shouldn't wake sleeping dead. I give her my hand and stammer vague thanks. Kisses are reserved for Western relatives. I beg your pardon, Cousin, my cousin, I didn't want to . . . Shit. She shakes my hand. A serious little girl. Farewell, Cousin. See you again, under other skies, in another world. Better. Or worse. I'm on the doorstep. She pulls at my sleeve. Serious and shy. She hands me a box.

Oh Cousin.

Turkish delight.

I had a bad case of the blues when I got off the bus. On top of that, with all my empty thoughts, I had missed my stop.

At the time, I was rather pleased with the electrifying, quick-witted way I was telling Stérile about all the trouble I *didn't* have getting a ticket.

Compared to me, Homer was nothing.

But I was a flop. All she said was that only I could have made such a circus out of so little.

Should I paint my nose red and walk on my hands?

And when was I leaving, by the way, she wanted to know.

'Hmm?'

'I asked when you're leaving.'

'The eleventh,' I said.

She nodded and counted something on her fingers. I thought I saw her lips draw themselves into something like a silent 'phew'.

But I don't know how to paint.

Not that it matters, since I didn't leave.

Here's why.

Shortly before my departure date, one evening vigil when Stérile and I, both of us wan and mute, were contemplating the television with its wan and blaring images of gangsters pumping each other full of lead, the telephone rang.

'Who could it be, at this hour?' Stérile asked.

'You'll find out soon enough,' I said without taking my eyes off the screen.

'I suppose that means that I'm the one who should answer?'

'Ah,' I said, 'ah, ah, ah.'

It was very unusual for us to speak directly to each other.

'It's for you,' she said when she came back. 'A woman with a horrible foreign accent.'

How about that?

She was exaggerating, of course. As usual. The accent was light and the unknown woman spoke with the refinement, precision and preciousness that only foreigners who have learnt our language have mastered. Louis XIV would have been delighted to hear it, even if a bit surprised, I'd imagine, that a human voice could come from a piece of Bakelite. But let's assume he'd have deeply appreciated the way in which she stuck the imperfect subjunctive onto every third verb and exhumed from the depths of time words whose existence I had completely forgotten.

C . . .

Cou . . .

Cousin ? ? ?

I'll be damned. It was my cousin. She just happened to be on a little tour of Europe, had gotten my address from the lawyer in Switzerland, and was, unfortunately, for only the most fleeting of intervals, waiting for her next train in the

Buffet de la Gare de Lyon. Since she didn't know the city well and only had a few minutes, she very much hoped, assuming I was amenable to her suggestion, that I might rejoin her so that we could at last make each other's acquaintance.

Well, knock my socks off.

Trying to clean up my lorry driver's vocabulary, I answered that I would be delighted. Absolutely delighted. Don't move, Cousin, I'm on my way. But how would I recognize her.

'I'm with my husband,' she said. 'He has a black beard. And with our daughter who has about four springtimes.'

Tweet, tweet.

Obviously. I can't picture her telling me she has a fat arse. And a faint moustache.

But I'm anticipating.

She ended the conversation with 'Until later, then, Sir.'

Sir? 'My honourable cousin' probably stank a little too much of the Comtesse de Ségur and plain old 'cousin' must have struck her as obscene.

I returned to the room where Stérile, lying on her stomach, chin in hand, was still watching television. We left the set on the floor in the hopes that dust would eventually cover it completely and we would forget about it. I sat down cross-legged next to her and put my hand on the back of her neck.

'It's crazy,' I said, 'you know who that was? The famous cousin who . . .'

'Save it for your sister,' she said, squirming away from my hand.

Which fell to the floor.

'No kidding. It really was her. I'm going to the train station to meet my little family for a drink.'

'Oh,' she said.

'Responses don't come much drier than that . . .'

She raised her head to look at me, her face at a very attractive angle. Her face was very beautiful in the flickering half-light of the cathode ray tube.

'And what exactly am I supposed to do when you announce that you're going to have a drink with some distant relative—faint?'

Ouch. Maybe I'd gone looking for that one.

I don't know why I then said what I did, that if she didn't want me to go, I could skip it. I could call the restaurant back and . . .

'Don't be an idiot. You were about to travel thousands of kilometres to . . . But now that I think of it . . .'

She frowned, then knelt and turned off the television.

I was already in the living room doorway.

'Bye,' I said, 'see you later.'

'Hang on. Wait a second,' she said.

I was already on the front doorstep.

'Wait,' she cried, 'does this mean that . . .'

I was already at the top of the stairs. She was on the landing. I turned round. Her thin silhouette and her white bathrobe stood out against the red light on our landing. I thought she looked beautiful.

Is there a law against it?

What was wrong with me tonight and what the hell was that lump in my throat?

Stop or I'll cry.

'Obviously I won't be leaving,' I said. 'Since the mountain has come to Mohammed, there's no point in me giving that metal bird a chance to crash into the Mont Blanc or Mount Elbrus or wherever.'

Our door slammed just as the light timer went out.

And I groped my way downstairs in the dark.

A little overdone, as symbols go.

My cousin was a strong woman with a faint moustache on her upper lip. Where else would she have one, by the way? In the bashi-bazouk vein, her husband wasn't bad. Not bad in the obstinate, suspicious, hostile vein either. Jealous, or what? Not once did he speak to me—it is true that he couldn't speak our language—and he kept his hands on his belt for our entire meeting, as if he had a concealed *yatagan* or some such weapon. As for Four-Cherry-Trees-Blooming, I didn't see much more than the not particularly clean bottom of her bloomers. Standing on the seat of the banquette, she kept trying to climb up the back, almost knocking down the vase of flowers on top of it three times.

A few good smacks, yes.

Instead of which he or she settled for taking the girl gently by the arm and seating her back down while stuffing her mouth with sweets by the ton.

Starting off well, the new generation.

Hardly saying a single word, my cousin and I spent the first minutes celebrating our meeting and eyeing one another intently while carefully trying to avoid looking at each other.

One hell of a warm welcome.

So then, the man in the white coat had a brother, younger or older, I wasn't quite sure, who one day had taken a wife. Or had no choice but to take the woman reserved for him from the cradle. Such marriages are surely no worse than others. It's a lottery one way or another, so you might as well cheat if you can. In any case, I had in front of me, in the flesh, and quite a bit of it at that, the result of this union.

Not exactly brilliant.

'Imagine,' I said, 'I don't even know your first name.'

I had to repeat it a few times because at the next table a couple rather drunk guys were reminiscing about their military service at the top of their voices.

'Leila,' she said.

I don't know why, but that name immediately made me think of belly dancing. The unbridled belly button of my unbridled cousin dancing on a table in the Buffet de la Gare de Lyon. The stunned spectators. And her husband, mad with rage, brandishing his cut-throat razor and decapitating everything that moved. Tssst.

'You don't seem very interested in your family,' she said.

Was she kidding? Not sure, I didn't answer. I stammered that her uncle had shown me her picture one day.

'He was such a generous man,' she said.

He was?

'Tell me about your parents,' I said. 'I don't know anything about them and . . .'

'They're dead. Both of them are deceased. And you, you're married, I believe?'

I nodded. Best not to go into too much detail.

'And your . . . our grandparents?' I said. 'Your uncle never told me about them.'

'They also died when I was quite young.'

In that case, well . . .

'But . . .' I began.

She interrupted me, 'And you have a little girl, I think, who must be about as old as my Rachel?'

Said Rachel was trying to plant the white flag of her bloomers triumphantly upon the back of the banquette. They made her get down and she started to scream, her mouth full of sweets.

'Yes,' I yelled, 'Stephanie.'

'That's a strange name,' my cousin said.

A thousand apologies, dear cousin, next time I'll send a telex to find out your opinion before I . . .

The next time?

'And your brother,' I asked, 'what's become of him?'

'My brother? My brother? I don't have a brother.'

'I beg your pardon. I thought that . . .'

'Maybe you're confusing me with Miriam?'

'Maybe . . .' I said doubtfully. '*Who* is Miriam?'

'She was my sister. She died of diphtheria about a dozen years ago.'

Oh.

'Otherwise, that's it?' I said.

'I don't follow you.'

'Besides you and me, there are no close relatives left?'

'No,' she said. 'You weren't aware?'

'It's just that . . .'

'You never spoke about us with Uncle Ben?'

'Never.'

'That's strange . . . He was very fond of us, after all . . . Do you know that throughout his entire life he remitted a monthly pension to my uncle without fail?'

First I'd heard of it. The man in the white coat, immigrant worker, supporting the entire tribe back home.

'Of course, he could certainly manage that, after all,' she said. 'He could earn a good living in this peaceful country, whereas we . . .'

Funny tone, all of sudden, Cousin. You're reproaching him of what, exactly? Of having deserted you? Of having taken off? Of betrayal?

'And you?' she said.

'Me?'

'Your living, are you making a comfortable one?'

'So-so,' I said.

'I see,' she said. 'I see . . .'

There was a long silence that the neighbouring table disrupted by braying a drinking song. Rachel looked at them with wide eyes, then, so as not to be left out, tried to harmonize with them by bellowing just as loud. She almost managed.

'Just look at that. Would you look at that,' one of the guys said. 'Did we frighten the little cutie?'

He stretched his arm out towards her, probably to stroke her cheek. My cousin's husband's hands dropped the sheath of his *yatagan* and grabbed his daughter by the shoulders, pulling her to him. Then he gave the men a look . . . whoo whee.

'Take it easy,' the man said. 'We weren't going to eat your kid.'

Silence.

'They are . . . well, they are strange, the people in *your* country,' Cousin said. 'Have you gotten used to them?'

'You know,' I said, sheepishly, 'I'm not really French. It's just my adopted country and . . . Besides, I . . .'

The advantage of not coming from anywhere in particular is that you can always pretend to be from somewhere else.

And I recalled another train station and walls decorated with enormous frescos depicting the greatest moments in the history of Switzerland. The paintings were decidedly on the primitive side, naive as well, especially if you compare them to those of Lascaux or Altamira. I was Swiss and Switzerland's past was my only real past.

It seems.

Her mouth all sticky, Rachel had started climbing again and reached base camp two. Cousin's husband was speaking to Cousin. I couldn't understand a word. His voice staccato and bitter. She answered him with the same tone.

I can leave if I'm in the way.

Cousin then turned to me and hesitantly said that Uncle Ben's financial assistance had been a lifesaver for them.

'For me too,' I said stupidly.

'Yes, but you,' my cousin says, a little surprised, 'you were his son . . .'

Who was denying it?

'He was a very generous man,' I said.

Seriously.

'Yes,' she said. 'Yes. And you . . . Maybe you could . . .'

I interrupted her, saying now that we've met, we should write to each other often. Very often. Occasionally. Now and then. At the New Year.

Never.

'Of course,' she agreed. 'We'll keep each other up to date. Let's stay in touch. We're family, after all . . . I mean . . .'

I understood.

Silence.

Cousin checked her watch. Then her husband.

'It's about time for us to leave if we don't want to miss our train,' she said.

Her husband was already on his feet, helping Rachel on with her coat. Rachel didn't want to put on her coat. Rachel screamed and thrashed.

The bag of sweets was empty.

Cousin was standing up.

Wait, for God's sake, you idiot. There are so many things I would have liked to ask, so many things I'd like to know, so many . . .

'What time does your train leave?' I heard myself ask.

Even though I didn't give a shit.

And she said, 'In fifteen minutes.'

And I said, 'Have a good trip. Get home safely. And if one day I were to make it to her country, I'd be sure to . . .'

And she said something about her poor country and that she'd be delighted.

Then she tapped herself on the forehead.

'I almost forgot . . .'

She said something to her husband, who grumbled, put the suitcase back on the banquette, unzipped it halfway, groped around inside it and pulled out a box which he handed me as brusquely as if it were a grenade with the pin pulled out.

Oh, Cousin.

Turkish delight.

You shouldn't have.

But of course, of course.

Farewell, Cousin.

Farewell.

When I got home, not exactly happy-happy, Stérile wasn't there. She had packed her bags and buggered off.

With Stephanie.

Kind of rotten to make a little kid get up in the middle of the night like that. Especially since it's cold outside.

Inside, too.

Marranos: *Derogatory name (meaning pork) for crypto-Jews in Spain who had accepted baptism in order to avoid death or expulsion, but continued to practice the Jewish religion in secret.*

It's night when I wake up. That is, it seems to be more night-time than usual.

Because with the size of the window . . .

I stretch my hand out towards the switch of the lamp on my bedside table. I encounter only emptiness. *Mister Emptiness, I presume*? Good God, it's true—I moved.

Shit.

There's nothing like thinking 'shit' on waking up to get you ready to face the day.

Everything is calm.

If it weren't for this pressing need to piss, there is no doubt that Morpheus would drop all the snoring chin-dribblers in this damned city in his arms just to make a little room for me.

No way out of it. Gotta go.

I can't remember where the switch for the ceiling light is—somewhere over there, on the other side of the room. And between the other side of the room and me, hidden in the shadows, there are two dozen volumes, jaws open and ready to bite, scattered all over the floor.

Fortunately a book bite is not deadly. But still, my ankles are black and blue by the time the light goes on. Not to mention the noise. I've absolutely got to find somewhere to fit these books. After all the trouble I went to to bring them with me . . .

In the meantime, I open my front door. The light from my room paints a little triangle on the landing. Beyond that extends the dark tunnel of the hallway. *Terra incognita. Persona non grata* setting off to relieve his bladder in the heart of unknown lands.

Where is the goddamn switch for this bloody hallway? I grope along the length of the wall outside my door. Aha. A button. Without thinking, I push it.

A shrill ringing resounds inside my studio. I jump backwards, quickly close my door and press my back up against it, heart beating wildly. Who could possibly be ringing my doorbell at this hour? I hate unexpected visitors, especially early in the morning. Some insurance salesman, maybe? Everyone says it never takes them long to sniff out a tenant who has just moved in. They grease the concierge's palm.

I hold my breath and listen carefully. Not a sound behind the door. I picture my visitor, on the other side, a perfect double, making the exactly the same gestures as I am, as if there were a mirror between us and not a door. At least he's not from the police. He would have already kicked the door in, after the customary warnings. Or *without* the warnings, if I were suspected of having a few grams of hashish rotting in some old pocket. 'Aren't searches in the middle of the night against the law?' 'Where do you think you are, arsehole, with the porridge-eaters?'

Silence.

Is he going to leave or what?

Two hundred and fifty thousand centuries ago, already laughing, my ancestor stops Abraham passing by for the business at hand.

'See any blood there?' he asks, pointing to his forehead.

'Nnno . . .' the chief answers warily.

'That's strange because my bladder's so full it's splitting my skull.'

Ah. Ah. Ah. Silence. There's always the sink? No, not on the *first* day.

Silence.

Must have left, on tiptoe. Or I was just dreaming. I open the door a crack, with the tips of my fingers.

Nothing. No one. Silence. Really?

The advantage of having only one eye is that it takes half as long to get used to the dark. A few fumbles and I'm here. I made it. A world premiere of sorts—I hadn't yet seen the crapper.

I have to admit that I happened upon the ad for this room rather by chance. It was pinned to the door of the sacristy in the archbishoprivy . . . Tssst—archbishopric. Because it pretty much corresponded to what I was looking for, I rang and asked to speak to the archbishop.

'There is surely no need to aspire so high, my son,' the brother doorman told me, still rather nicely.

Then he explained the owner had entrusted him with separating the wheat from the chaff and choosing the next tenant himself.

I regretted not having put on a tie.

He asked me lots of questions about who I was, where I came from and where I was going. The fact that I work in a bank—I didn't mention that I was on probationary status—seemed to please him, although the owner would have preferred a classic domestic employee, Spanish or Portuguese. 'First of all, they're Catholic, of course, and then they're not the kind to call in a lawyer when we throw them out.'

Nice.

'Speaking of which, Catholic—you are one, naturally? Or at least Christian?'

Looking him straight in the eye, I quickly reassured him that yes, of course, naturally . . . This made me think of some of my Jewish ancestors who, it seems, around five hundred years ago, had three months to convert or, well, *adios*, they'd have to leave Spain. So two lines formed, one led in a chain gang to the baptismal font, the other to overcrowded ships whose captains couldn't think of anything better to do than increase the normal fare tenfold. Even then . . . Wasn't it in connection with this that I was told all the children aged twelve and above married among themselves so that, in exile, each girl had the protection of a husband? I vowed to track down the details in my encyclopaedia, trembling at the thought that I would have already been married twenty-four years.

Seeing me hesitate, Brother Doorman thought it best to let me know that a half-dozen people, as Catholic-worthy as I, were waiting only for my refusal to rush into this deal. Certainly, I had the opportunity to be the first, but that would require that I not waste any time and that I sign *hic et nunc*.

Fine.

Only when I was leaving did I dare mention that we hadn't spoken about . . . Did he know, was he was aware of some rather . . . trivial . . . details, the . . . well, the . . . was there a . . . were there any . . . what I mean is, does the room have a . . .

He finally understood what I was getting at.

'On the landing, of course, my son. With that rent, you can't afford many dreams, you know.'

I'm not dreaming. I'm even pleasantly surprised. I don't know why I expected some kind of Turkish squat, with a little heart cut out of the door, a stinking wooden box buzzing with thousands of blue-and-green flies, the round cover never put back on properly, the newspaper cut into rough squares and the never-ending stories of kids who fell into it and slowly sank, choked, drowned.

Obviously it doesn't compare to my previous ones, with little green faïence tiles, gleaming chrome fixtures and some kind of host always floating in the toilet water, turning it practically Hollywoodish hues. But it's reasonably clean, and larger than expected. It's true that when I'm on the seat I can touch the door with my leg out straight, but there's plenty of space to my left and my right that tells me no real-estate developer has washed his hands here for a long time. If one had come, he'd have found a way to lodge five or six immigrants in the space.

Dirty Frenchmen.

OK, I'm exaggerating a little. But not that much.

In short, I do what I have to do in this place and, just when I'm about to pull the chain, I freeze, petrified. I clearly heard creaking behind the door. Could my mysterious visitor have followed me here? I've got my left hand clenched round the handle at the end of the chain and, stupid reflex, I pull. Where do I think I am, for Chrissake, *where*? In a hotel, ringing for a chambermaid or a detective? As always, for several minutes you can only hear the noise of the water rushing through the pipes and then the wheezy, spitting noise of the reservoir refilling. I use these minutes to ensure that the bolt is set. Even though it doesn't look very solid, it's better than nothing. A bit more whistling, some glugs, some hiccups, and a thick silence settles back in.

A war of nerves. I'm cold. My head hurts. Leaning against the wall, eye fixed on the door, I await my adversary's next move. It doesn't take long.

There's a knock on the door.

Reassuring, in a way. Why would someone out to get me bother to knock? That he would knock on *me* I can understand, but on the door?

There's another knock.

'Yes?' I say very softly.

Too softly, no doubt, since there's a third knock, a very loud one.

'Yes?' I say again.

Almost normally.

'Are you dead, or what?' says a voice outside.

Why do they all ask me if I'm dead?

'Who are you?' I ask.

'I'm the one who should be asking who you are. Don't you know that this toilets are only for the tenants on this floor?'

'*I'm* the new tenant on this floor.'

'That's what I thought,' the voice grumbles. 'I'm the neighbour on your left. And now, would it bother you to get out and let me piss? It's urgent.'

Maybe it was urgent, but still not quite pressing enough to keep him from taking the time before locking himself in for his turn, to explain that I can receive whatever visitors I want at whatever hours I choose—there's no law against that yet—but then for Chrissake give my visitors a key when they're going to show up at four in the morning because, if I hadn't noticed with the nutcase on my right, the walls aren't ten kilometres thick and the doorbell a little while ago had jolted him awake.

So I didn't dream it. Who could it have been? Stérile? C'mon, man, get real: she refused to visit you at respectable hours at an address she knew. Is she going to show up at four in the morning at an address she doesn't even know? At this point some might add, 'With women, you never know . . .' I don't add anything: with women, I *know*. But now I think that, still, I probably should have left an address with the new tenant in my old flat, in case she did decide to call. I'd be surprised if she called but with women, you never know . . . In any case, the concierge has my new address.

Sbritski—I still don't know how to spell his name—seems surprised, even a bit shocked, to bump into me on leaving the toilet. He quickly rebuttons the three buttons on the fly of his pajamas. He probably leaves everything open when he thinks he's alone. It saves time when he wants to dip his wick in his fat old floozy. That's not fair—I've never seen her.

'Why are you still here?' he asks.

I motion towards the door behind him with my chin.

'I have to go back.'

'Already? Are you sick or what? Got the runs?'

I want to shake my head to say no, but then wham, it hits me again all of a sudden. My knees buckle and I have to support myself with a hand against the wall. 'I'll admit anything you want me to, but for the love of heaven, *Lord Torquemada*, take the red-hot irons off me.'

'Are you sick?' he asks again.

I stammer that no, I'm not, I just need to go back in, that's all.

'Fine,' he says, 'fine. It's your business. But don't forget that the toilet on this floor is for everyone, right?'

I promise to keep it in mind and rush to barricade myself inside.

Twice in two days, good Lord, what's wrong with me? And that cretin, pompous and pontificating, who's going to put on his long rubber gloves and stick his Vaseline-covered index finger inside me or else, I don't know, a wand with a little light on the end, and on the screen, or whatever other apparatus, something will appear that will make him say, 'You see, sir, I can be frank with you . . . In my opinion, the sooner we operate, the better . . .'

I'd rather die.

I'm sitting on the lid, head in my hands. I feel better. It has passed. It's over. The good old doc took off his gloves and, with that almost paternal smile I'm so fond of, told me that I was worried over nothing and that he hadn't detected anything abnormal—it must all be psychological: moving, disruption of your habitual surroundings, etc. Keep talking. I know all the psychological trump cards, including when you break your leg skiing. Would I have planted myself in a snowbank like that if I hadn't had the meeting next week that I'm so worried about? C'mon now. The only difference is that instead of me going to the meeting, the meeting came to me. I must have had a temperature of ninety-eight degrees and change when Stérile's lawyer arrived and at least a hundred and two point five when he left.

Enough.

I study my surroundings once again. I had an idea earlier, while I was pissing. Yes, while pissing! Why not think when you piss? Why should you only be allowed to think when you're seated at a table, a pipe in your mouth, glasses pushed up onto your forehead and surrounded by stacks of scholarly books? Hunh? Hunh? I don't have any recent statistics, but I'm sure that a load of brilliant ideas have come to guys standing there with their right hands lost between their legs, left hands scratching their heads. The idea, for example, that it was not particularly clean, not to mention unhygienic, to piss everywhere in the halls of Versailles, that it tarnished the mirrors in the Gallery and so having a place set aside for just those purposes wouldn't be bad at all. Two centuries later, it was done. The problem at that point was that there was no one left at Versailles. Just tourists who weren't disgusted. And some incompetent archaeologists wondering where the hell those arseholes in wigs could have put their crappers.

Iraklion (Heraklion): *City in Crete* (*cf under this name*).

Good Lord, in the time I've been paging back and forth, Crete would have had time to adhere to the coast of Africa. Crete . . . I twist round to reach the third volume, 'C'. After 'A' and 'B', there's no 'C', but 'W'. I don't give a shit about 'W'.

I'm not playing scrabble here. I'm trying to educate myself . . . I alphabetize them every time before I leave . . . Aha, here's the 'C'.

It falls open to **Cancer**.

Shit.

On the way back to my digs, I passed a large blonde woman with dyed hair. There are times when my intuitions terrify me. Without saying a word, she gave me a dirty look. 'There he is, the cretin who wakes my husband up in the middle of the night, who then wakes me up when he goes out to take a piss and comes back anew with a tool this big and I have to put out when all I want to do is sleep.' That's my interpretation, how I read her look. Maybe I'm wrong. Especially about the 'anew' part. What I'd like to know is whether she's come to the john on her own or if he sent her. 'Getting laid, getting laid, good Lord, is that all you ever think about? Me, I'm dead tired. Hey, I know, how about going to the can, instead? It'll shake the new guy up a bit. He seems way too comfortable in there.' That's the scenario I picture. One of my greatest shortcomings is that I can never imagine anyone ever saying anything flattering about me, or even just something nice. Of course, it is true that I haven't done *anything* to earn it.

Speaking of getting laid, my neighbour to the right started up again round seven. Unless of course, as Asparagus suggested, she was, in fact, dying. In that case, it would be what's called a beautiful agony. A beautiful war, a beautiful agony, a beautiful death, a beautiful burial, a beautiful bastard. Everything ugly is beautiful.

Which is to say that a little later, in the concierge's lodge, I was yawning with every second or third sentence. She noticed right away.

'You'll get used to it,' she snickered. 'You'll get used to it or leave. There are some who don't. The previous tenant took off after . . .'

'Who don't get used to what?'

An enormous cat was doing figure eights round her enormous calves.

'Oh go on, don't play the choirboy. You know exactly what I mean.'

Maybe. Maybe not. I'd rather not specify, or I'll blush.

'I came to see you,' I said, 'because I have a problem with my encyclopaedia.'

'So does my son. It's very hard for him to sell them. In the circumstances . . . People don't want to educate themselves. They just want to stuff their faces. Speaking of which, would you like to subscribe? Twenty per cent cash down and . . .'

'Absolutely not. Mine is enough. And speaking of which . . .'

'Yeah,' she said, 'but Cabbot and Ostello, they're not in yours.'

I don't answer. I don't want to admit that I still don't know who they are.

'My problem is that my room is so full, I have no idea where to put my encyclopaedia.'

'That's your problem. Sell it.'

'Not a chance. I'm too attached to it. Besides, who would buy it? Didn't you say your son . . .'

'My son is a very bad salesman. He's too shy to knock on the door of anyone he doesn't know and . . .'

'*My* problem' I said a little precipitously, 'is the room my encyclopaedia takes up and . . .'

'That's your problem.'

'Yes,' I say, 'that's what I just said. And to solve it, I'm wondering if, until I find a permanent solution, I couldn't store my encyclopaedia in the toilet?'

The enormous tomcat misses a turn and flips, all fours in the air. 'Ooooh' from the audience. Impassively, the ten judges hold up their scores. There are nine zero point zeros and one nine point five. That judge is the female cat.

'In the toilet?'

'Yes, there's some extra room and if it were piled up in two or three stacks, the encyclopaedia wouldn't . . .'

'In the toilet?'

'Yes. You often find almanacs or travel guides or dirty books or just about anything to think on while squeezing your guts. So why not an encyclopaedia?'

Silence. Giving me a funny look, she seems to be thinking it over.

'It's not my problem,' she finally said.

'Oh really, I thought that . . .'

'I'm a concierge, you know. Not a librarian.'

'Of course, but . . .'

'Work it out with Sbritzky.'

'Sbritzki?'

'Not Sbritzki—Sbritzky. The neighbour on your left. He's been on that floor the longest. Longer than anyone in the whole building, I believe. He came before I did. In a way, he's the one who makes the laws on his floor. I almost I have to ask permission to sweep *his* hallway. The emperor of the sixth floor, you see?'

I see. And what I see doesn't look very good.

'After all,' I say, 'he's just another tenant. I don't have to ask his permission to . . .'

'And he won't ask yours to set your books on fire, or to throw them out of the window, if he doesn't like them.'

'Oh,' I say.

'Besides, he's not just another tenant. He's the former bodyguard for the owner's children. Took them to school and all that. Now they've grown up and he's grown old, so . . . But the owner still uses him occasionally for extra jobs, like when they want to come into an inheritance or things like that.

'Oh,' I say again. 'Oooh. A gun permit and all?'

'I would think so. Also jujit-something and kara-whatsit.'

'Buddies with all the cops, I bet.'

'With *almost* all the cops. Seems that the honest ones don't care for this kind of private police.'

I returned to my room, deep in thought.

I went round and round in circles until noon, trying to square them. I could easily slip a few volumes in under the sink in my room, but the rest would stick out and make a sort of wall around it and would keep me a good foot from the washbowl. That wouldn't work: in three days they'd be covered with water, soap and toothpaste. It is true that in the toilet . . . But I still had enough faith in man to hope that he would piss straight. Along my walls there was no room to be found, the space under the bed was full, and what is the point of having a table if I can't sit with my legs underneath it? Similarly, what is the point of having a table if it's loaded with twenty-five voluminous books? Like a complete and utter idiot or a little kid missing only the bars of a playpen and a rattle, I even tried stacking them all in the centre of the room. It could be an attractive look—why not—a colonnade, Greek temple, Ionic or Corinthian. Fucking moron. Once it reached hip height, around volume 'R' or 'S', the pile kept collapsing. The end of a civilization. Run for cover, guys, here come the iconoclasts. Shit. It was just too stupid.

Depression: *Depression is not an illness. It does not follow a regular progression, nor does it have one particular or specific origin. It may be ephemeral or permanent, deep or superficial. The level of intensity determines if a depression is pathological or not. Nonetheless, depression presents a certain number of particular traits that differentiate it from all other emotional states and represent a reaction to a profound sense of emptiness: a lack of interest in the external world, for example, lack of activity, lack of the capacity to love, loss of self-esteem, lack . . .*

Right, no interest. Let's move on.

Depretis, Agostino (1813–87): *Italian statesman known for the most part as the primary proponent of the parliamentary method known as 'transformismo'* . . . I picture myself in a room buzzing with thousands of conversations, desperately waving my placard: 'Would any one be so kind as to drop the name of Mister Depretis so that I can show off my knowledge?'

Sometimes, I make myself laugh a bit. Not more than that. It's cold. Onward.

Dera Ghazi Khan: *District and municipality in eastern Pakistan . . .*

I close volume 'D'. I've forgotten what I was looking for. In any case, it won't be long before one of the two comes knocking on the door. As usual. The sanitary version of 'harassment'.

Yes, shit, it was too stupid, so around noon I went to knock on the door of my neighbour to the left. Surely it's evident that there are doors I've knocked on with more enthusiasm. Like the dentist's, for one . . .

Through their door I can hear, slightly less distinctly than in my flat, the gentle sound of their television. A stupid game show. There's a pleonasm. A lady has twenty seconds to say how many stars a divisional general has on his hat. If you know that, and you also know the etymology of the word 'oasis', the name of Henry IV's assassin and the gender of Conon de Béthune, you can easily become a millionaire in this damn country. That and the lotto . . . Last time, the winning numbers were seven, eleven, twenty-three, twenty-five, thirty-two and forty-nine. I was angry with myself for not having played. Once the numbers are announced, they always seem so simple, so stupid, so *obvious*, that I'm sure I could have figured them out in advance . . .

God, they're taking a long time . . . I'm ready to knock again when the door opens.

Abruptly.

There he is, in front of me, wiping his mouth with a napkin.

'Oh, it's you,' he grumbles.

'Mr Sbritski,' I say with a light stammer.

'Would it kill you to call me Sbritzky like everyone else?'

We're off to a good start. I start again.

'Mr Sbritzky . . .'

And I stop, terrified. Behind him, some enormous monster, like a St Bernard, has appeared. The thing is advancing slowly along the hallway, drooling.

I swallow.

'Don't make any sudden movements,' I say softly, trying to keep perfectly still.

He stares at me, confused.

'What's the matter with you?'

'Listen, right behind you there's some kind of gigantic dog that . . .'

He looks over his shoulder. 'There something wrong with you or what? It's just Yela, my dog.'

Just Yela, his dog.

Who came to rub her slimy muzzle on his trousers and raise her vacant eyes towards me. He puts his hand on her head. Charming picture.

Revolting.

'I thought . . .' I say. 'I thought . . . you said yesterday that dogs and children, that . . .'

'Obviously,' he says. 'Can you see your mutt fighting constantly with Yela or knocking her up? Can you see your kid getting one of his arms or legs eaten? Because she's very gentle, my little pet, but you can't get her worked up and you know how kids are . . . That said, what do you want? I'm in the middle of lunch and . . .'

I explain.

'In the john?'

'Yes.'

'An encyclopaedia?'

'Yes.'

'What for?'

Is he a moron or what? . . . I just got done . . . Come on, kid, stay calm. You don't want to get him worked up, or his monster.

I explain again. The skimpiness of my room. The collection's cultural interest for the community.

'You know,' he says, 'when I go to take a piss, I don't give a shit who succeeded Louis XIV. I've got a television for that.'

Mmmm. He's thinking. So is Yela. While slobbering.

'An encyclopaedia, you say? One?'

I nod, sensing a misunderstanding. So does the dog, who starts to growl.

'Maybe you could hang it on the door knob with string? We did that with the *Farmers'* almanac.'

No. Terribly sorry. We couldn't hang it, not even maybe.

'On the floor, then?' he asks.

'Yes,' I say. 'In stacks.'

'What do you mean, "in stacks"?'

'One on top of the other. Neatly aligned.'

'One *what* on top of the other *whats*?'

Yela gives a sharp bark. I take a step back.

'An encyclopaedia consists of several volumes,' I say.

'How many?'

'Oh, about twenty, approximately.'

'About twenty? . . . Then no, absolutely not. You picture us doing gymnastics just to get to the shitter?'

'No, of course not,' I say. 'Stacked up against the wall, I'm sure that . . .'

'And if I say yes, who's going to stop the other tenants from doing the same and unloading their, I don't know, skis, old televisions, trunks.'

'You will,' I say. 'You'll stop them. *Who's* in charge on this floor?'

'I am and I don't want your stuff in my thing.'

Shit—to hear him, you'd think he really was in charge of the floor.

'Just let me give it a try,' I say. 'You'll see that once they're put in place, you will barely even notice them.'

All right. He takes a bit more pushing and his monster almost bites my hand off when I try to do the same to her. Then he gives me permission.

But only provisionally, revocably, until I find another solution.

Thank you, my liege.

So I spend the rest of the day arranging my room and moving the encyclopaedia to the toilet. Just as I thought: in three even stacks, lined up against the wall, it doesn't take much space and leaves plenty of latitude for the occupants to move. As for longitude, it's still not customary to lie down in the loo.

Or on it.

. . . the largest disaster in the history of Armenia began with the outbreak of the First World War. Despite numerous proofs of loyalty by the Armenians, starting in 1915, Turkey accuses them of complicity with the enemy (who had just launched an attack on the Dardanelles) and feared they would support the Russian army's advance on the eastern front. That is why they decided to deport the entire Armenian population (approximately one million seven hundred and fifty thousand people) towards Syria and Mesopotamia. The operation was carried out with abominable barbarity and some six hundred thousand Armenians were massacred or perished en route . . .

Dirty Turks.

I passed a little boy in the hallway. About ten years old. When he saw me, he jumped back and pressed himself against the wall to let me by. Maybe my eyepatch scared him. It happens. And not just with children. People who have never seen the sea in their lives, people who live in a country that doesn't have the tiniest opening onto the least of oceans, sometimes take me for a Barbary pirate. The all-powerful imagination. Over my pile of books, I smiled at him. 'Hello.' He didn't answer. He was staring at me, wide-eyed, lips trembling. Then he mumbled some incoherent words, spittle forming at the corners of his mouth and ran away with a strange, sort of rolling gait.

Oh? OK.

That evening, I collapsed onto a chair. I looked around me and saw that all was well. If I followed the traditional pattern, all that was left for me to do was notice that I felt a bit lonely. And create a woman.

More than a little crazy, right?

The pharmacist was friendly. And rather cute, in her white coat.

'I'm having trouble sleeping,' I told her.

'Me too.'

Nice smile.

'And what do you take?' I asked.

'The hand I'm dealt.'

If there's one thing I'm absolutely immune to, it's other people's sense of humour.

'I was talking to the pharmacist, not the philosopher,' I said.

Shrugging, she handed me a container of yellow pills.

'How many do I take?'

'One or two, if you're counting on waking up. Otherwise, two dozen.'

Well now.

She saw my astonished look. 'I was speaking as a pharmacist, of course. Not a philosopher.'

I'd made myself another friend.

In any event, they were very effective and I fell asleep before finding out who the murderer was in the movie at the Sbritzkys'.

Too bad.

Among my short-lived careers, I was also a petrol pump attendant. Yep.

Full time.

In the mornings, I filled tanks. Because a man's got to eat.

And in the afternoons, I posted the latest rise in prices on the sign.

Because I had a degree.

I tripped and fell through the air: I blame it on Voltaire.

The chair sent me to St Peter: I blame it on Voltmeter.

You can laugh later.

Still, if I catch the bastard who thought it was funny to stretch this nylon rope across the hallway . . .

Pretty soon I'm going to need a mine detector just to take a piss in peace.

My right knee hurts a bit. To compensate, and to show some invisible spectator my complete contempt for procedures like these, I raise my left shoulder.

Thus did Quasimodo, lame and misshapen, reach the door of the toilet and lock himself in.

'Victor Hugo was not pleased with his sentence and rummaged around in his beautiful white beard: Wouldn't readers think that his hero locked himself *in the door*? He shrugged and, to unwind a bit, went up to the sixth floor to his ancillary loves. With a not-at-all unattractive black woman.'

The sixth floor, I live there too. That's handy.

'Excuse me for a second, Victor, I'm right in the middle of a fascinating piece on the Balkan Wars.'

. . . *Nonetheless, discord soon spread once again among the Balkan allies. Tensions in Macedonia pushed the Greeks to form an alliance with the Serbians to divide the region, an alliance negotiated on different terms from those agreed upon between the Serbians and Bulgarians in their accords of March 1912. At the same time, the Greeks opened negotiations with the objective of forming a definitive alliance*—definitive, my ass—*with Turkey and in the hope of receiving Turkish assistance against Bulgaria, which had laid claim to Salonica, while the Serbians claimed the towns of Prilep, Kicevo and Ohrid—even though they had ceded these cities to the Bulgarians—under the false pretext that the Bulgarians had not properly respected military conventions. Attempting to calm the situation, the Russian Tsar himself sent telegrams to the kings of Serbia and Bulgaria, asking them to attempt a reconciliation.* ARE ALL OF YOU ABOUT DONE ACTING LIKE ARSEHOLES?—STOP—YOU WANT THE BACK OF MY HAND?—STOP—IT'S MY . . . Tssst. *The Bulgarian Cabinet showed themselves favourable to appeasement but King Ferdinand and his Major General, Savoy, demanded that the Russians adhere strictly to the treaty of 1912, and gave them one week to declare their intentions. The Russians refused to help the Bulgarians any longer, but Ferdinand, confident of a quick victory and convinced that Austria–Hungary would come to his aid, ordered Major General Savoy to launch an attack against the Serbians and the Greeks in Macedonia. The Bulgarian Cabinet, however, which had not approved the order, enjoined Savoy to stop and he did even though he had already begun his advance into Macedonia. Furious, Ferdinand dismissed him for disobeying orders and named another general to take his place. But it was too late and, deprived of reinforcements, the Bulgarian army was at the Romanians' mercy when they advanced into the country in July. At the same time, the Turks, violating the terms of their armistice, invaded Thrace and recaptured Adrianople (Edirne) . . .*

Well, how about that.

And you, Grandfather, tell me, you, when you read your newspaper, wearing a fez or a skullcap on your head, maybe sitting under a plane tree with a tiny cup of coffee and a huge glass of water, you, Grandfather, we're not going to get all teary-eyed but tell me one thing, Grandfather, when you were reading the newspaper, did you understand anything about the political situation there?

Someone knocks on the door.

It could be Victor, his spirits now becalmed,—a gentle euphemism, a charming way of taking the . . . parts for the whole—who has come to teach me the art of being a grandfather.

Apart from a few devoted fans, will I surprise anyone when I say that it could have been, but wasn't?

All this just to give me time to think.

I was caught with my hand in the bag.

The tube of lipstick in my hand, rather.

On the wall in front of me stretched the words 'Sbritzky is an a . . .' that I had just scribbled. That I had just laboriously spelt out, that is. We'll discuss this later when you've had time to try 'scribbling' anything at all with a tube of red lipstick.

I had thought I would have a moment alone. Both of the Sbritzkys just went and . . .

Someone knocks again. Timidly.

I quickly erase my inscription with a piece of toilet paper rolled up into a ball. It leaves a big red smear.

I could always claim I'd swatted a mosquito.

A giant one.

'Timidly?' Someone knocked again '*timidly*'? But then . . .

I open the door.

The kid jumps back and tries with both hands to hide the large wet spot spread across the front of his trousers.

Shit. I stammer that I'm very sorry. I didn't know it was . . . I thought that . . .

His lips tremble. It's a mania with this kid. He stares at me for a second, opens his mouth wide enough to show that the reserve of spittle has not run dry, then flees as fast as his limp allows.

I call out to him to look out, look out! for the . . .

Too late.

Now, at least, he'll know why he's limping.

When nasty remarks like that pass through my head, I'd like to replace them with a 7.75 millimetre bullet. Or .76.

I let the waves of regret wash over me, but not for long. I lock myself back in the can, where I meditate on those serial battles, about which I never understand the first thing.

Earlier, I did what anyone would have done in my shoes. I'm not the type who tries to call to attention to himself whatever the cost.

Earlier, when I felt the need to learn more about this or that subject—Wilhelm I, for example—I would go to the toilet to get the appropriate volume and take it back to my room to read. It's certainly true that if another need arose simultaneously with my thirst for knowledge, I killed two birds with one stone and urinated while reading the article that interested me. But that was rare. You can't control nature.

I soon ascertained, alas, that the almost uninterrupted noise of my neighbours' television—not to mention the other nutjob's moaning—made concentrating on anything nearly impossible. Nothing is harder than trying to understand what separates two ethnic groups than a journalist's booming voice describing live—he has no choice but to yell so he can be heard over the sounds of gunfire—the battles the two groups are waging against each other. At first, I dug my heels in and put my hands over my ears. I knew that my encyclopaedia was my Bible and would help me understand the ins and outs of such confrontations. I knew things were never as simple as they wanted us to believe. Only extensive research that didn't omit a single detail or fact, however trivial, would authorize me, at last, to form an opinion. They slaughtered each other and I retraced the centuries. By the time I had at last reached the end of my labours and when at last—I did it!—I was convinced I understood everything, the wars I was researching had usually been over for months and my pedantic explanations of the conflicts' exact causes all but earned me the accusation of trying to rekindle them.

'And the back of my hand, is that going to rekindle anything?'

I'm a pacifist, but let's not push it.

Fortunately, if I may be so bold, so much . . .

I'm not so bold.

Unfortunately, so much hatred and fanaticism seethe under the cold ash of our planet that a new conflagration was never long in flaring here or there. In order to better appreciate the causes, to understand the effects more deeply, to try and determine, during my tête-à-tête dinners with myself in town, which side should get my vote—which of the two teams I should cheer when it scores a goal—I dove back pronto into my encycllococus . . . Tssst: encyclopaedia.

Sometimes I got lucky and didn't even have to change volumes when a new war started with the same letter as the previous one.

Nifty.

Thus, in a very short period of time, I learnt all sorts of things about China, Cambodia, Chile, Cyprus and the Congo.

But my luck ran out with the Congo. A footnote sent me to Zaire.

Oy.

Still, as luck would have it, the final volume covered 'W', 'X', 'Y' and 'Z'. And the war that followed not long after Zaire's took place in Yemen.

Amen.

Someone knocks on my door. I know that that's what doors are made for, but still, when I'm home, I just want my goddamn peace and quiet. It's not for nothing that I cut the doorbell wire after that incident the other night.

For a second I think it could be Stérile. 'My dear, I had such a difficult time tracking you down. I've missed you so much . . .'

Look, here's some money, go buy yourself some celebrity gossip rag.

I open.

It's Sbritzky and Yela. In alphabetical order—not biggest to smallest.

'Yes?' I said, since nothing else occurred to me.

'Someone wrote on the wall in the john that I was an arsehole.'

'No!'

'They did. You know who it could have been?'

'Nn . . . no. Not the slightest idea. Unless it was the kid, you know, the one who . . .'

'The retard? Are you kidding or what? Can't even write his own damn name.'

'By the way,' I said, 'did you notice someone wrote "Dirty Jew" the other day?'

'No?'

'They did.'

One all. Serve to Sbritzky.

'Alexandre Dumas, at least, had the excuse that he was paid by the line,' the referee thinks in a flash of inspiration.

'Maybe it was the little bugger, after all,' Sbritzky says.

Out.

'Maybe,' I say, good sport, fair play, deflated.

All of a sudden, the deafening wail of an accordion invades the room. *Maaddaam* Sbritzky and her quarter-hour of popular music. Yela is drooling buckets.

'No one can hear a damn thing in your flat,' the husband bellows.

As though he's reproaching me.

Happy, at least, that he realizes.

''Scuse me,' he says.

He pushes me lightly with the palm of his hand, crosses my room and pounds on the wall that separates our flats. The wailing stops.

Her master's fist. She recognized her master's . . .

Above all, make yourself at home.

'By the way,' he asks coming back towards me, 'did you figure out a solution yet, for your books in the can?'

I answer that no, as a matter of fact, not yet, I . . .

'You'll have to get on that,' he says. 'I told you it was provisional and . . .'

Yes, yes, yes.

They're leaving.

'Watch out for the rope,' I say in a conversational tone.

They look back.

'The rope? What rope?'

'Nothing,' I say and close my door.

As soon as they close theirs, the accordion starts squalling again at full throttle or at full whatever it is that an accordion has.

Oh Jesus, let my joy remain.

Yesterday, I read in the newspaper my lettuce came wrapped in—well, what did you think? That I live on air alone?—that in a small town in the United States, some journalist who wanted to know which candidate the citizens preferred but didn't have time to do a telephone poll asked the public in a radio broadcast to flush their toilets at precise moments and at successive intervals. Sitting in the water tower, the journalist was able to calculate each candidate's level of support according to the amount by which the water level dropped in association with each name.

Uuhhh . . .

That gave me an idea. I ran to the toilet and flushed it nine times. Three short, three long, three short.

A message in a bottle, so to speak.

Small cause, big effects—a bout of constipation led me to the solution. Forced by circumstances you can imagine and upon which I will not have the bad taste to dwell, I dwelt on the toilet longer than usual and thus realized that the john was by far the quietest spot on the whole floor. 'Eureka!' Archimedes exclaimed, watching his excrement sink straight to the bottom.

Since it's a small world and you should always close your circles, this reminds me of those early morning hours when, after endless pointless discussions, I would tell Stérile that if she didn't close her mouth, I'd go lock myself in the water closet, yes ma'am, in the *WC*.

A hundred million for the first one to invent a machine that can extract memories.

Not running much of a risk there . . .

In any case, from that day on, I got more and more into the habit of studying on site. The peace and quiet that reigned in the john more than made up for the relative discomfort of the seating. And the fact that I occasionally had to make way for others was a small price to pay for the silence that I enjoyed in-between.

As long, at least, as the needs of the floor were normal. That is to say, as long as the Sbritzkys didn't feel they had to play tag team in bugging the shit out of me as soon as I shut myself into this reeking haven of peace.

The letter the concierge slipped under my door did not come from Stérile—you can always dream—far from it. The letter was from . . .

'Slipped under my door?' Good Lord, what on earth are you thinking? That the concierge climbs the stairs every morning to bring me croissants, coffee, newspaper and mail on a tray? Like in the movies? I wake and stretch languidly as she draws the curtains? 'Beautiful morning, sir,' and I grumble that maybe it is but I have a splitting headache. And she impishly answers, 'Sir should not go to bed so late.' To which I say, 'Why don't you come a bit closer,' and I then untie the strings of the white apron hiding her bare essentials and lay her down on the pillows, and she 'Sir, oh sir, ooohhh sir, sirrr, you sh-sh-shouldn't . . .'

The letter my concierge spitefully handed me on the doorstep of the lodge was a bill. For the telephone.

The one I don't have.

A telephone number for complaints was printed on it.

I went to the corner telephone booth and dialled the number for complaints.

'I received a telephone bill,' I say, 'even though I don't have one.'

'Yes, of course,' I was told, 'that's right. And right now we're communicating with smoke signals, perhaps?'

It took me a moment to understand what he meant.

'No, of course not,' I said. 'A phone booth. I'm calling from a phone booth.'

'You are trying to tell me,' the voice answered, 'me, a telephone company employee, that you were able to find a public phone that works in this goddamn city?'

'I swear to you . . .'

'Call it in.'

'I beg your pardon?'

'Call zero-one-one. That's the number that's supposed to have a list of all working public telephones in the city. If you have the slightest sense of civic responsibility, that is. As long as you're not one of those arseholes who spend their time sabotaging the . . .'

'I am public-spirited. But about this bill, what should I . . .'

'Pay it, my good man, pay it. Believe me, it will be for the best. Unless you want us to cut off the phone you don't have? And how will you call us then, tell me that? From which phone will you be able to report the service failure?'

He hung up, choking with laughter. If only it could have been with the cord of his phone . . . I could picture very clearly one of the girls in the office pushing open the door, horrified to find him like that, cold and stiff with his big purplish tongue licking the receiver like an ice-cream cone . . .

The things I can picture most clearly can never be realized. Maybe that's because I only have one eye?

Fine, I dialled zero-one-one. Among the sound principles the man in the white coat instilled in me, solidarity was one of the most important.

Besides, it was amusing to keep the excitable man who was constantly drumming on the phone booth waiting. Shit, it's each man for himself.

It must have rung at least twenty times before someone answered on the other end of the line.

'Yeah?' said a sleepy voice.

'I have the honour of informing you with this call that I have found a working phone booth.'

A little pompous, but you do your best.

'Pah!' the voice replied. 'You must think you're very funny. If you knew the number of times people have played this sophisticated prank on me.'

'You think,' I said, not quite mastering myself, 'we're communicating through smoke signals?'

It took him a while to catch on. Not the brightest bulb.

'And how do I know you're not just calling me from your own phone?'

'You don't. You can take my word for it or you can go—'

'OK,' he said, 'don't get angry. You see, we so often end up going to a lot of trouble for nothing that . . . Fine. I'll send a team over for a report. Please be so kind as to stay and keep an eye on the booth until they can get there, all right?'

And what else? That's the kind of thing that will land you in the police station. All witnesses are presumed guilty and all those who are presumed guilty run a high chance, upon leaving these gentlemen's headquarters, of benefitting from at least a week's leave from work.

Go figure.

So I promised, I swore I'd stay and I rushed out of the booth without even hanging up.

Ten metres on, I turned back and saw the excitable guy from earlier leaning over the phone. A knife in his hand.

A world of lunatics. Are you surprised I go out less and less?

Anyone object to a brief journey round my room?

I think that what would first strike any chance visitor—aside from my fist which I would slam into his gob to show him just how much I hate chance visitors—is the irritating way my books always seem to spread themselves out everywhere. Where are my shelves of yesteryear, smelling so sweetly of dust and furniture polish?

In fact, no matter how often I try to push my books into neat, stable piles up against the walls, they never stay. After a few hours, my stacks collapse. If at first you don't succeed, try and try again.

And I do have to try again, a hundredfold.

I have to try and try again. And.

And I have to . . . OK, OK. All right already.

It got to the point where, certain mornings, it looked to me as if it had snowed books. As if the narrow paths I had carved out with such difficulty to reach the sink, the window or the door had been filled in once again during the night and obstructed with fallen books. As if yet again and once more, stupid, goddamn Sisyphus that I am, I'll have to spit on my paws and clear out this mess, at once blinding and dark, formed willy-nilly by the letters, words, lines, spaces and paragraphs. Contemplating them from my bed, my eye still half shut with slumber, I sometimes have an extraordinary vision, especially considering the person having this vision only has a quarter of a normal person's sight. (*cf Table IV in the appendix*). Thrown higgledy-piggledy onto the ground, on their spines, legs in the air, face down, nose in the dust, or sprawled in thirty-six other bizarre positions—not to mention those that seemed to be leafing through themselves in the drafts of air—my books seemed to have reverted to a state of wildness. Yep. Dangerous. Capable of anything. It would have only been a small step for me to start comparing a bookcase to a cage or a prison, but I didn't go there. It was too close to blasphemy. With all my talk about taking steps, I figured I might as well get up. It was time, for Chrissake. Wading up to my calves in literature, I went to the window to check on the weather. Judging by the lighter or darker colour of the interior courtyard's cement and the presence or absence of a sheen, I could tell whether it was raining. And it wasn't without a certain melancholy that I recalled the time, not so long ago, when I could look out at the sky—that's right, the sky—and give Stérile meteorological readings about which she didn't give a shit.

Sic transit . . . *Miss Gloria Mundy, in transit to the Tarpeian Rock through the Capitol, is* kindly requested *to report to ticket window number so and so* . . . Tssst.

Leaning out of the window, I also see the corrugated iron roof of the flimsy henhouse of a structure they use to store dustbins, old newspapers and dead children. Every night at the same time, the concierge pants as she drags it all out to the street for the rubbish men. If I listen carefully, I can hear her grumbling each time that there's no point in passing laws on abortion if everything is just going to go on like before. That's one point of view. Every morning she returns at the same time, her heart a bit lighter, and puts the empty dustbins back in the henhouse. The dear soul's routine is so precise you could set your watch by it.

Like who?

Kant.

Years and years of philosophy and that's the only thing I can remember. And then only in connection with dustbins.

There must be a philosophical conclusion to be drawn from this.

Another time.

. . . because, in fact, the Swiss authorities' stance on the right to asylum fluctuated over the course of the centuries, at times displaying positive aspects, at others negative ones. Throughout the nineteenth

century, for example, the country generously welcomed exiles of all origins. On the other hand, during the Second World War, the official stance with regard to Jewish refugees which could be summed up as 'The boat is full' was not only glaringly insufficient but, in certain respects, downright scandalous.

'The boat is full . . .'

Dirty Swiss.

My eyes are still brimming with tears. However, nothing comes from nothing, and I did it—I managed to tear out the necessary several dozen hairs. At least now I'll have a good excuse for my premature baldness.

One after the other, I set a trap on each volume of my encyclopaedia. A drop of glue on the front cover and a second on the back allow me to fasten a hair over the front edge. I've seen it done a hundred times in detective and spy movies. It's a very clever way to tell if a door has been opened. Or a suitcase.

Or a skull.

Invisible seals, as it were.

It's not that I'm insisting on splitting hairs, but if the volume or volumes with broken seals have more torn, wrinkled or smudged pages than I remember, I will have proof that someone is out to hurt me.

Of one thing I am already absolutely convinced—some wise guy is having a good time wreaking havoc on my alphabetization. What an arsehole. I have, in fact, never left the toilet without having put my volumes in strict order from A to Z and whenever I return, I always find my ordering undone. If only it were limited to slight inversions, 'N' before 'M', for example, or 'J' before 'H', I'd have resisted succumbing to paranoia and wouldn't have considered it particularly malicious. Anyone can make a mistake like that, especially the gang of illiterates who run rampant on my landing. And yet you might ask yourself—excellent question and thank you for asking—'Why the hell are these illiterates messing with my encyclopaedia?' But once you start asking questions like that, you end up seeing men with swords behind every bush, just waiting to skewer you.

And then one day, I found my books put in proper order, but *backwards*, from Z to A.

My teeth started chattering and I thanked heaven that there weren't any bushes in the toilet.

Last night, the Sbritzkys' television informed me that after a period of relative calm 'furious battles' had broken out again in my cousin's country.

The nutcase next door just moaned louder.

Hold on little cousin, I've got my gun and I'm on my way!

But first, before doing anything precipitous, I consult my encyclopaedia to learn a bit more about the region in which the battles are raging. You don't just rush in to a war zone, head down, butt up. A question of logistics and all. Obviously, if the man in the white coat were still alive and if, when he was alive, we had been able to talk about more than the weather, I would have asked him, for example, for information about the rainy season which was about to start in his native country. Wasn't it likely, for better or for worse, to stop the fighting? Maybe we would even have philosophized over a glass of the cognac he saved for special occasions—and which he'd never brought out again after the day of my birth—about those ancient, modern and tribal wars that only wind, rain, snow or sandstorms could interrupt. 'You, sir,' I would have said—forgetting, in the strength of my feelings, that we'd addressed each other informally for twenty-five years—'you, whose profession claims to understand mankind and who—for once let us be frank and direct—

earn most of your revenues from that understanding, don't you think it extraordinary that in the middle of the twentieth century, only the forces of nature unleashed—for which mankind, you must agree, is only *very indirectly* responsible—are able to suspend, even if only for several months, the unleashing of human violence? Tell me, is it disrespectful to smile at the thought of so many politicians, diplomats or other eminent negotiators whose key words, as they put away their documents and push in their chairs after one of their endless deadlocked conferences, whose key words, as they stand with their hands on their hearts and flocks of doves fluttering around them while men eviscerate each other outside, are something along the lines of "if only the rain would come soon"?'

Tell me, oh Father, what the *weather* was like in your country—surely you remember that? Or is meteorology *another* state secret?

Sniff.

These cogitations lasted exactly as long as it took for me to cover the distance from my door to that of the toilet.

Which I ran smack into.

Ouch.

Occupied.

Fortunately, I have proof that I'm not the one inside or it could have been a long wait.

Doubtful.

Since there is no way I'm going to miss my turn, I lean back against the wall, cross my arms and wait. And wait. And wait.

What the hell are they doing in there?

And I wait.

I know putting your ear to the door is just not done, but I do it anyway. To piss for that long, you'd have to be the Niagara at least. And the Niagara is loud. It's another of those sublime things Mother Nature has thought up to prevent too many absent-minded ninnies from falling in.

Not a sound from inside. Total silence. What is going . . . ?

'Anything interesting?'

This startled me so much I must have a set new high jump record.

Old man Sbritzky, obviously, in his slippers and his old dressing gown. He shuffles over in my direction with a sarcastic smile.

I don't answer. It's hard to talk when you've got your heart in your throat.

He gently pushes past me and plants himself in front of the door to the loo. A plant, by the way, that doesn't lack for manure. Tssst.

I manage to stammer something about the toilet being occupied. And afterwards, it will be my turn because I was there before him.

'Yeah, right,' he says. 'Sure.'

He takes a key out of his pocket, sticks it in the keyhole, opens the door, goes in, closes the door behind him and locks the door. Shtlok!

'I'm sorry to disturb you while you're reading, but have you seen my bearings?'

I've lost my bearings.

I started drumming with both fists on the door, yelling that it was a dirty trick and he didn't have the right . . .

And, wham, it hits me again. A few spasms to start, near my anus, that make me clench my teeth and my buttocks. My knees buckle, and then a half-dozen shocks in quick succession—isn't there anyone, I beg you, who can unplug the goddamn wire?—that leave me on the ground, eyes watering. Oh God, oh God, *oh God.*

Sbritzky almost trips over me on his way out of the can. He leaves the door ajar. It stinks in there.

'Just a warning,' he says, 'That's just a little warning.'

'Listen,' I manage to say, 'I'm not well and—'

'That'll teach you not to monopolize the crapper for hours,' he continues. 'And if it happens again, I'll lock the door again and you'll have to come and ask me for the key when you need to go. *Supposedly* need to go. Is that clear? And don't forget to get rid of those books one of these days. It's taking too damn long and it's becoming a pain in my arse.'

Yeah, and what about mine?

He disappears down the hallway and I drag myself into the toilet. Once again, volume 'C' is on the top of the pile and once again, on its own, it opens to a certain page. You can guess which one.

No point in waiting for cancer to get you. Best to leave in time.

Tssst.

So I pull my trousers up quick, like you'd throw a sheet over a corpse lying on the side of the road and zoom out through the door.

There are some days, you see, when you just don't feel like educating yourself.

For several days, thanks to my neighbours' television set, I was more or less able to follow the course of the fighting. Even though Old Lady Sbritzky—'I don't give a shit about politics over there and all that'—kept changing the channel—just like you yank the chain?—every time a news bulletin, special announcement or not, interrupted the usual mindless pap she was watching. However, since she didn't have one of those little gadgets that let you instantly change the channel without moving, she always needed a few seconds to complain, get up, go to the set and push another button. That usually took long enough for me to hear the essential part of the announcement, that is, the number of casualties left by this or that attack or counter-attack in the fields or in the foothills. In any case, since the war between the various TV channels was limited to a battle over which one would be the first to broadcast new developments in the war fought between men, each new programme my neighbour chose was soon interrupted by a news flash almost identical to the one we'd just heard. The whole rigmarole was branded with the exact time in hours, minutes and seconds. (I could picture the blinking time stamp in the screen's upper left-hand corner.) Because later, when it was time to take stock, what would be more important than knowing who won or lost the battle, and at what cost, would be establishing, with numbers to prove it, who first reported it. That's how it goes . . .

And so, sitting on my bed with my hands knotted so I wouldn't bite my nails, I followed, in this somewhat random and incoherent fashion, the no less random and incoherent conflict that was engulfing my cousin's country with blood and flames. Just as the situation there was more than a little dramatic, you have to admit that my situation, too, did not lack for a certain piquancy and there is no doubt it would have amused my beloved ancestor.

Which is to say?

Oh, that's just to say that, for example, sometimes a special news bulletin described the siege of a city in my cousin's country—and wouldn't it have been fitting, in that looking-glass world, if Leila had been named Alice instead—and the resulting famine that was endangering the inhabitants. So far, nothing unnatural. On our beautiful planet, millions die every year. And by the millions, the smiles of children—wearing T-shirts that have become much too large for them, sometimes printed with messages along the lines of *If I smile to you, do you smile to me?*—rotted alongside roads furrowed by tank treads amid the smell of diesel, dust and dried blood. By the millions, men and women, rarely white, who had devoured everything that still had more than just skin on its bones within a ten-mile radius, chewed up the last root, sucked dry the last blade of grass, vomited up the last handful of dirt, these men and women burped up their sole remaining cell of protein, fat or carbohydrate into God's face and sighed their final sigh. By the millions, this cohort with their swollen bellies and wire-thin limbs adorned the grotesque tableaux of which every day we hang more in our showcase of horrors.

Fine.

But it all became truly ridiculous when my neighbour would get up, grumbling, to change the channel and the reports of war and famine would be replaced with some unctuous quack holding forth, offering his chubby audience advice on the best way to lose weight. 'Watch out for sauces, laaadies, and avoid sugar, laaadies, and bread, laaadies, and starchy foods, laaa . . . What?' And the nice moderator would apologize for interrupting the professor's brilliant exposé, but current events had priority and they would have to switch to . . . And the channel turned to the same newsreader as the previous channel. Then my neighbour would get up, grumbling, to change the channel. It was time for commercials.

Cat and dog food. Big industry. Millions and millions worth of revenue involved.

Woof.

And the other nutcase, the one to my right, was still moaning.

That reminds me of one night when, having had, I admit, quite a bit to drink, I couldn't take it any more and I let loose with my fists on both of the walls that separated me from my neighbours. The lunatic's moans briefly changed into a kind of hiccuping and then she started in again, louder than ever. As for the Sbritzkys, they didn't turn a hair or lower the volume on their television in the slightest. But one second later, a volley of hoarse barks echoed outside my door along with the sound of nails scratching against wood.

Bleib still, du Schweinehund!

I open the door cautiously, millimetre by millimetre. I never quite know what I'll find in the hallway. Another solution would be to fling the door wide open and throw myself to one side after tossing a grenade through the opening. Or thrusting a spear.

Flames.

Some kind of pale crazy-arse Pierrot with his singsong, 'My candle has gone out, I no longer have a . . .' takes the blast full in the face and, howling, starts to burn like a torch.

People wonder where I get this kind of thing.

The same place I found this: 'Alfred de Musset, deeply moved, opens the door to the auditorium for the free lecture course bearing his name and is thrown out by the doorman with a swift kick to the arse. "What's the meaning of this? This is no place for long-haired drunks." '

Enough.

Between one yawn and the next, since I slept so poorly the night before, I can see through the yawning gap that the coast to the toilet is clear. At least up to the corner where the hallway turns. After that . . . I don't have a periscope or one of those guns that shoots into corners.

The shot pans to a little boy as he furtively slips out of the toilet. He's holding something that looks like one or more brightly coloured sheets of paper. Not enough time to look more closely. Pan back to me as I make my way down the hall. (I hired myself to act in the movie I'm also directing.)

Pan to the kid who, still on tiptoe, heads towards the bend in the corridor.

Pan to me advancing in a parallel and symmetrical fashion, skirting the wall.

Pan to him.

Pan to me.

To him.

To me.

Him.

Me.

H.

M.

The damn film editor is having the time of her life.

And then, what was meant to happen happens. He and I turn the corner at the same time and stop short, face to face. Fortunately neither of us was going fast and we freeze, trembling, centimetres from each other. He panics and drops what he was holding. I notice it's a half-dozen illustrations representing the female anatomy torn out of my encyclopaedia. Since these illustrations, printed on clear plastic, are made to be viewed in layers, you can leaf through them and see, on page after page, the same idiotic redhead with her hair cut too short and her lips painted too red, while delving deeper and deeper into the centre of her body: smooth at first, as soft and silky as you'd see in any nightclub, then skinned, as if in a butcher's shop, muscles, ligaments, veins and arteries, and finally wide open, obscene, revealing with every detail large and small, the totality of her organs, including the most intimate and the large intestine. It's all depicted in loud colours, oxblood, purple, vomit pink, dirty green and goose-poop brown. A real treat.

We stand there for a moment and stare at each other without speaking, then I bend down to gather the ones on the floor.

But moving faster than me, he falls to his knees, grabs the scattered pictures and stands up, clutching them to his chest. 'Honh,' he grumbles. 'Honh.'

Honh?

I'd like to say something nice to him, to let him know I'm not angry and that if he's interested in the redhead, he can take her home and study her at his leisure. 'What do you want to be when you grow up? A doctor?' But given the state he seems to be in, a question like that would not be very tactful. Supposing he even understands it.

Besides, I've never known how to speak to children. Ask Stephanie. She started to cry every time I opened my mouth.

So I don't open it and instead he's the one who, still clutching the pictures to his heart, stammers a word I think I can make out.

'Beautiful?' I say. 'You think she's beautiful?'

'Honh?'

'The . . . The lady, you think she's b . . . ?'

And the light timer goes out. Groping blindly, it would take me at least ten seconds to find the switch and turn the light back on. Since I only have one eye, I just need five.

But five were all he needed to disappear. Just like that. Ppffft.

Fine.

I close the toilet door behind me and examine the volume 'A' (**Anatomy**). The seal hasn't been broken. My hair is intact.

Who said the kid was an idiot?

As long as I've got the 'A', I stick with it. I settle in and leaf through the book, looking for something interesting to read. But I don't find anything.

You can't win all the time.

But there is this:

Street scenes in Albania: *picture top left, the city of Gjirokastra, southern Albania, perhaps on the site of the ancient Adrianople.*

In Albania, now? I thought that . . .

My patronymic fluctuates.

As does my ancestors' native city.

All is flux.

Et mergitur. Like the city of Paris, it all fluctuates but doesn't sink.

Let's yank the chain. Chain of events in Alb . . . Tssst.

'. . . a pitiless manhunt was launched in the city's southern districts by the most fanatical faction, sorry, most fanatical *fraction* group of the MALEV after it had bombarded the site with mortars for more than three hours in retaliation, it seems, for the bombing by the YRC of a bus trapped in the south of the city, an attack which was itself, according to the latter group's spokesman, a retaliation by the YRC for the MALEV's decision to encircle the city's southern districts. This containment leaves them with no options other than revolt or famine, which the MALEV categorically denies. The MALEV, as reported earlier, claims instead that they have merely implemented a *cordon sanitaire* to stop, or at least limit, the flow of arms that was posing an increasing threat to the entire community. The cellars in the southern districts have become veritable arsenals and . . .'

The evening news, uplifting.

I hated it when the man in the white coat sent me down to the cellar. And the bottle I brought up was never the right one. Why didn't they ever send the maid, rather than someone of my vintage?

In my cousin's house, on the other hand, I imagined her saying to the kids, 'Go down to the cellar and get me a Kalashnikov 1947, a Mauser 1953, two Beretta 1962s, three of last year's 7.65 calibre, five grenades and a bottle of mineral water to cool the barrels.' They must have loved that, those sweet little blond boys. At their age, I only had a miserable little pop-gun. And even then, the man in the white coat, specialist in paediatric psychology, never missed an opportunity to go on and on about the harmful effects of toy guns.

In retrospect, Professor, you will perhaps agree that the pop-gun did not make me all that militaristic? Though to do you justice, I have to admit that I was definitely far from amusing when I ran in circles round you, shooting you in the chest and yelling, 'Bang, you're dead!'

Aiding Oedipus, in anticipation.

Now you're dead, as is the one who came from your deathbed to tell me you had passed. And the first two people I told of your death are dead as well. And dead, too, probably, are half the people in your funeral procession.

You didn't exactly spread happiness, Professor.

There was a knock on the door. At least, I thought there was. I automatically reached out to turn down the volume on the television. But it's not up to me.

There was a knock. That time, I heard it clearly.

So what did I do then?

Quick, quick, I erase the lipstick I'd smeared on my face. I must not have gotten it all. She gives me a strange look.

Who is she?

I have no idea. It's the first time I've seen her. She's holding the illustrations from my encyclopaedia. Dirty, crumpled, torn.

Thin, delicate. Not bad at all.

Jeans and a thick turtleneck.

About thirty.

She says something I can't hear. My God, that television.

'I beg your pardon?'

'I'm Sebastian's mother,' she yells slightly.

'Oh? You're the mother of . . .' Then I yell that she should come in where we can hear each other better. Good old pat phrases, there when you need them. Movie or novel. Because inside, it's just as loud as it is outside.

She hesitates for the fraction of a second that makes the difference between a glorious gold medal and complete anonymity. And then she enters.

'I don't like to leave him alone for too long,' she says, raising her voice.

'I'm sorry,' I say, 'this room is a little . . . It's not very good . . . Anyway . . .'

She doesn't answer. Her eyes sweep over my lair. Sweep, honey, while you're at it, given the God-awful mess in this place, you'll be most welcome as soon as . . .

Macho.

I say, 'I suppose Sebastian is the little boy who . . .'

'Yes,' she answers. 'Yes, he . . .' Then she rather brusquely hands me the illustrations.

'I am so sorry. He doesn't . . . You see, it was so tempting, especially for someone like him who . . . What I mean is . . . And I had a hell of a time getting them away from him. He . . . Besides, nothing would have happened if you didn't leave your . . . books lying around. Anyone could . . .'

'Yes, I know, ' I says, 'but you see . . .'

With a vague gesture, I sweep my hand round the room.

'But still . . .' she begins.

If she doesn't finish, it's because the television next door suddenly grants us a moment of silence. Someone important must have died. Someone *very* important. Because at least a hundred bipeds on our planet must die every minute of starvation alone. There'd be no end to it if we had to commemorate every single one, and those goddamn gossips on the news broadcasts would get paid to stand there at attention all day long and not say a single word.

You can give them the idea with my blessing.

In any case, the fact that we didn't have to yell to be heard strikes both of us dumb. It's the kind of silence that makes the room shrink even further.

She takes a step back.

I'm still holding the gaping body of the skinned woman.

Haaanngghaah rhaaaahnngghhh.

She freezes, her hand on the doorknob.

'What . . . what is that?'

'My other neighbour,' I say, trying to smile.

'But what is wrong with . . . ? I mean, is she not well, or . . . ?'

'Or what?'

Haaanngghaah rhaaaahnngghhh.

'I don't know,' she says and takes a step back towards me. 'I mean that if she . . . if they . . . you must have heard . . . the other, after all. There must be someone else, no?'

'No, never.'

Haaanngghaah rhaaaahnngghhh.

'Oh, you mean that . . .'

I realize she is standing very close to me. Between us, there are only the encyclopaedia illustrations I'm holding with both hands.

Haaanngghaah rhaaaahnngghhh.

Am I mistaken, or are her eyes shining?

The pages tremble in my hands.

'What you mean is . . .' she begins again.

Haaanngghaah.

'Listen,' I say, trying to control the tremor in my voice, 'Listen, I don't mean anything at all and . . .'

Rhaaaahnngghhh.

I don't know where to look.

'And it just comes over her . . . Is she often like this?' she asks.

'Yes, quite often. In fact, it seems to me like she never stops . . .'

Haaan-ngg-haah. Rhaa-aanng-ghhh.

Without taking my eye off her moist lips, I place on the table the dissected and garishly painted cadaver that separated us. The way is clear. One step and . . .

Ha-aan-ngg-haah rhaa-aahn-ng-ghhh.

We're almost touching. I should . . . I really should . . .

Ha-ha-ha-hah-rrrrr-haaaaa.

Silence.

'It's done,' she says without moving.

'Yes, for now.'

'Unless . . . Unless she's really dead?'

'That would be too good . . . In the beginning, the first time, I also thought that . . . No, believe me, it won't be long before she starts in again. If you'd like to stay for the next show, you're welcome to.'

'Sebastian . . .' she begins, then shakes her head and moves away from me. 'What makes you think I have the slightest interest in a crazy woman's moaning?'

'Nothing. Just a thought, that's all.'

There might be a touch of sarcasm in my voice.

Again, her hand is on the doorknob.

'What happened to your eye?'

A kick in the teeth.

'An accident,' I say.

'That's what I thought, you know. What kind of accident?'

'Are you married?'

'Why do you want to . . . ? Divorced. He . . . My husband can't bear it that Sebastian is . . . that he isn't . . .'

'I see.'

'No, you don't see anything. By the way, you didn't answer about your eye?'

But from the Sbritzkys', the football game starts with fanfare. National anthems. Sirens. Horns. Firecrackers. The teams are introduced. Shouts. Yelling. Bellowing. They must have observed a minute of silence pre-emptively. Just in case.

For the referee.

In the meantime, she has opened the door.

'Could we maybe . . . see each other again?' I say.

She answers without much conviction that she lives with her son in the studio at the end of the hall.

Yelling to be heard, I ask her what her name is.

I think she says something. I see her lips move. But the game is at such a pitch in the opposing team's penalty box that I can't hear a thing.

Not even with the door closed.

Ciao bella ciao.

The Technicolor autopsy is still spread out, yawning on one corner of the table. *201) Vesica urinaria. 166) Ureter. 168)*

Vagina. 167) Uterus. 130) Os publis. 148) Rectum. 175) Vasa ovarica. 168) Vagi . . .

'Walsh passes to Ford . . . Who gives it back to Walsh . . . Who passes to Lang . . . Lang shoots and . . . Goal! Goal! Goal! A superb goal! . . . A picture-perfect goal!'

What could I do?

I went and locked myself in the toilet.

I know from experience that I've got a forty-five minute half of complete tranquillity. I know from experience that the Sbritzkys would rather piss in their slippers than miss a second of the match. I also know from experience that I'll have to watch the clock and leave the scene a bit before half-time. Because at that moment, they'll race to the can, sucking on their lemon wedges and woe, woe to anyone who delays them from taking care of their personal business as fast as humanly possible so that they can flop back down in front of their screen without missing the slightest instant of the second half.

'Tell me,' the man in the white coat would say to me when I came home from the stadium suitably covered with dirt and, overflowing with pride and enthusiasm, wanted to tell him about the superb goal I'd made, 'tell me, surely you don't intend to become *one hundred per cent* an athlete?'

To be fair, it is true that at the time men with white coats and stethoscopes earned a better living than those in shorts and cleats.

My predecessor had been in such a hurry not to miss the kick-off, that for a kick, he didn't bother to flush.

Wrinkling my nose, I do it for him and think, how fitting for a business card: 'Godfrey Stool, Ordure of the Gutter/Professional Flusher, licensed and certified. By appointment only.'

I never claimed it was funny.

But I'm not in the kind of place where the mind can breathe free.

Speaking of breath, the stench is so vile in here, I'm about to lose mine as I try not to breathe through my nose.

This is the sort of detail that makes a literary coterie swoon with admiration.

I settle in as best I can, trying to remember who said somewhere that because gold is immutable, it should be reserved for the construction of lavatories. Whoever it was, no one seems to have heard him. Can you imagine the face of a customer in a bank who needs to take a piss and is told his precious little ingots have been used to construct the bidet . . .

Why does the bare light bulb hanging from the wire and covered with cobwebs always remind me of a prison hallway or a condemned man's cell?

'You who are waiting to be executed at sunrise, do you have a final request?'

'Yeah, a parasol.'

Tssst.

Things aren't right in my head. Still, it wouldn't take much, just a few details, to make the place feel more intimate. A side-table lamp, a small rug, two or three paintings on the wall, a camp-bed. And, once a week, Sbritzky would knock on the door and yell, 'To the visiting room!' Stérile would be waiting there for me, with a kilo of oranges and eyes brimming with tears. Sweetheart, my love, are you doing all right? I'm all right, and you? All right, and the little one? Oh, she's fine . . . she misses you. Give her a kiss for me, of course . . . Oh sweetheart, oh my love, time goes so slowly without you. I know, honey, for me too . . . And then much later, early one foggy winter morning, the enormous, creaking prison doors would open, and there I would be, on the pavement, hesitant, suitcase in hand. I would take a few steps and notice you, sitting behind the wheel, smiling and crying, with your raincoat collar turned up, hair unkempt, and then, stifling sobs, you would say something like, 'Hey there, handsome soldier, you want a ride?' and I would sit next to you and you would throw yourself into my arms. I would smell your perfume and feel your tears and your body's warmth under the icy raincoat. I, in turn, would want to cry like a baby. In a strangled voice, I'd say, breathing you in as deeply as I could, 'Never again. It was too hard. Never again will I eat meat during Lent . . .'

No, things are not right in my head. Come on—get a grip.

I glance at my watch and see that I still have half an hour before half-time. The problem is that I'm so stressed, I can't remember which encyclopaedia entry I'd wanted to look up. Something about cooking or war in this country. But what, exactly? I don't have the slightest idea.

Too bad. I put the 'C' volume to the side and grab another randomly. 'S'—why not the 'S'—and I open it at random.

Slavery: *From the sixteenth to the nineteenth centuries, between one and three hundred million Africans, according to different authors, were torn from their native lands and transported to the United States, primarily to the southern regions (due to the climate and culture). Around 1860, there were approximately four million slaves working on the plantations. The price for a strong Negro between twenty and thirty years of age could be as high as two thousand dollars. To protect the owners and to increase revenues, slaves were subject to a number of rules. They were prohibited from carrying weapons, from owning any possessions, from learning to read or write (although they were required to learn English), from assembling outdoors in the presence of a white man, from bearing witness in a suit of law in which charges were brought against a white man, etc. When the northern abolitionists denounced these rules (and their motivation was often simply to ruin the southern* *plantation owners), the supporters of slavery responded by citing the Bible and ancient Greek history. Furthermore, they claimed the 'Negro' was a congenitally inferior being, incapable of rising above the state of servitude. The suffering and horror that resulted from this stance were irrelevant. Their sole concern was reaping ever-greater profits . . .*

By virtue of the singular paradox according to which the less employment there is in general, the better those minor occupations flourish which are dedicated to monitoring, denouncing and punishing those whom said unemployment occasionally pushes so far—misery, despair—that they violate norms, I found myself engaged as a security guard in a large Department Store.

Oh! It didn't last long.

The guy opened with a complete circus about my eye. 'A one-eyed security guard, imagine that . . .' I asked him, who better to keep an eye on shoplifters than I? This didn't make him laugh. It made him thoughtful. After all, a one-eyed security guard might seem so incredible, so outrageous, that maybe those I was hired to spy on might drop their guard in front of me.

A real ace of counter-espionage, this guy.

He walked all the way round his office and stood alongside me, somewhere to my left. On the side of my bad eye.

'Don't turn your head,' he barked, 'and tell me how many fingers I'm holding up on my left hand.'

'Three,' I said, and added that he was picking his nose with the index finger of his right hand.

He grumbled that he was not talking about his *right* hand, but in any case I managed pretty well with just one eye.

And the mirror behind his desk.

Then I was treated to an entire lecture on long-haired young people, the n . . . Blacks and the rag . . . Arabs. Because they were the primary cause, like it or not, for the loss of merchandise. And I shouldn't call him a racist because all he was doing was citing statistics. If one day they showed that elderly bald white men were stealing more than other demographic groups, then he wouldn't hesitate to call them out on it just as forcefully, you see?

I pulled my hat down to my eyebrows and agreed. Seriously.

And one more thing: What about that outfit?

That outfit? I remembered my ugly mug in the mirror that morning before I left, my best and only suit, my most attractive and only tie, my hair cut nice and short, the shoes I'd spit on at least a dozen times . . . What was wrong? Was something missing? A swastika?

Then he explained that I was to look as much as possible like those I was hired to monitor—surely I had an old pair of jeans and a jacket that wasn't quite clean.

Give me a break—that's all I've got.

As for my hair, too bad, it'll grow back.

But there wasn't enough time for that in the end . . .

'Excuse me for asking,' he concluded rather hesitantly, 'but your eyepatch. It . . . I . . . I don't suppose you could take it off?'

'Of course I could, but when I take it off, it looks even worse.'

'Oh?'

It seemed to me that he jumped back slightly.

Wheeling a trolley through the Department Store's aisles wasn't exactly brain surgery. And yet . . .

'Are you an idiot, or what?' the boss yelled after summoning me to the small room behind the cash registers. 'Do you think it's normal for someone to wander through the store for almost three hours with nothing in his basket but a tiny container of *plain* yogurt?'

'It's not just yogurt,' I stammered, 'it's Greek yogurt.'

He roared that it made no difference. Yes, there was a difference—the taste. Had I been hired, goddamn it, to sample the snacks?

'No.'

'No, who?'

'No, boss.'

When they caught the very pale young woman, that very pale young woman who had stuffed a bottle of whisky and a tin of foie gras in the pocket sewn onto the inside of her large coat, they dragged her into the small room behind the registers. She came out just as pale, though her right cheek bore the red mark of a hand.

Merry Christmas.

When they caught the kid with the plaid scarf, that kid with the plaid scarf who had stashed three plastic toy cars in the pocket concealed between his shirt and chest, they dragged him into the small room behind the registers. He came out in tears, his hair wild and his shirt hanging out of his trousers.

Merry Christmas.

When they caught the frail and dignified seventy-year-old woman, that frail and dignified seventy-year-old who had slipped on three pairs of gloves, one over the other, they dragged her into the small room behind the registers. She came out, her fingers bare and numb—they must have had a heavy hand—her eyes were fixed on the ground and she was trembling from head to toe.

Merry Christmas.

When they caught the man with the very Mediterranean features, that man with the very Mediterranean features who had surreptitiously stolen an empty detergent barrel near the front entry and then filled it with packets of butter, salami, chocolate bars, various cheeses and a dozen multicoloured combs, they dragged him into the small room behind the registers. He came out haggard and stumbling, only to fall into the police van that was waiting for him outside.

Merry Christmas.

When they caught the man with holes in his socks, that man with holes in his socks who only declared two slices of boneless frozen cod at the register but who had on his feet, would you look at that, a pair of shoes so brand-spanking new they shone with a thousand flames, like mirrors, they dragged him into the small room behind the registers. The shoe salesman from next door, who remembered the customer with holes in his socks, came with his testimony, but he came too late. 'How could you not suspect someone with holes in his socks?' my boss grumbled as an excuse. And many were those who felt relieved not to be in his shoes. In any case, the man left having trouble breathing and with a black eye and a bottle of bad champagne, all for having found cheaper prices elsewhere.

Merry Christmas.

When they caught the ageless Portuguese woman, that ageless Portuguese woman who didn't even give a shit about learning how to speak French properly, was too stupid, the dimwit, to notice that the costume-jewellery necklace was sticking out of her pocket, and who kept begging, 'No tell to Madame . . . No tell to Madame . . .', they dragged her into the small room behind the registers. When she came out, her vocabulary had been enriched with two nice words in our beautiful language. Whore. And bitch.

Merry Christmas.

When they caught the old executive, now out of work, that old unemployed executive who had been hired to dress up as Santa and clown about by the front door in order to lure in little children and their gracious mothers but had shown up so appallingly sloshed on rum—they found the bottle in his sack between the dolls that wet themselves at the slightest annoyance and futuristic machine guns that spit long tongues of blue flame—that he began bellowing lewd barrack-room ballads at the surprised blond children and insulted any of the mothers who dared protest.

Merry Christmas.

And when, *alleluia*, when, *laudate domine*, they caught me, me personally, ten days after they had hired me, ten useless days, ten barren days during which I hadn't seen anything, heard anything or denounced anyone ('Either they've all suddenly turned honest—and you'll never get me to believe that—or you're a complete imbecile that any two-bit suburban thief can put one over on, or, unh hunh, maybe you look away *on purpose* when any . . .), when they caught me on that fine afternoon of the twenty-fourth of December, *hark the herald angels sing*, one, two, ten customers had complained that they couldn't hold it any longer, not to mention their little girls who were sitting along the wall and, blushing, peeing for all to see. But is it my fault if the pictures on the wall are so difficult to distinguish, so androgynous somehow, that I mixed them up and landed in the women's? By the time they caught me after having searched high and low—their insipid music resounding in the johns, their announcements of special offers, their two-for-ones, their blue-light specials penetrating even into the johns, along with their increasingly urgent calls for Security Monitor Seventeen—after they stumbled onto my trolley, overflowing with lettuce and abandoned in the beauty-product aisle, by the time they caught me, the women and children, tired of drumming on the door, had invaded the men's room while the men, completely confused and afraid that they themselves were mistaken, fearing who knows what charges of public indecency, quickly closed the door while babbling excuses and rushed out to piss in the car park between stranded trolleys and soaked cardboard boxes. It didn't do any wonders for the Department Store's image to have all these guys pissing all over their shoes in the open air as horrified mothers slammed on the brakes, ordered their kids to look away and drove off, pedal to the floor, to finish their errands with the competition. The managers didn't know which way to turn and, even on Christmas Eve, fights threatened to break out in the corridor to the toilets, as bipeds of both sexes, hands pressed between their legs, insulted each other over the gender of the little sign nailed to the only open door and began, with all due respect, to splash about in urine, and rumours spread through the store and so did the hubbub. The madding crowd, *alleluia*, the mob come to make its final purchases, for those colourful little packages to place next to Uncle Pierre's plate or Cousin Elizabeth's, between the *boudin blanc* and the non-drip candles, the crowd, as I say, didn't understand at first what exactly was going on. The word 'toilet' flew from mouth to mouth, inspiring an urgent need 'to go' in dozens of people of all ages who would otherwise never have even thought of it, and the managers grew more and more nervous. Inevitably, there was talk of a bomb in the toilets and that created a lovely onset of panic which some wise guys took advantage of to slip past the cashiers. Merry Christmess to all and peace on earth . . . When they caught me—one of the managers, looking the other way and trying to avoid the little girls and their mothers squatting along the walls, had finally come to bang on the door and yell, 'Come out now whoever is in there, are you sick or what?'—when they caught me, some benevolent souls had begun to pile up the store's stock of chamber pots and organize a chain so that the pots would reach those in need, 'Open up or I'll have to break down the door,' another manager was still wandering through the mob looking for me, you can't have too many security monitors with imbeciles like these getting all excited and running around in all directions,

Messy Critters, the speakers crackled everywhere, mixing laundry detergent with calls for calm and missing-person announcements, when they caught me, they had to call the firemen, an icy night was falling on the coloured lights outside while the fallen Santa whose fake hair and beard had been torn off snored, bald and wrapped in his red coat on a pile of old papers, when they caught me, a semblance of calm had been restored in the store, the managers, with the assistance of a riot squad, had brought the looters to heel and the head manager—it was Christmas, after all—Messy Critters, dear customers, offered to open his personal toilet to his most faithful shoppers, when they caught me, the only ones left in the hallway were the firemen, the head manager, a cleaning woman busy mopping up the urine and a dozen customers for whom blood or scandal were far more fun than the risk of falling off a shaky stool while hanging electric candles on a plastic pine tree, *hark the herald angels sing*, when they caught me after the usual warning, 'Go ahead, men,' the captain said, 'My door,' the head manager moaned. Ccccrrrraaaackkkk.

When they caught me, they froze on the threshold of the half-demolished door. I don't think they saw me at first, on the floor, curled into a ball, hugging my knees, I was on the floor, way in the back between the toilet bowl and the wall, when they caught me, they didn't see me at first way in the back, curled up in a ball in the darkness, knees under my chin, unable to stop trembling, I felt at bay, at the end of my rope, my rope was completely strung out, like the strands of toilet paper I'd hung here and there, on the flushing handle, over the coat hook on the door, I had woven my splendid spider web and had retreated, panting, to one of its edges, and now, with the door open, it covered me almost completely, like a hygienic shroud, scented and resilient.

'What on earth is that?' the fire chief said, entering my lair and, like an explorer in the jungle, parting with his hands the tangled pink vines that barred his path.

'What? What's going on?' the head manager bellowed behind him.

Then the fire chief's enormous boots slipped on a tube of red lipstick and he had to lean on the wall to keep from sprawling on the floor.

'What's going on? What is it now?' the head manager still bellowed behind him.

Trying to regain his balance, the fire chief put his foot down quite inopportunely on the other tubes scattered over the ground. This threw the poor man further off balance and he staggered backwards all the way to the door, where he bumped into the head manager who was still yelling and trying to find out what was happening.

'Nothing,' I said standing up, 'nothing. It's just me.'

Their faces, when I emerged into the light with a forced smile and blinking a bit in the sudden glare.

It must be said that the Department Store was well stocked with lipstick. I'd stolen tubes in all the different shades, from pink to mauve, passing through black, purple and even green. What's more, since there were no mirrors in the toilet or, rather, since the management, fed up with seeing one mirror after the other disappear, had eventually refused to replace them, I had had to work blind, if I dare say, by trial and error, mostly error.

Their faces, oh, their faces.

Right up to my eyepatch, I could now see in the mirror over the sink in the lavatory, right up to my black eyepatch which hadn't escaped a few vermillion smears.

Their faces, oh, their faces. And the scream from cleaning woman who, still on all fours, dropped her floor cloth.

I went over to the mirror. They stood back to let me through. No one had yet said a word.

Not even 'Merry Christmas.'

Looking at myself closely in the mirror, I guessed I'd done good work, since it had been guesswork. Only a few narrow furrows that ran down from my eyes, along my cheeks and petered out somewhere below my chin, slightly disrupted the full effect.

Dazzled, I leant with both hands on the sink.

That's when the head manager managed to collect some of his wits.

'You . . .' he said, 'you . . .'

Looking at him in the mirror, without turning round, I said I supposed I was fired?

'No . . . No . . . What gives you that idea?'

But from his tone of voice, I knew he was joking.

Merry Christmas.

It is on 9 March 1923 that, at the appointed time, he puts the barrel of the gun to his temple and fires. A short time later, he comes to, drenched in blood, and goes to knock on the door of his neighbour who is a doctor. Perhaps at this very moment he remembers the adventure that befell him on his return from the United States. His boat was attacked and a sailor near him was shot in the head by a bullet. He threw himself to the ground and, once he got over the shock, he realized he was spattered with the sailor's brains and he wondered how a living person might feel his own brains. In any case, the doctor determined that only one piece of buckshot had wounded his eye but could not say whether or not it had entered his brain. The pain, however, was unbearable and he begged the doctor to finish him off. Nonetheless, two weeks later, completely recovered but for the loss of one eye, he was back at work. He would survive for more than two years.

To return to Saint-Simon's political tract, The Parabola, *let us say that . . .*

Greetings, colleague!

If the one-eyed of the world all agreed to put out their remaining eye, stock prices for manufacturers of white canes would go through the roof.

I remember something I read somewhere: 'Would the Church modify its stance on condoms if it held shares in latex companies?'

Tssst. That's enough, son.

I close the 'S' volume I'd opened at random earlier, it was beginning to weigh heavily on my lap.

It's coming.

Plop.

As I straighten my clothes, I remember that other saying, whose author I've also forgotten and that I wish I had come up with myself: 'The day shit is worth anything, the poor will be born without arseholes . . .'

I open the door at the very moment Sbritzky is about to knock. Instinctively I pull my head back between my shoulders.

'Stick your head back out,' he says. 'I need to talk to you. Although it may be your right to refuse to open the door of your room to me—and I'm not entirely sure about that—it is mine, my right, that is, for Chrissake, to tell you that if you don't get your goddamn books out of there by the end of the week, it's gonna be war. Got it? And I mean *war*.'

Because up until now, it's been what? Milk, honey and flower garlands?

With a wave of my hand, I show him the toilet behind me.

'Do come in,' I say politely, 'we can speak more comfortably inside.'

He takes a step forward . . . and then catches on.

'You're a wise guy, always the wise guy. But I'll make you swallow your wisecracks.'

He pushes past me and slams the door behind him.

If you can't even joke around any more . . .

Only once I'm back in my room do I realize that, distracted by the story about the buckshot, I'd forgotten to look up the article that interested me in the encyclopaedia.

Diphtheria.

Since I don't know how my family lived, I'd like to learn more about how they died, if you don't mind.

It can wait.

On the end of every branch in my family tree, the higher ones as well as the lower ones, there hangs a gagged corpse. And life's circumstances, in their very oddness, were such that not once in more than twenty years, if you don't count a brief mention of Leila, did the man in the white coat—the last living twig at the time, the last thread that still tied me to this array of rotting corpses, skeletons and dust—find it useful or necessary to mention them in front of me, even in an anecdote. 'Did I ever tell you about the time my grandfather, that is your great-grandfather . . .'

I would have fallen off my chair.

What I can't remember is whether I asked him questions that he avoided or flat out refused to answer, or whether some instinct told me there was no point in trying.

And besides, who gives a sh . . .

Someone knocks. My poor front door. Everyone keeps pounding on it.

I ask who it is. I yell, rather.

'Sbritski.'

Without a 'y', as if to butter me up.

But it doesn't work. And I yell at him to go away, that I'd already told him I wouldn't open the door, that he should leave me the hell . . .

His wife bangs on the wall.

'I just wanted to let you know it was free,' he yells from behind the door.

And he leaves.

Let me know that it was free? That would be the first time he . . .

Suspicious, very suspicious.

I roll some toilet paper into a ball and try to erase the 'Dagos go home' written with black marker in letters this high. My attempt leaves a blackish streak on the well next to the red smear my lipstick left the other day.

If we keep this game up for a while the damn wall will be an abstract painting.

Then I clean the volume on which he—deliberately?—pissed. I retrieve it from the little puddle of urine in which it's been marinating and wipe it dry as best I can. Speaking of marinating, the cover will probably split its sides.

I can't even make myself laugh.

The bastard.

The piece of shit.

I should go grab him by the scruff of his neck and rub his nose in the mess.

That's it, and his dog, hmm? What about his dog, did you think of his dog? It's easy to be a hero with your butt comfortably parked in a chair, but . . .

Tssst.

Then I notice, as if by chance, that it's the volume 'D'.

But still, rationalist that I am, Cartesian and all that, I don't believe in chance any more. There have been too many coincidences in my life for me not to suspect the influence of some snickering *deus ex machina* pulling the strings.

Like a bad novel.

Like *all* novels.

That said, since it is volume 'D', let's assume the die is cast and, as we bob gently upon the waters of the Rubicon, we'll see what this book of books has to say about the death of some dear little unknown cousin.

Even though there is no direct relation between the growth of the membrane and the gravity of the infection, as a rule, the expansion of this membrane towards the tonsils and its gradual invasion of the soft palate, the uvula, the pharynx and the larynx indicates a serious condition. The swelling of the lymph nodes and oedema of the periglandular tissues sometimes causes what is called a 'bull neck'. Symptoms can also include foul-smelling nasal discharge. The membrane develops in three stages: in the first it resembles egg white, in the second it still resembles egg white but in a more coagulated form, and in the final stage it becomes rubbery and takes on shades that run the gamut from grey to reddish-brown. There are known cases of diphtheria in which this membrane forms in the eye or in the vagina . . .

Yum-yum.

'Will we make love tonight, my sweetheart, my Stérile?

'Not tonight.'

'Oh, do you have your . . . thing?'

'No, dear, I don't have my . . . thing, as you call it, I've got diphtheria.'

In the last months, we didn't make love once. She curled up on the far side of the bed with her back to me, turned off her light and good night Irene. If I reached my arm out too far under the sheets and tried to caress even just the curve of her bottom, she shrank back like an oyster does when you touch it lightly with a fork. 'Get lost, would you?'

Sigh.

When I went back to my room, the Sbritzkys' door was ajar. I'd had the feeling they were watching me. At the top, the dog's drooling muzzle, underneath that, one above the other, their two faces.

Just like in a pie-toss stand.

Tonight, in honour of some deceased head of state or orchestra or head chef, my dear neighbours' television is broadcasting a classical music concert. Perhaps because the other channels are on strike, the Sbritzkys don't have any choice and they stick it out sullenly. I think they've fallen asleep. The strings, in any case, aren't inspiring the usual ear-splitting commentaries that accompany their favourite boxer's slipping through the strings round the boxing ring.

Mozart.

Miraculously, the other nutcase is silent too.

Thus does life, my brothers, consist of such privileged moments when, in a state of grace, bone-headedly and blissfully blissful you burp, brothers, folding your delicate hands over your rounded bellies and reflecting that outside, cold, hunger and death reign. And who knows, my brothers, if we don't require the suffering of others, distant, strange, elsewhere, to fully appreciate the advantages provided to us by our artificial and provisional disguise as white Northern European men?

He missed a step climbing down from his pulpit and ended up in the hospital without the slightest idea how he got there.

End of the first movement. And it's that moment when all those in the concert hall who have even the slightest cold, cough or chronic catarrh hurry to hawk furtively and clear their throats before the second movement begins, that precise moment, you will have guessed, when there's a knock on my door.

Finally, my love, we are together again. Happy New Year.

Tssst.

Remembering the time when, to my great distress—I so loathed doing it, he literally had to push me into the hallway—the man in the white coat sent me to apologize in advance to the neighbours below us for the noise we would make when we grimly threw confetti at each other later, I did the same with Madame Sbritzky.

'Oh, oh,' she said mockingly, holding her monster back by the collar, 'oh, oh, noise? Are you planning on throwing a little party?'

'No. I'm planning on biting my nails.'

Some guy shows up, frighteningly thin. Dressed all in black. A black suitcase in his hand. Black gloves. A black scarf covering the lower part of his face like a mask.

'Listen,' I say, raising my voice over the noise of the music that has started again next door. 'Listen, if you've come to commission a requiem, it's no good. I can't even draw a G clef.'

There's no way to tell if he's smiling, under the scarf.

'I'm an inventor,' he says in a hoarse voice.

I tell him I'm happy for him.

'I invented a machine,' he says.

I say really? Like Papin?

'I could show you my machine,' he says.

And I tell him a thousand thanks, sire, but I really don't need anything whatsoever. My neighbours, perhaps . . . ?

'A machine that can extract selected memories,' he says.

A machine that can . . . ?

I threw him out, but quick. Not, however, before he could tell me I'd regret it.

Growling and snapping at his calves, Yela chased him down to the fourth floor.

Right in the middle of the divine Wolfgang Amadeus, a news bulletin castigates those regions incapable even of respecting the ceasefire between Christmas and New Year's and announces the invasion of my cousin's country—how many times already throughout history?—by one of its neighbours.

A question of re-establishing order.

The Really Big countries, apparently, protest. The Big ones don't give a shit. And the Little ones pay the piper.

Business as usual.

A towel draped over my neck and soap in hand, I head down the long, icy and poorly lit hallway to the shower shared, like the toilet, by everyone on the floor, although at the other end of the corridor.

The Sbritzkys' mutt growled when I passed their door. It probably doesn't like the scent of my soap.

From Marseille.

For once, I'm lucky. Someone is coming out of the shower just when I get there. In the fragrant cloud of vapour steaming out the doorway, I can't see who it is at first. Then, as the steam clears, I recognize Sebastian's mother. When she notices me, she jumps and automatically tightens the belt of her bathrobe. Then she pushes back a wet strand of hair hanging over her eye.

Don't worry, my lovely, I'm not much of a sight either, in my old sweatpants and worn T-shirt with the number one hundred and eighty-seven printed in large black numbers.

Boy, it smells good.

We exchange 'hellos' that each of us considers suspiciously, as if wary of being taken in by fake sincerity.

'How are you?'

'I'm OK,' she says.

'And your . . . and Sebastian, how is he?'

'He's OK . . . The school doesn't want him any more. They say he's holding the others back. But aside from that, things are OK.'

'Oh . . . And what are you going to do? I mean . . .'

'I don't know,' she says. 'Try to find another. Especially since your neighbour, Sbritzsomething, is doing everything he can to get us evicted. Claims our rent is too low. But the truth is that it's Sebastian who . . .'

'I see,' I say, 'I see. The bastard.'

She doesn't answer. She shivers slightly. I tell her she should go home, that it's cold in the hallway and that one of these days I'll come say hello, to both of them.

'If you want,' she says. 'If you want, but . . .'

'But . . . ?'

Casually, with a raised eyebrow. Very *Actors Studio*. Moronic.

'Nothing,' she says, 'nothing.'

Then in much the same tone, she asks if I keep my eyepatch on in the shower.

They're all the same.

It's warm inside. And the cloud of steam that hasn't yet dissipated swallows me completely. As soon as I'm naked, I'm covered with millions of droplets of sweat and lavender that she had left behind. Not bad, as far as sensations go.

Crazy lunatic.

She forgot her soap. A long blond hair is encrusted in the pink foam that covers the bar.

I decide to use it instead of mine.

Lunatic *and* thief.

Then, after a mistrustful look at the showerhead, an ancient relic, I turn the taps.

I wasn't wrong to be mistrustful: she must have used up all the hot water. The stream is barely warm.

Brrr.

But misfortune is good for something, and this one shrinks my hard-on to its usual dimensions.

That's enough, isn't it?

During the Second World War, the man in the white coat, being a medical doctor, was hauled into the Swiss Army as an officer. He kept watch along our beautiful and inviolable borders for I don't know how many months or years with his weapon at his feet—or, rather, his handgun in his belt. When the slaughter in neighbouring countries was at its height, in this one he no doubt had to treat a few head colds and twisted ankles and, men being men everywhere in the world, see to a handful of cases of the clap. There's no need to go over that again. Nevertheless, there were times when I wondered if at least once, on some dark and lonely evening, an evening, for example, when everyone round him in the officers' mess was yelling, playing cards and ordering beer or cognac, or an evening, perhaps, alone in one of those tiny rooms over the stables requisitioned from the proprietor, an evening when he might have put his copy of *Don Quixote* in Old Castilian Spanish on the bedside table that also held an enamel pitcher and bowl and might have gotten up from the bed on which he'd lain, cigar in his mouth, and gone to the window to watch one of those pathetic assemblies, parades or other exercises punctuated by hoarse commands that were our most admirable contribution to the war effort, yes, there were times when I wondered if, on such an evening, he had ever considered, oh so fleetingly, dropping all his titles, comforts and respectability, crossing the privileged borders of happy Helvetia, and joining up with—getting himself killed with?—the hounded, panic-stricken cohort of Jews, yesterday his brothers, who at the time, step by step, centimetre by centimetre, by train and truckload, were drawing ever closer to the gas chambers?

The question would never be asked.

And only, ladies and gentlemen of the jury, only for the valid and excellent reason that no one gives a shit.

'*However, Mr Foreman, I do have one more comment if you will allow?*'

'*Yes, Mr Prosecutor?*'

'*I find it unseemly, to say the least, that this individual who owes so much to his father's decision to settle in Switzerland obstinately and coldly insists on calling his father "the man in the white coat," this very individual who reaped the benefits of being born and spending his entire childhood in the coziest possible cocoon, while at the time—need I remind you?—men, women and children, and not just Jews, were being massacred by the hundreds of thousands within gunshot of the cradle in which he peacefully wailed. I find his snivelling, whining attitude unseemly and—how should I put it?—provocative, with regard to . . .*'

All right, arsehole, we get it: *The boat is full.*

I push the door open and expect the worst. Who knows how far things will escalate?

And yet, everything ooks
norma . It a seems to be in
order. The encyc opaedia
vo umes are carefu y stac-
ked against the wa   in neat
pi es, which a   ine up . . .

In neat piles? All lined up? . . . Still, one pile seems shorter than the others. As if . . .

I bend down to check.

That's it: the 'L' volume is missing roll call.

Sbritzky wins another round. What could he have done with it, the idiot? Did he take it home to brush up on lichens? . . . Unless he . . .

But these amenities aren't exactly conducive to hiding things. The only place . . .

At great risk, and almost slipping off ten times, I perch on top of the bowl and feel around on top of the tank.

There it is, I've got it. If he booby-trapped it, now is when it would blow up in my hands.

He didn't booby-trap it. Drawing a swastika on the cover and shredding all the four-colour illustrations was enough for him.

'Be like the sandalwood tree that perfumes even the axe that fells it,' I think to myself.

Are you out of your mind or what?

I tell myself that when he was climbing on the seat to stash the book up there, he, too, could very well have slipped and split his skull in the bottom of the bowl. Or drowned, being too weak to stand up and swallowing the stagnant, polluted water in huge mouthfuls.

You're too kind.

I lower the lid without thinking and sit down. I'm still holding the 'L' volume.

Laurestinus: *popular name for the flowering shrub, Vibernum tinus* . . . thrilling.

Lauria, Roger of (1250–1305): *A Sicilian-Aragonese admiral and the most important military commander in the naval war that followed the Sicilian Vespers revolt* . . . is that so? Next time, I'll sing it for you.

Laurier, Sir Wilfrid (1841–1919): *Canada's first francophone prime minister* . . . I'm learning all sorts of things today. But since they've given him three pages, let's skip ahead . . .

Laurium: *A city in ancient Greece located in the* nomos (*prefecture*) *of Attica, forty-two kilometres SE of Athens. This city was renowned for its silver mines, exploited from the sixth century* BC *and at first not particularly productive. In 483, however, a very rich vein was discovered and Themosticles persuaded the Athenians to use the unexpected revenues to expand their naval fleet significantly. This enabled them to defeat the Persian at Salamis* . . . Really? Didn't know that . . . Funny thing is, all you have to do is change 'silver mines' to 'oil wells' to make the entry topical.

Lausanne: The name reminds me of something . . . What was it again that led me to this entry? Let's see . . . Hmm . . . *Capital of the canton of* . . . Hmmm . . . *Two rivers, the Flon and the L* . . . Hmm . . . *the Cathedral of Notre Dame, a superb example of primitive Gothic* . . . *Several buildings on the Rue du Bourg have facades dating from the 17th* . . . Hmm . . . *University founded in 1537, the first in which theology was taught as a* . . . Hmm . . . *Roman Museum built on the site of an ancient Gallo-Roman settlem* . . . Hmm . . . *Many famous writers including Voltaire, Rousseau, Hugo, Dickens, Shelley, and Byron spent time in* . . . Hmm . . . *In 590, the Bishop Marius* . . . Hmm . . . *Since 1536 under Bernese* . . . What the hell do I care? That's not what I was . . . Ah! Here we go . . .

Lausanne (Conference of): *The peace conference in Lausanne opened on 19 November 1922 and concluded on 23 July 1923.* Bon appétit, you honourable ministers! Tssst . . . *The Turkish delegation arrived crowned with glory from its recent victories and negotiated with the allied nations on equal footing. Although Turkey ceded its claims to the ancient Arab provinces, it recovered all the territory possessed before 1914 including Eastern Thrace* (*up to the Maritsa or Evros River*) *and the city of Edirne* . . .

Hmm.

'The young medical intern carefully replaced the issue of the *Feuille d'Avis de Lausanne* dated 25 July 1923. Then, on the envelope that held a letter to his parents written that very morning, he crossed out the word GREECE in the lower right-hand corner and replaced it with TURKEY.'

Me, I think it's funny. But he probably didn't.

However, when Grandmother replied to him several weeks later—I assume she was still alive at the time—and enclosed, along with her letter offering traditional advice about being prudent, the traditional sticky jar of rose hip jelly and the traditional box of Turkish delight, Switzerland, praise Allah, was still Switzerland.

In fact, it's been so for seven centuries.

Nevertheless, there are times when it makes me furious that I don't know why the man in the white coat—*pace* that moron of a prosecutor—chose Switzerland rather than another country or rather than no country at all, rather, that is to say, than staying in his own country and taking up his father's work, whatever that was. Someone—who?—deep in the heart of the Jewish quarter of Edirne must have fed him with false hopes by describing the advantages of said distant country and that evening, at the dinner table he announced, in front of my appalled grandfather—'Switzerland? First of all, *where* is this country *Switzerland*?'—that he wanted to go there to study. Or was it, instead, the tradition in this bourgeois Jewish family that the most gifted (?) child be sent abroad to study—Swiss diplomas conferring, who knows why, additional prestige on the holder—and did Grandfather Whatsit have to insist, rage, threaten to convince the future man in the white coat to go while the latter had absolutely no desire to leave, but nurtured instead dreams of some sort—I have *no alternative* but to guess that they were of *some sort*—like, I guess, becoming a sailor on the Bosphorus or a grocer in Constantinople. And if, at first, it was only a question of studying abroad, why did those stays turn into a veritable exile, why did he change his citizenship, why his refusal—as far as I know—to return to his native land?

I'd gotten to that point in following my vacant train of thought, much like a grain of pollen trying to figure out which way the wind is blowing, when I am so startled, I almost drop my book.

I hear whispering in the hallway.

In the very next second, there's a hard knock on the door and I hear: 'Police! Open up!'

Po . . . Police?

I jump to my feet, pull back the bolt and open.

There are three of them in the hallway. Sbritzky and two men I don't recognize.

'Look how he's dressed,' Sbritzky yells, 'Look how he's dressed! He's got all his clothes on and didn't have the time to . . .'

'Hold on a second,' one of the two interrupts. 'Just hold on. Let's follow the proper procedure.'

They shove a card in my face. He tells me he's Commissioner Stalun and this is Bailiff Hiltler.

I can't vouch for the correct spelling, but when strangers introduce themselves, you rarely know exactly how to spell their names.

'We were summoned,' he continues, 'by Mr Sbritzki here present . . .'

'Tzky,' says Sbritzky.

'. . . by Mr Sbritzky, here present, to issue a ticket for prolonged and undue occupation of . . . a location associated with the communal spaces in the building.'

On top of it all, they don't look like they're joking.

'And we have been able to confirm,' the bailiff says, 'that you have occupied these toilet facilities for . . . (he consults his stopwatch) . . . thirty-nine minutes and eight seconds . . .'

His fob must not measure down to the tenths and hundredths of a second.

'Furthermore,' Bailiff Hiltler goes on, 'and as has been stated by the plaintiff, your apparel is not in the condition of someone in the process of . . . well . . . what I mean to say is . . .'

'I could have been pissing, ' I say. 'A fly can be zipped up as fast as lightning, you know.'

'You don't . . . one does not urinate for thirty-nine minutes,' he announces sententiously.

'Drop by drop,' I say.

He looks troubled.

'I have to say, Bailiff,' the commissioner jokes, 'this must be the first time you've had to confirm that someone has his trousers on. Usually, in adultery cases, it's rather . . .'

'Commissioner, please . . .' Hiltler says.

'If he pisses the way he says he does,' goes Sbritzky, 'then we'd be able to see, right? He didn't flush and . . .'

'Do your duty, Bailiff,' the commissioner says.

'You mean that I . . . That I have to . . . ?'

'Unless you see another solution?'

'Nn . . . No, I don't.'

But the perspective still hardly seems to enchant him.

We can't all be Uccellos.

'Do you want me to look?' asks Sbritzky who, on the contrary, seems delighted by the prospect.

'That would have no legal validity, 'the commissioner says. 'Let's go, Bailiff, to work.'

'Listen,' I say, 'this kind of harassment—persecution . . . is utterly ridiculous and . . .'

'You, shut your trap,' my neighbour says.

'Come, come, gentlemen, let's maintain a minimum of civility,' Hiltler intervenes. 'Let me through, please, and I will make my determination.'

He goes in to the crapper and right up to the bowl. With two fingers, he raises the plastic lid and leans over.

I burst out laughing. I can't help it.

'What is so funny?' he asks.

'Nothing,' I say, 'nothing. Just the look on your face, the look when you . . .'

'Should I cure him of his urge to take the piss out of us, boss?' Sbritzky asks the commissioner.

The commissioner says no. Not in front of a witness. And Sbritzky grumbles that they didn't always handle dead meat with kid gloves. The commissioner agrees, but reminds him with a hint of nostalgia that times have changed.

During this exchange, with a deep sigh, the bailiff has knelt down next to the toilet bowl. With his head stuck out over the bowl, he looks like a man in a bad way after a heavily irrigated wedding reception. As he gets into position, the ignoble black scrap that he calls a tie slips out of his vest and straight into the bowl. He gives a plaintive little cry, flips it to the side and stands up, dusting off trousers.

'Well, Bailiff?' Stalun asks.

'Impossible to determine anything whatsoever! You can't see a thing in these toilets. I'd need a flashlight . . .'

'I'll get one,' Sbritzky says and rushes out into the hallway.

Time passes. Leaning against the wall, I don't quite feel my best.

'You see what a pain in the arse you're giving us?' the commissioner asks me.

I shake my head without answering. Sbritzky is already back, his monster at his heels. In his hand he's holding a powerful torch pointed, involuntarily, I'm sure, right in my face, while Yela is busy coating my shoestrings with drool.

I have, on occasion, lived through more pleasant situations. All the more so since, oh good God, not again, I'm starting to be shaken by the precursory spasms of . . .

The man in the white coat wrote his thesis—I learnt by chance five years after his death—on the psychosomatic aspects of some disorder or other. He could just as well have laid me out on the examination table and had his examiners prod me. 'Nurse, how is the patient in Room Twenty?' 'He died at dawn, Doctor.' 'Oh, he's just high-strung.'

Once my eye readjusts from the glare, I see the bailiff shining the light into the bowl.

'Well?' says the commissioner.

'Nothing,' says Hiltler. 'Nothing in the colour, or in the . . . well . . . odour to make one think this toilet was . . . used recently.'

'You're not required by law to eat asparagus at every meal . . .' I manage to mumble between two grimaces.

'Or to piss in Technicolor,' I add.

'You know where you can stick your editorial comments?' Yela barks.

And if it's not her, then it must be her master.

In any case, even if I were a skilled contortionist and able to put my comments where he suggested, the spot was taken. It was taken by a red-hot corkscrew digging its way, spiral by spiral, towards the exit. Unless it was moving inwards. Difficult to diagnose.

Through a haze, I see the three of them bickering endlessly over the toilet bowl. Lying at their feet, head on her front paws, the dog doesn't take her eyes off me.

The light bulb's wan, yellow glow. Their dark silhouettes detach themselves from the clinically white walls like shadow puppets. The chain of the flushing lever a vertical black line.

'I . . . I demand . . .'

They turn towards me and say 'What?' in fine unison.

I manage to stammer again that I demand an analysis of the water . . . That only a chemical analysis done by a qualified laboratory . . .

'Would you look at that? My lord demands,' the commissioner snickers. 'And would it inconvenience my lord terribly to stand when he speaks to us?'

Only then do I realize that I am, in fact, sitting on the ground. I mumble that I would like to stand, but I'm in pain, a lot of pain . . .

'That's irrelevant,' he cuts me off. 'This isn't a hospital.'

Then Bailiff Hiltler leans over me and announces that he will write up his report which will state that, without valid cause, I occupied the toilets for a period of time significantly exceeding the accepted and conventional use of the premise by a responsible citizen. He alerts me to the fact that this report will be included in my file and that I have two days to request a second, independent evaluation should I wish to do so. However, considering the rather . . . well, unusual nature of this matter, I must inform him immediately whether I wish to request a second evaluation. Should that be the case, he would, indeed, be forced to seal the premises. He adds that while he cannot advise me in the matter, in his opinion I've already caused my neighbours sufficient disruption to forego imposing on them this additional annoyance which would require them to beg Tom, Dick and Harry for permission to satisfy legitimate and natural needs.

During this elevating lecture, Yela constantly sniffed at my face, drooling and with her fangs half-bared, as if she were deciding which part she would eat first.

'Call off your dog,' I say. 'Please tell your dog to back up and . . .'

On a discreet sign from the commissioner, Sbritzky calls to his monster, who curls up at his feet—if, that is, a pygmy elephant can be said to *curl up* anywhere whatsoever.

'Well?' the bailiff asks. 'What have you decided?'

I tell him I don't give a shit and that they should get lost and that I'm in serious pain, for Chrissake, can't they see I'm in pain?

'Very well,' he says. 'I'll clearly note that you have renounced your right to request a second, independent evaluation.'

And they leave.

I manage to call after them, 'My file? What file?'

They don't answer. They don't come back.

I'm alone, sitting on the ground, still in the pool of yellowish light coming from the toilet. In that damn light, I must look half dead.

I don't know how long I sit there like that, waiting for the shockwave to dissipate. And what if, one day, it didn't go away? If it lasted night and day?

Morphine and again morphine and morphine times ten.

For the last ten days.

Such was the man in the white coat's end.

The apple did not fall far from the tree.

'. . . the same leaves to the above-named: (1) A bonsai-sized genealogical tree in its original pot, which he will care for to the best of his abilities. (2) A box of Turkish delight. (3) The complete edition in five volumes of *Vida Y Hechos Del Ingenioso Cavallero D. Quixote De La Mancha, compuesta por Miguel De Cervantes Saavedra*. (Barcelona: Por Juan Jolis Impressor. 1755). (4) A *Handbook for the Traveller in Switzerland*: A work containing all the information necessary to find and savour all the delights available to a foreigner travelling through this country (Orell, Fussli & Co., 1810). (5) All remaining, still-edible jars of rose hip jam. (6) One cancer or tumour, its location to be chosen by the legatee . . .'

Are these waves of pain or laughter washing through me?

In any case, that's how Sebastian finds me when he comes into the corridor and stops dead. Of course, it must have frightened him to find this figure, legs extended, laid out on the floor in the middle of the hallway.

'Don't be scared, ' I say, 'it's me. You know, the one with an eyepatch.'

He takes three steps towards me and stops again. I pull my legs in to let him pass. I feel better. One more reprieve. A few more wrinkles and several handfuls less of hair.

'Hello, Sebastian,' I say. 'Don't worry. I'm going to get up. I was just a little . . . sick.'

He's very close to me now. The kid's huge eyes.

'S-s-s-sick?' he stammers.

'Yes, but it's over.'

'Over?' he repeats. 'Over?'

'Yes, over. And you? You doing OK?'

He nods.

'Pretty . . . pretty la-dy,' he says.

'Yes, very pretty.'

Suddenly he digs his hand into his jacket pocket and leans towards me. He takes hold of my arm, opens my hand and sticks something in it. Then he runs off to the toilet in his funny, limping gait.

A little red plastic bus. A little red plastic bus with a few wheels missing.

'Bye, Sebastian.'

According to my neighbours' television set, things don't look good in my cousin's country. It's so bad, in fact, that if I took up arms and went I wouldn't know whom to shoot. Alliances broken as soon as they're formed, fierce street fighting, a complete lack of certainty about the position and intentions of the neighbouring country's army, which is 'too deeply engaged at present to retreat, yet continues to meet with greater resistance than it had expected,' the new Foreign Minister's strong objections, 'named that very morning by a government now all but unrecognizable and that accuses . . .' 'And now, Madam, your time is up and we need your answer: Is Uyghur, U-y-g-h-u-r, (a) a species of monkey native to Java, (b) a dance with ape-like movements from the Ubangi-Shari territory, or (c) a Turkic language spoken in Central Asia?'

My neighbours have changed the channel.

I wonder if anything is being broadcast this evening in my cousin's country. If so, and if they haven't started spearing each other with their antennae, I doubt they are showing the usual programmes. Instead it's probably just a static shot of, oh, I don't know, government buildings, or a military parade, things like that, accompanied by blaring marches interrupted now and then by the national anthem. It can hardly be a barrel of laughs, but it's got to be better than the anchormen's ballet, each one succeeding, replacing, contradicting, insulting, even shooting the next, depending on who has control of the broadcasting building at any given moment.

I don't wish them ill, but for Chrissake, if only we could have one of those dances here once in a while . . . Every twenty years, say . . . Just to refresh the corps.

Hands on her hips and a winded cat at her heels, the concierge announces that I'm wanted on the phone in her lodge.

'Don't make me do this every day,' she says. 'It kills me to climb all these flights, because the lift is broken, for a change.'

Every day? It's the first time.

'And I thought I'd be kept waiting,' Stérile says in response to my hesitant 'Hello?'

Sté . . . Stérile?

'And I thought I'd break my neck at least twenty times. My stairs are steep, you know.'

'No, I don't know.'

That's true.

'By the way,' I say, 'how did you find me?'

'Your old concierge. She was supposed to forward your mail, wasn't she?'

'Supposed to' is exactly right. Unless no one wrote to me.

'Yes, she was . . .' I say. 'How are you?'

'I'm fine.'

'And the little one?'

'That's just it. I'm calling about her . . . I . . . You haven't exactly abused your visitation rights.'

No, I haven't. That much is true.

'It just so happens,' she continues when I don't answer, 'that we'll be passing through town and . . .'

'Town?'

'Oh? You don't know?' she says. 'The three of us now live a little outside the city, a small house in the suburbs . . .'

'Which one of you counts as two?'

'Which what?'

'You said "the three of us", didn't you?'

'I see. His honour hasn't lost his gift for sarcasm, it seems?'

Let it go, man, don't take the bait.

'So then,' I say, 'you're in town? . . .'

'Yes, and if you have a minute to spare, we could meet for a drink. At the Buffet de la Gare de Lyon, for example. Stephanie would like that.'

'At the Buffet?'

'Why not? It's central and . . .'

'Fine, if you'd like. Just one more thing . . .'

'Yes?'

'How will I recognize you?'

'Ahaha,' she says.

Then she hangs up.

Taking advantage of the fact that the concierge has her back to me, I give a friendly kick to one of her cats that was playing with my shoelaces.

Pushing open the main door of the Buffet, I realize that I haven't been this far from home in a long time. As for my women, either they've really changed or they're not here yet. I find a space near the bay window overlooking the platforms and ask the waiter to bring me a, oh, I don't know, how about a little Calvados? This is the right weather for Calvados, isn't it? He answers drily that in this weather he'd drink chicken broth and that there's no point in coming up with lame excuses if I want to destroy my stomach and the rest of my insides with rotgut like that . . .

Oh? Another lefty earning money for his education.

Torrential rain is pouring down on the station. Through the window, I see several trains champing at the bit, steam pouring from their nostrils, impatient to tear through the curtain of rain hiding the horizon. A woman with a fur coat under each arm hurries by and yells something to the porter who, with his cap on crooked and cigarette butt in the corner of his mouth, follows her down the platform pushing a trolley piled high with suitcases. On a leash, the woman pulls a hideous little Pekinese, invisible to the naked eye. She's obviously not the kind of person who travels in second class. And from the number of her suitcases, it's clear that she won't be getting off at the next stop. Unless someone pushes her.

After my parents' divorce, I would take the train to visit the man in the white coat, sometimes on a Sunday, sometimes for a summer holiday. Occasionally, he would drive part of the way and meet me at some intermediate station. I was so afraid I'd miss the stop, I'd repeat the name over and over again to myself for the entire trip. He would be waiting at the end of the platform. The rules of the game dictated that I go into raptures over his new car, whenever he had one, and that I feverishly try to come up with something to say when he didn't.

Just as the waiter brought my drink, the loudspeaker announced that the Orient Express bound for Istanbul, via Lausanne, Milan, Venice, Trieste, Belgrade and Sofia, would depart in a few minutes.

One day the Turkish consulate in Switzerland sent me the man in the white coat's passport. Below indecipherable Turkish characters, it said:

IN NAMEN SEINER KAISERLICHEN

MAJESTAET DES SULTANS

AU NOM DE SA MAJESTÉ IMPÉRIALE

LE SULTAN

Ausgehändigt dem

Ottomanischen Untertanen . . . . Monsieur . . . .

Délivré au sujet

Ottoman

. . . . Nissim Benoziglio . . . .

Inside the passport there was a kind of transit visa delivered by the Prefect of Adrianople. Below indecipherable Cyrillic characters, it said:

IN THE NAME OF THE GOVERNMENT
OF
THE KINGDOM OF GREECE

> We request all civil and military officials in the Kingdom of Greece and those in friendly countries to grant free passage, without hindrance or molestation, to Mr Nissim Benouziglio, en route to Switzerland through Bulgaria for his studies. We further request he be granted assistance and protection in case of need.

And inside this *laissez-passer* was a large sheet of parchment, folded in four. Under indecipherable Hebrew characters, it said:

CERTIFICATE

Constantinople, 16 May 1916

I, the undersigned, Director of the Jewish school, certify that the young BENOSIGLIO (Nissim David), born in Adrianople, attended our school from 10 September 1915 until the present date in the ninth class.

He earned the following mentions in his last report:

TURKISH LANGUAGE . . . . Very Good
HEBRAIC LANGUAGE . . . . Very Good
GERMAN LANGUAGE . . . . Acceptable
ENGLISH LANGUAGE . . . . Very Good
FRENCH COMPOSITION . . . . Good
FRENCH GRAMMAR . . . . Good
FRENCH SPELLING . . . . Very Good
GENERAL HISTORY . . . . Satisfactory

JEWISH HISTORY.................... Good
GEOGRAPHY........................ Good
PHYSICS .... Good
CHEMISTRY .... Good
ALGEBRA .... Good
GEOMETRY......................... Good
BIOLOGY .... Good
ACCOUNTING .... Satisfactory
PHYSICAL EDUCATION .... Good
DRAWING .... Acceptable
CONDUCT .... Good
CONSCIENTIOUSNESS.............. Good

These papers and the one dated 18 August 1937, consecrating Mr Norbert Benoziglio (known as Beno) a Swiss citizen, are all I own: four documents and four different spellings of his name.

'Lost in thought, as usual? . . .'

I jump, startled.

Stérile. And behind her, a small, water-logged figure in a red raincoat, hood pulled down to her nose, clutching an enormous blue elephant with its legs in the air and its trunk hanging down almost to the ground.

'Sorry,' Stérile says, 'we're a little late, but Stephanie insisted that I buy her a new elephant . . .'

I argue with the people at the next table over two chairs. They claim they're waiting for two people. I tell them, maybe so, but for now they don't need four chairs for the two of them. Voices are raised a bit. Stérile looks embarrassed and Stephanie whines that her elephant wants to sit down. The waiter appears from God knows where and literally shoves two chairs into my arms and, as the neighbours triumph, asks what the two ladies would like to drink.

'I don't know, a coffee,' Stérile says, busy taking off Stephanie's hat. 'And you, Steffie?'

Steffie?

'A Coke,' Stephanie says, trying to find a little room next to the elephant on her chair.

'Steffie, listen, I've already told you a hundred times that Coke is poison,' Stérile says.

'Just for once . . .' I say.

'Would you mind not sabotaging my efforts, please?'

'Oh come on. Letting her have a Coke just the *one time* isn't sabotage . . .'

'I'm waiting,' says the waiter, arms crossed.

'A coffee,' Stérile says, 'and . . . a fruit juice for the little one.'

'I don't like fruit juice,' Stephanie says as the waiter walks away.

'Steffie!'

'What's with the nickname, "Steffie"?'

'It's Marc,' Stephanie says brightly. 'Marc always calls me Steffie.'

'Oh? And who is Marc?'

Stephanie blushes slightly and turns towards her mother. Then she tries to dunk her elephant's enormous trunk in my shot glass of Calvados. 'He's thirsty,' she says.

Silence.

'How's school?'

'It's OK . . . Daddy,' she says. 'For Christmas, I made a napkin ring for Mommy and a key ring for—'

'And you, what are you up to?' Stérile asks.

'This and that . . .'

'Have you found a job?'

'A few things, here and there . . .'

'What does that mean, a few things?'

The waiter returns. He puts a coffee and a juice on the table. And a Calvados.

'I didn't order another Calvados,' I say.

'I brought it on the off chance,' the waiter says. 'I figured I'd spare you the trouble of finding another lame excuse for ordering a second one.'

Arsehole. In front of my daughter, too.

'Should I take it back?'

'No, I . . . You might as well leave it, now that it's here.'

Stérile gives me a look full of innuendo.

Silence.

'Funny,' I say, 'earlier they announced a train leaving for . . .'

'Da . . . Daddy?' Stephanie interrupts, 'Is—'

'Don't interrupt your father,' Stérile cuts her off.

'Don't interrupt my daughter,' I say.

Stérile shrugs and our young one isn't sure if she should laugh or not. It's true that she's too young to remember our bitter repartee.

'What did you want to ask me?'

'A riddle,' Stephanie answers, 'do you want to hear it?'

'OK, miss, I'm listening.'

'All right. Why can you never starve in the Sahara Desert?'

'I don't know, why?'

'You lose! Because you can eat the sand which is there. But how did the sandwiches get there?'

'I still don't know. How?'

'You lose again! Noah sent Ham and his descendants mustered and bred!'

'Mustered and bred? . . .'

'The condiment,' Stérile cuts in, seeming slightly aggravated, 'mustard, and bread. For the king of puns, you . . .'

'Oh,' I say, 'Oooh, mustard, mustard and bread! Oooh, excellent Stephanie, very funny, very, very funny . . .'

She looks at me through her glass, still full of fruit juice.

'You're overdoing it, Daddy,' she says. 'Daddy?'

'Yes?'

'I . . . Your eye, does it hurt?'

'No, it doesn't. Not a bit. I'm used to it now.'

'How can you see?'

'Hmmm?'

'How can you see with just one . . .'

'Steffie,' Stérile says.

Silence.

Stephanie stares at each of us in turn then puts her ear to the elephant's trunk.

'He wants some of my juice,' she says. 'He's a very special elephant who *loves* fruit juice.'

'Drink it up,' says Stérile.

I give all the signs of someone about to speak. I keep my big mouth shut.

Silence.

'Where was the train headed?' Stérile asks. 'The one you mentioned earlier? Steffie!'

Bending forward with her nose in the glass, Stephanie is trying to drink with her arms crossed behind her back.

'Istanbul,' I say. 'Do you . . . do you remember?'

Stérile nods but her face doesn't exactly light up.

'Where is Isbantul, Mommy?' Stephanie asks.

'Tanbul,' I say. 'That's where your grandfather was born. Somewhere near there.'

'My grandfather?'

'Yes, of course, your grandfather . . .'

Her funny little face darkens with thought but clears as she tells my that it's strange, she knows she has one, a grandfather, that is used to have, of course, but that sometimes she thinks that . . .

'That what?'

'It's not like Grandpa Charles, you know?'

'Yes, of course, Dad . . . you never knew my father and . . .'

'Yeah,' she says, 'yeah . . . You used to tell me about him when I was little? Did you tell me stories about my grandfather from Istan-wherever?'

'Is-tan-bul. No not really.'

'That's why, then . . . Sometimes I close my eyes, you know, and I try to . . . But I don't see anything. Anything at all.'

'Oh. And me?'

'What about you?'

'When you close your eyes, do you . . . ?'

'Oh, please!' Stérile interrupts. Then looks at her watch and says that OK, it's about time they . . .

Silence. Stephanie brings the glass to her lips and blows on the sticky, pink surface.

'Boiling,' she says, 'my drink is boiling hot.'

'Don't be silly, Steffie,' Stérile says. 'Just drink it.'

I drink my Calvados.

'And you,' I ask Stérile, 'what does he call you?'

'What?'

'What does this great guy, Marc, or whatever, call you? What's his special nickname for you?'

'He . . .' Stephanie begins, then notices the look her mother's giving her and goes back to blowing on her drink.

'You just can't help yourself, can you?' Stérile says between her pretty teeth. 'You're just not satisfied until you make some cutting remark? Until you try to poison everything?'

Without answering, I flag down the waiter and tell him to bring another Calvados and . . . wait! A Coke. To my astonishment, he makes no comment.

'Goody, goody, goody,' Stephanie cries, bouncing up and down in her chair.

'We're leaving, Steffie,' Stérile says.

'But Daddy just ordered me a . . .'

'We're leaving,' Stérile repeats, already on her feet. 'Come on, let's go.'

She takes a piece of paper out of her bag and hands it to me, saying that it's her new address and could I please at least *try* to be a bit more regular with the child support . . . I nod.

Stephanie looks at me. Her eyes seem moist.

I don't say anything.

Stérile is already helping her put on her red raincoat. Then she ties the hat strings under Stephanie's chin and tells her to give Daddy a kiss.

Her kiss is furtive. Wet.

I don't say anything.

Then Stephanie hands me her elephant and tells me that it wants to say goodbye, too.

I squeeze its trunk. Gravely.

'I'll call Mommy soon,' I say. 'And, if you want, we could spend an afternoon together. I . . . We'll go to the circus, or anywhere you want, OK?'

'Yes . . . yes, Daddy,' she says in a very small voice.

They're standing next to the table, holding hands.

'Delighted to meet you,' I say to Stérile.

She gives me a strange look, then shakes her head several times, gives a soft sigh and leaves, pulling Stephanie along behind her.

I watch them weave through the crowd.

I didn't want this. I swear I didn't want this.

'A Calvados and Coke,' the waiter says when he finds me alone at the table. 'A Calvados with Coke—now I've seen everything.'

Much later, as I leave the Buffet a bit unsteadily, I laugh for a long time, without quite knowing why, at a little sign posted on the door that says, 'HAVE YOU FORGOTTEN ANYTHING?'

I got home in such a state—I can't remember if it was that evening or another, it doesn't really matter—that I locked myself in the loo to look up something that had been on my mind for a while, on the off chance there was an entry.

But there was nothing between **Benoni**: *A city in the Transvaal noted for the southern European aspect of its main road, Prince Street* and **Bensberg**: A *city in the Federal Republic of Germany, a bedroom community a few kilometres outside Cologne.*

There was no one between them either.

As you'd expect.

In novels based on movies and movies based on novels—in other words, in anything that can be adapted from something else in order to make a maximum amount of money with a minimum of ideas and intelligence—the protagonist returns to his room in a Moscow hotel and deduces from minute details that unscrupulous persons have searched his room with a fine-tooth comb.

Not to mention the scenes in which he finds the body of a naked woman hanging from the showerhead.

In my case, my hovel was already such a mess that I only realized I'd had a visitor when I saw that my mattress had been sliced open down the middle.

As if I were the kind of person who would hide gold napoleons in my pallet.

As for the last memento I still had of the man in the white coat—a platinum watch, one hundred thousand carats, rubies, diamonds, the whole shebang—I never wore it.

Out of some kind of filial modesty.

A present from a patient he had cured of megalomania.

Go ahead, laugh, all of you.

I ensure there's no naked woman hanging anywhere, on the reasoning that only when it's too late, once the damage is already done, does anyone regret not being insured.

I loathe the thought that someone put their dirty paws on my things. Especially on my books. But so many idiots hide banknotes between pages of the Bible or Marx's *Capital* that I can't fault my burglar for trying.

For a second, as if it were still the good old days, I naively consider reporting the break-in to the police. For a second, the idea lets me have my way with it, then it elbows me hard in the stomach.

Fine.

I quickly try to restore a sense of disorder in my room and then, trying my luck, because you do have to venture something sometime, I go knock on the Sbritzkys' door.

On their television set, some guy was explaining in a booming voice that if the track is not too heavy and if a few of the favourites would just get the bright idea of breaking a leg at the start, then *Lady Spittle* has a fair chance of reaching the finish line tomorrow.

Only after the horseracing commentator recapped the situation and reminded his fellow bettors that of the fifteen starters his favourites were the numbers four, eleven, five, eight, fourteen, three, one, twelve, seven, thirteen, six, ten, with the two or the fifteen as outsiders and very bad odds for the nine, even though you never know and the trainer does appear disturbingly optimistic when he mounts nine, only then does Sbritzky deign, with a pencil stub between his teeth and a piece of paper covered with numbers in hand, to open the door.

The conversation begins over the sound of a report about a 'catastrophic earthquake in El Salvador, in which numbers one to twenty-five thousand are believed to have perished, and with figures getting worse by the hour, numbers twenty-five thousand and one to thirty thousand are outsiders . . .' This report was cut short in turn by—'we appreciate your understanding, but we have come to the end of our programme and . . .'—a commercial for some awful-smelling product for cleaning toilets. Not a word, this evening, about my cousin's country. This is reassuring insofar as it signifies that today's fighting must have resulted in the same number of victims or fewer than yesterday's.

You don't want to bore people by always telling them the same thing is happening in the same place. Or they'll turn away from their screens, people will. And then how, please tell me, will they flog their stinking crap, their toilet cleaner? No one ever considers that side of things, Missus Jones, you start worrying about other people's lives, you know, and what does that change? Then all of a sudden—bam!—a few hundred more on the dole . . .

'Yeah, and?' he yells.

Then he smacks his left palm with the side of his right hand and says that as long as the bastards don't have to worry about the death penalty, you shouldn't be surprised at what happens. But he bets that I'm against the death penalty, aren't I?

I answer that if his bets at the races are as sure as that one, then he'll be a millionaire.

'Well in that case, don't come crying . . .'

'I haven't come crying to you,' I say. 'I came to ask if, by any chance, you might have seen or heard anything?'

He grabs my wrist and pulls me towards him.

'I don't like what you're insinuating,' he says putting his face up close to mine.

The pencil stub he was chewing must have been made of garlic.

'What insinuation? And let go, you're hurting me.'

Reluctantly, he loosens his grip. I rub my wrist. Then I box his ears.

In my mind. Then I stammer again that I don't know what he means . . .

He tells me to stop being an arsehole and that I know perfectly well what he means.

If he says so . . .

Behind him, his wife—or his dog—screams at him to hurry up if he doesn't want to miss the beginning of the movie.

'Coming!' he yells over his shoulder.

And to me he says very quickly, now that he's got me—I take a step back—he advises me to read very thoroughly the classified ads for studios to rent.

With a soft thud, my question mark hits his slamming door.

. . . and there are numerous examples of the extraordinary 'fraternization', of one people with another, so to speak, that reigned between Christians, Jews and Muslims from the twelfth to the fourteenth centuries throughout Spain, fittingly known at the time as the 'Land of the Three Religions'. Meals and baths were even taken communally and . . .

The sound of footsteps makes me raise my eyes. Eye, that is. At the end of the hallway I see the bulk of Old Lady Sbritzky advancing towards me. She notices me at about the same moment. She seems startled. In any case, her gait appears to become much more cautious. Sitting on the lid, I scoot back so that I can lean my back against the wall more comfortably, I cross my legs, very relaxed, hold the open book on my knee and watch her approach.

She stops on the threshold and stares at me, hands on her hips.

'Well, I never,' she says. 'Honestly . . .'

My only answer is to give her a smile. As friendly a smile as I can.

'But,' she says, 'but you're not even *pretending* any more? . . . You leave the door wide open and . . .'

She stands there, gaping.

'Would you care to take my seat, my dear Madam?' I ask, standing up and closing the book.

She closes her mouth, too. Finally. Then opens it again.

'I'm going to tell him,' she says. 'I'm going to tell my husband about this . . .'

I put volume 'S' back in its place, still without answering her. I adjust my trousers and slip out. I take three steps and turn back:

'If you would care to lift the lid, my dear Madam, you will be able to confirm that I did not make use of these amenities exclusively as a reading room.'

I erupt in laughter that I myself don't recognize and return to my room.

As fast as I can.

Thinking that I'm very funny.

And completely out of my mind.

Thinking of Stephanie again, I remember that when I was living with the man in the white coat, he would, on occasion, get up very early in the morning to turn on the clinic's electroshock machines and to count how many of his patients had escaped during the night. Or committed suicide. Lying tensely in bed, I strained my ears to follow each of his movements. His razor, the noise of crockery, the toilet flushing, the clinking of keys. He opened my door slightly. 'Are you asleep?' he whispered. I mimicked as best I could—in other words, badly—the mumbling of someone still groggy. I don't know if he was taken in or if, like me, he was relieved that this pathetic strategy spared both of us an awkward goodbye ceremony. Our etiquette was not exactly Fontainebleau calibre. 'Goodbye,' he would add. 'See you tonight. There's tea in the . . .'

And I'd go, 'Mmmmm.'

The front door was barely closed when I'd jump to my feet and rush to the kitchen window to watch him drive out of the garage. The toilet bowl was still filling, and throughout the flat floated an odour of shit and aftershave. *Eau de Colon* and *Colic Number Five.*

Enough!

And only after his car had disappeared around the corner, leaving behind a small cloud of carbon monoxide, did my tension finally ease and I breathed freely again. I was rid of him until evening.

Pretty stupid, life is . . .

If everything repeats itself—and if I live long enough there's no reason everything shouldn't repeat itself—then Stérile will probably have to say at least once a month to Stephanie: 'It's been a long time since you called your father . . .' 'Mmmmm,' Stephanie will answer and then change the subject. Then, the following day, Stérile will bring it up again, 'Don't you think you should . . . ?' And she'll probably have to hammer it home over several days— 'He's your father, after all, he's your father, all the same'—until resigned, nervous, faltering, incapable of saying anything more than, 'Hello, Daddy, it's me, how are you?', the little one, and later the adolescent, finally decides to call me.

Just like in Balzac.

'I . . . I just wanted to bring you your soap,' I say. 'You forgot it in the shower the other day.'

She takes a step back and stares at me with a frown.

'You . . . You could have used it to clean yourself up a bit,' she says. 'What is that on your face?'

'I thought . . . I thought it might be fun for your . . . Sebastian, I mean . . . You know, like a clown and all that?'

'You're more likely to scare him out of his mind. It doesn't make you look very reassuring, you know.'

'It's only lipstick,' I say. 'May I come in for a minute?'

'Well . . .'

Just then Sebastian, wearing yellow pyjamas and holding a miniature ambulance with its tailgate half loose, slips between her and the wall into the corridor. When he catches sight of me, he freezes, raises his eyes to his mother who is still standing motionless on her doorstep, looks at me again and, hiccuping, ecstatic, nodding his head up and down, he drops down to the ground and sits with his back leaning against the wall. A little drool drips from the corners of his mouth.

'You see,' I say, 'he . . .'

'Sebastian!'

He wipes his mouth on his sleeve.

I still have the slimy bar of soap in my hand.

'Listen,' she says, 'I'm sorry but . . .'

'Just for a second . . .'

'I was ready to go to bed. No, really, I'm very sorry . . .'

'Or you could come have a drink at my place? I'm a little . . . tonight, I'm very . . . Well, a little lonely and . . .'

'No,' she says. 'Goodnight. Let's go, Sebastian, stand up! You're in the way and I can't close the . . .'

He shakes his head, drops his ambulance and grabs on to her skirt.

She's wearing smoke-coloured stockings. A shade of woodsmoke. A shade of come lie down in front of the fireplace on my sheepskin rug. A shade of isn't this Mozart divine? A shade of amber-coloured cognac. A shade of red-painted fingernails digging into a back. A shade of all the bullshit and sorrow in the world.

'Please,' I say.

'No, no, and no,' she says, bending down and trying to loosen Sebastian's grip. 'Don't insist . . .'

'Haaannrraah rhaaahhnghh.'

It just slipped out.

She cringes, straightens up and looks at me, furious and blushing.

'Haaannrraah rhaaahhnghh,' I say, louder.

'You . . . you . . .'

'Haaannrraah,' Sebastian echoes, half laughing, half sobbing.

'Be quiet, Sebastian!' she yells. 'Be quiet!'

'Haaannrraah,' I'm almost yelling.

'Rheurrhaaoohh,' Sebastian joins in at the top of his lungs.

'Are you happy now, you . . . you . . .' she screams. 'You see what a state you've gotten him into . . . ?'

'Rhaaahhnghh,' I say more softly.

Something between a gargle and a pigeon cooing.

'Aaah-rrhaaa-ooouuh?' Sebastian asks in the same tone.

'Raahhaaa-ha-ha-ha,' I solemnly confirm.

Trembling all the while, with clenched fists, she swung her head from one of us to the other, looking at each in turn.

'That's enough now!' she screamed. 'Enough, got it?'

She frantically grabs hold of Sebastian's arm and drags him backwards, still sitting, along the floor. He writhes, kicks his feet and moans softly.

Her doorway now clear, she slams the door in my face with all her strength. 'Insane, insane, insane . . .' she hisses.

I return to my flat singing 'in-in-in-insane / in-in-in-insane' to a samba rhythm.

I still have the slimy bar of soap in my hand.

Of course there's the inevitable photograph.

The only and inevitable photograph.

Dated 3–16 January 1908. One hell of a long time to pose.

On the back of the inevitable photograph, written in French and in Turkish, printed in gold letters or scribbled in pen, the inevitable accumulation of inevitably picturesque inscriptions.

The photograph consists of an inevitable group portrait, shot in front of the inevitable backdrop depicting a forest or some other bucolic scene. Six people in all. Inevitably, a corpulent, middle-aged man with a moustache and wearing a fez sits regally in an armchair that one would guess is red with gold embroidery. Greetings, Grandpa Whatsit! Inevitably, a little girl about two years old is perched on his left knee, her two tiny hands gripping the man's enormous mitts. Greetings, Aunt Whatsit! To the man's left, her right hand resting gently on his shoulder, standing perfectly straight and very beautiful—it's inevitable—her hair drawn into a large bun and wearing a tailored jacket fitted at the waist, yoohoo! It's Grandma Whatsit. Hello there! A little girl of four or five sits on a cushion or a stool completely hidden by her lace dress. Her hair, drawn into a single braid tied with a ribbon, hangs over her left shoulder. Greetings, Aunt Whatsit Two. Finally, on either side of the group, both standing, one about a half a head taller than the other, dressed exactly alike down to their tall side-buttoned boots, and both wearing the same inevitable expression, simultaneously tensed and relaxed, the one on the right leaning his left elbow negligently against a small column made of plaster or cardboard or stone decorated with carved acanthus leaves, the one on the left holding a closed book by the binding in his right hand and leaning the front edge on a small wall made of the same material as the column, his right hand probably on the back of the armchair and his left arm cut off by the man's shoulder, which gives him a slight air of being infirm or deformed, finally, then, at either side of the photograph are two young boys who are roughly and respectively seven and nine years old.

Six typical Turkish Whatsits.

What is perhaps less inevitable, is that seventy years after M. D. Michaïlides 'Photographer in Adrianople (Koulé-Kapou) across from the theatre' shot this portrait, and fifteen years after the death of the man in the white coat, I still don't know which of the two boys is him and which is Uncle Whatsit. Because of the book and the taste for bibliophilia he later developed, I arbitrarily decided one day that the future Swiss citizen was the one on the left. But if, just before the sitting, he had given in to his brother's pleas and lent him the book—such things happen even in the best of families—then it's a wash and I've been staring at the wrong child's smooth brow, trying to uncover its secrets.

Avunculate (*from the Latin* avunculus, *uncle*): *The rights and duties assigned to a maternal uncle with regard to his sister's son, including the authority over both of them invested in him by society . . .*

No: that's not it. And yet, it seemed to me that the Jews did have a rule concerning uncles who . . .

In any case, he's dead. As is Felicity, his honourable wife.

Also dead, no doubt, I haven't the slightest idea, are Aunt Whatsit One and Aunt Whatsit Two. In their seventies or eighties. Even so, it is possible that one or the other is still alive . . . But where could I find her? And how?

Help me, encyclopaedia, just two words!

Here's volume 'G'. Hmm . . . Hmm . . . Ah ha!

Genealogy (registration): *In the first stage, the researcher asks a certain number of people to name, one by one, as many of their relatives as they can recall, immediate or distant, and, if possible, the exact relation of kinship between the individual listed.* I don't understand a thing. *This information can be easily* ah! *transcribed using the following symbols:* O *for woman;* Δ *for man;* = *for alliance or marriage;* | *for descent and* ┌───┐ *for siblings. According to this system, a married couple with two children (daughter and son) would be represented in the following manner:*

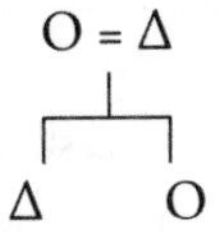

```
  O = Δ
    |
 ┌──┴──┐
 Δ     O
```

OK, and? *The name of the individual represented is listed next to each circle or each triangle.* Oh?

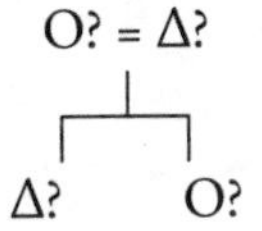

```
  O? = Δ?
     |
  ┌──┴──┐
  Δ?    O?
```

Obviously it's much clearer this way.

Just as I reach my door, Sbritzky comes out of his flat in a dressing gown. He gives me a dark look.

'You missed,' I say graciously, 'not by much, but you missed.'

I slam the door in his face at the very instant he charges, horns first.

FLASHBACK

Might I not have come to the conclusion, rightly or wrongly, like a confused child, that he didn't consider me worthy of carrying the family torch? (And if, in fact, he didn't, then, seen in hindsight, this astute psychologist was a hundred times correct.) That he would not have hesitated to confide at least a part of his and his family's past to a son more worthy of him, to offspring better suited to I don't know what wishes? That, even if he couldn't deny it, biologically I had come from his thigh, God's gift—Oh, thunderbolt-brandishing Jupiter—and if he couldn't disinherit me legally, thanks again, thanks *all the same*, nothing prevented him, on the other hand, from avenging (?) himself in some way for the offense against nature and society that I represented, and creating a void round me, placing a thick, dark veil between us, a towering wall of silence? That by allowing himself to fade, to become all but disembodied, to become nothing more than the image of a father, to become both as small and as distant as possible, as mysterious as possible as well, his goal—perhaps subconscious—was to have me fully grasp the fact that on the long, millennial procession of the sons of Ben, I was but a minor accident or historical mistake?

Because, perhaps—there's this aspect, too—perhaps I alone represented the concrete proof, the tangible result of a certain number of difficult decisions, of painful rejections and, why not, of badly borne renunciations?

I don't know. Because, of course, you can always see things in a different light and believe that the man in the white coat's demeanour grew from the legitimate concern that I believe as deeply as possible in this land, in this Switzerland where he thought I'd have to dig my foxhole, one day, and find my place in the sun, believe that it had always been our country, without friction, conflict or upset. He might have thought it one way of easing my integration and of sparing my young, supposedly impressionable spirit the vaguely schizoid risks of misguided paths between civilizations, customs, languages and religions. A way, in other words, for him to fit in with the fathers of my little school-friends who, gentiles twenty generations back, didn't even know the meaning of the word 'pogrom' and followed in the footsteps of their ancestors one century after another and thanked their lucky stars every night for having been born in so beautiful and peaceful a country.

I don't know.

I really don't.

If that's the way it was, though, it might have worked. For many long years, in fact, the question of my origins never even occurred to me. I was Swiss and neither proud nor ashamed of it. And if a swarm of cassocks sweated blood to turn me into a little *converso* with style and class, they had no more or no less trouble with me than with my fellow students. In any case, in the middle of the church, drowned in the crowd, I was far from being the only one yelling, with an angelic smile on my face: 'Hell Mary, full of grease, the Lord says achoo . . .' To be sure, my family name, usually shortened, sounded no more exotic than most others, since in Switzerland there were plenty of Luginbühls, Waschmuths, and Pelligrinis. Also, to be sure, there were details that didn't fail to catch my interest—the half-opened box of Turkish delight he received every Christmas, for example, covered with excrescences of stamps and seals, or the narghile filled with stagnant water left stranded in a corner. But more than membership in some tribe I knew nothing about, such minor details represented in my eyes an additional proof of originality—if not eccentricity—which the man in the white coat evinced in many other areas and of which, stupidly, I was rather proud, though I never admitted it to him. Furthermore, to be sure, I overheard snatches of conversation in which he repeatedly mouthed the word 'Jew' and, when the television reported on the nth war in my cousin's country, he would silence me more brusquely than usual. And finally to be sure, sure, sure, he occasionally dropped in a flash his usual Sphinx-like demeanour and let slip some confidence which he then seemed to regret immediately. One day, when he met me at the station and I was complaining about the discomfort of my trip—I'd had to stand for the forty-five-minute journey—he retorted that at my age, he had had to spend the entire trip from Istanbul to Switzerland propped on his suitcase in the train corridor. 'Istanbul?' 'Mmmh hmm.' He didn't say another word and so I went back to studying the rain-covered road before us. Another time, when I was criticizing the food served at school, I remember that he evoked, with a faint grimace, the beans he'd been force-fed in his Turkish school. *Beans*. Despite the distressing banality of these *revelations*, I no doubt remember them because of their rarity.

Whatever the case and even if it were just a game, for a long time I had no difficulty in playing along with my father's voluntary *Marrano* spiel, exulting over the Swiss Army's age-old exploits and weeping over the national football team's defeats. Nothing, not even a hooked nose, distinguished me from my schoolmates and I never had to endure the slightest remark about my distant origins. The discovery, made a bit later, that the man in the white coat had only recently been naturalized didn't change anything at the time in my frame of mind. The Jews, from what little I knew back then, were a people hardly more miserable than any other. And even when I later learnt about the fate that had been prepared for them in the concentration camps, if I were as indignant as everyone else or almost everyone else, I was, to be precise, *only* as indignant as everyone else. Or almost. As for the theological aspect of the issue, it never crossed my mind. For me, the Jewish religion was a religion like any other, in other words—I was at an age prone to a certain radicalization—it was stupid, unnecessary, and hypocritical.

It's also possible that during this entire period, the ghostly and glacial fog that enveloped that branch of the family tree was more than compensated for by the affection of my maternal grandparents. Even if they are not my subject here, it is probably time to pay them homage.

Their deaths and the death of the man in the white coat—those disfigured corpses that had begun to line my path like the crucified along Nero's route—and my arrival in France where I soon realized that Jews, like the Arabs, Senegalese, Vietnamese or Luxembourgers, were not always regarded very highly, as well as my meeting Stérile, all these marked the beginning of a long and subtle evolution. No road to Damascus, then, nothing frenzied. But the void left by the disappearance of so many and the new atmosphere in conjunction with Stérile's attitude prompted me, almost despite myself, to take a new look at the problem and to ask myself some questions now that all those who might have given me answers were gone . . .

About Stérile, I won't elaborate. Let's just say that, to my great astonishment, I heard her declare categorically, on every possible occasion, 'That one's a Jew,' about this or that name in the news. As if that were a normal, definitive and scientific way of characterizing an individual. Up until then and to this day, an epithet like that indicated, for me, at the very most, a person's nationality and/or religion, mere details, trifles of one's civil status which held almost no interest for me compared to other qualities—human, political, artistic, scientific, etc.—that the person in question may or may not possess. In Stérile's eyes, however, it didn't matter if our man was proclaiming his atheism loud and clear and waving a Swedish passport. 'That one's a Jew,' she would say all the more convincingly and almost alarmingly since there was no discernable contempt, no external evidence of racism. 'He's a Jew,' as if she were saying 'It's raining.' In short, it didn't take me long to understand that what meant almost nothing to me was highly significant to her and so self-evident that it would never occur to her that she might need to explain herself.

For all that, she knew about my family origins. I'd spoken of them two or three times, without elaborating much but also without trying to hide the fact that, despite everything, despite the fact that the man in the white coat's naturalization and conversion had made me entirely Swiss, I did occasionally daydream about who I was, where I came from and the usual bullshit of that nature. 'Oh?' she asked, raising an eyebrow, 'Oh, really?' That was all. But one night when I was talking about a writer I admired, she interrupted me. 'He's a Jew, isn't he, with a name like that?'

Possibly, indeed. I hadn't thought about it. It had never *occurred* to me to think about it. And I suddenly saw red.

'So what,' I said, 'So what? What the fuck difference does it make?'

My reaction seemed to take her by surprise.

'Why are you shouting?' she asked.

'I'm not shouting,' I yelled. 'I'm just sick of hearing you call people . . . as if . . . it doesn't make any difference . . .'

'Why are you getting all worked up if it doesn't make a difference?'

With a show of complete and utter innocence.

'Because . . . because it's always the same, it always starts the same way . . . First they start, angelically, to differentiate the Jews from the others and then . . .'

'And then, what?'

'Nothing,' I said, 'Nothing.'

Silence. She studied me. She was beautiful. You have to give her that.

'What are you playing at?' she asked.

'What am I . . . ?'

'Do you think it's amusing to . . . to act like a survivor of the catastrophe? To try and make yourself interesting by carrying on your shoulders the weight of millions of victims and bemoaning the fate of *your* People?'

'I'm not Jewish!'

'No point in defending yourself. I . . .'

'I'm not Jewish and . . .'

'So you're denying your own, now?'

'Holy shit, I'm not denying anything! I'm not Jewish, not officially, that's all, that's how it is! I could have lived in the Gestapo's headquarters and no one would have thought of bothering me!'

'Really?' she said. 'But I remember reading somewhere that in the Third Reich any one who had at least one Jewish grandparent was considered "Non-Aryan". '

I was taken aback.

'No,' I stammered, 'no, really, you think so?'

'Yes, I'm pretty sure. Do you want me to find the book where . . .'

'No, no! It's not worth it. I . . .'

I got retrospective cold sweats. And then, in the hallways, some piece of shit of an *Obersturmbannführer*, dressed all in black would call me in for questioning and ask, *Teufel*, who I was? And me, feeble, cowardly and in good faith:

'I'm Swiss, Sir, and Catholic.'

For once the damn religion is of some use to me . . .

'*Und Vater*?'

'Swiss, Sir, and Catholic.'

'*Und Mutter*?'

'Also Swiss, Sir, and Cathol—'

'*Grandparents*?'

'Umm . . . My mother's parents have Italian roots, Sir. But now they're Swiss, Sir, and that . . .'

'*Und was* other grandparents?'

'Other . . . grandparents?'

'*Jawohl!*'

Uh-oh.

Dirty Krauts.

Weep, oh Israel.

Vélodrome d'hiver: *Originally constructed in 1892 inside the building used for industrial exhibitions at the 1889 World's Fair and inaugurated on 30 October 1910, it was renowned for its boxing and cycling events. It was also an arena for political assemblies. The building was demolished in 1959.* Phew.

'Regardless,' I started in again, 'by systematically distinguishing them from others, whatever their ideas, religion, nationality, you . . . you keep . . . you start all over again with the . . .'

'Possibly,' she answered very quickly. 'Possibly. But me, I say it's too easy to play the prosecutor. Too easy for you, always slandering Switzerland and France, to dream up thrills of heroism or martyrdom after the fact!'

'I'm not slandering—'

'In any case, you don't miss a single chance to point out that you don't really belong, that you're only living here by chance—and to me that's the same as slander. Because, shit, it's my turn now, shit, shit, shit, in the Gestapo headquarters, you would have said to those who asked you where you were from, you would have said, in that tone you have that I despise—at once serious, afflicted and superior—you would have said, 'Yes, I'm Swiss, but . . . I haven't been for long. Because, our family history, as a matter of fact, is very complicated—of Jewish ancestry, you see, we . . .' That's what you would have said, isn't it?'

Exasperated, I shook my head and grumbled that she was mixing everything up. It was only later, after Stephanie was born, that all our conversations would end with 'Shut the fuck up.'

I hadn't wanted to go on about Stérile.

Ever.

END OF FLASHBACK

. . . and in a certain sense, the concept's meaning depends on the ideology, attitude and environment of the individual who uses the word. In a country where, for example, there are only moderate forms of anti-Semitism (the 'polite' exclusion from society, the tendency to use pejorative terms for Jews), such behaviour would be considered outright anti-Semitic. On the other hand, in countries where persecution and massacre are the order of the day, the more benign manifestations of anti-Semitism are rarely mentioned.

Let's say, as a general rule, that non-Jews assert that there is much less anti-Semitism than Jews claim, and the Jews assert that there is much more of it than non-Jews are willing to admit . . .

Thank you, oh goddamn encyclopaedia. Now I know so much more.

According to the scraps of information I was able to gather through the wall, things in my cousin's country were going along their merry way. Death was a daily occurrence, so were the bodies exploding into little pieces as they were sitting out on a cafe terrace, just as they were about to put sugar in their cold tea. Every day cars belched long, bluish flames towards the heavens when harried men turned the ignition key, every day the whistling sound of shells immediately preceded a shower of glass shards, plaster and rubble, from which the volunteer rescue teams, themselves under fire by the enemy camp, would have a hard time extracting you or your corpse, every day barrages of machine-gun fire burst out anywhere, anytime, anyhow and left a trail of disjointed puppets to rot there, drop by drop forming—unless they're piled onto a trolley—a stinking, sticky compass rose, every day shrill women beat their breasts and tore at their hair before a family member's mutilated body, every day our journalists cited contradictory and vengeful communiqués with detachment and solemnity, whereas the editorialists—priggish, permed, portentous—analyzed the stances of the various factions and speculated on the odds that the conflict would be extended. You'd have thought they all, such as they were, had drawn up once and for all a kind of discourse that was completely interchangeable and adaptable—like those professors whose lectures, down to the feeble jokes here and there, remain immutably the same over the years—in which only the names of the countries changed, according to developments.

Strange noises outside my door.

Shuffling. Whispering. Stifled laughter.

Then nothing.

Dead silence.

On tiptoe, in the best spy-movie tradition, I stealthily approach the door and open it suddenly and with full force.

The nutcase next door starts—*rhaaahhnn*—moaning at the very instant that a dozen volumes of my encyclopaedia, piled precariously against the other side of my door and topped with a old cardboard box full of junk, come crashing down on my feet.

Ouch.

And bing and bang and boom, the waltz of the empty tin cans.

And bam and bam and bam, Sbritzky's fists on the wall behind me. 'Can we have a little peace and quiet out there, for Chrissake?!' he bawls.

Nice warm atmosphere, you have to admit.

Jaws clenched, I clean up the mess as best I can and start carrying my books back to the toilet.

They can't beat me. I'll fight to the bitter end.

Just watch.

When I get to the door of the bog holding the first three volumes in my arms, it's standing half open.

'James Bond was about to elbow the door open and enter when, suddenly, he froze, as if alerted by a secret instinctive premonition. A sly glint lit up his eye.'

Good night, Irene.

I back up into the hallway and kick the door open, hard.

Badaboom!

I should have seen it coming.

One of them even ends up in the bowl of the crapper. That's what you get for not closing the lid when you're done. Luckily it's too big to sink all the way to the bottom and gets stuck halfway down with one upper corner just skimming the surface. *Upper rt corner lt water damage*. It's volume 'C'. Oh? Oooh.

I put it to one side, gather the other volumes, put them all back in alphabetical order, bolt the door, and sit down on the seat.

Volume 'C', hunh?

I had another episode yesterday. How many now over the last few weeks? Does it mean anything that they're happening more frequently?

Leaning forward slightly, I grab volume 'C' on the floor leaning against the toilet bowl. I've been avoiding it for some time now, going straight from 'B' to 'D'. It's the only one, in fact, with the seal I made from my hair still intact.

It looks like that hair has turned white.

Exclaimed Marie Antoinette.

And in their lodges, frozen in front of their television screens, twenty thousand concierges dissolve into tears.

Tssst.

It caught me in bed this time. I woke with a start, grimacing, as if suffering from cramps. But a cramp *there*? I couldn't hold back a faint whimper, or maybe it was a loud one. In any case, the bitch next door woke up and started growling, which in turn woke the bitch on my other side, who, as a result, moaned until dawn.

It was one of my nights of May.

Come, poet of mine, take thy lute and go get screwed.

Come, come.

The 'C' volume is now resting on my knees. I'm sorry to wake it so early, but one cannot escape one's fate and a man worthy of the name must looks things in the face.

Especially if it concerns his rectum.

Well, shit, if you can't even joke around any more . . .

Trembling a bit, I open the volume at random to the entry . . . to the entry? . . . to the entry??? . . .

Canning.

Well done!

Canning, George (1770–1827): *British statesman and politician, born in London. His father, George Canning, Sr, was the eldest son of a wealthy landowner in County Londonderry, Ireland. In 1768, Canning Sr married a beautiful but penniless woman named Mary Ann Costello against his father's wishes. The latter* *subsequently disinherited him. He died in 1771, leaving his wife and his one-year-old son, the future prime minister, in abject poverty. Mary Ann took up a career in the theatre and became the mistress of the actor Samuel Reddish, with whom she had five children.* Life is a novel. *Later, she was to marry another actor, Richard Hunn, with whom she also had five children. This new marriage, however, did not spare her from misery and disrepute. Her son was torn from these disastrous circumstances by a rich uncle who raised him alongside his own children . . .* What a beautiful story! How many more such stories are there in this encyclopaedia, how many eventful lives of which I know nothing, not even the protagonists' names? Hold on, just a second, let's look ahead a bit. It's always more fun than . . .

Cannizzaro, Stanislao (1826–1910): *Italian chemist and pioneer in the development of modern atomic theory. When still quite young, he took part in the Sicilian revolution of independence of 1848 and was condemned to death by the Bourbons. After the failure of the insurrection, he escaped to Marseille and from there went on to Paris in October 1849 . . .* Yeah. OK—one more, the next entry, and then I'll . . .

Cannon, James (1864–1944): *American Bishop noted for his virulent battle against alcohol* humpf *especially as leader of the international temperance movement. During the 1928 presidential campaign, he organized a relentless attack on the Democratic candidate Alfred Smith.* A drunk, should we assume? *In 1930, he was called before a Methodist church court to answer accusations of stock-market speculation.* Ah! *He admitted to his 'error', asked forgiveness and was not convicted. A short time later, he was called before a senatorial committee to explain his use of fifty thousand dollars with which he had been entrusted in 1928 to run a campaign supporting the Republican Party.* Aha! *He faced the committee, but refused to answer their questions . . .* The dear man—I love this kind of story.

I've backed up far enough, now it's time to leap.

I begin, slowly, to leaf backwards through the volume 'C', when there's a knock on the door.

Phew—finally!

I leap to my feet joyfully, slam my encyclopaedia shut, bang! And, contrary to my usual practice, I set it down on top of the pile instead of putting it in its proper place. Then I open the door.

Sbritzky is there, looking at me, his head tilted to one side. He must be disappointed not to find me half unconscious or covered with blood.

'I'm delighted to see you, ' I say. 'I was expecting you. Or Madame, your wife.'

Then I execute a kind of bow and head into the corridor.

I'd bet—I can feel a burning sensation between my shoulder blades—that he's glaring at me, mouth open, eyebrows drawn, for as long as he can.

Once in a while, on my neighbour's television set an eminent person, looking as serious as a pope—though this comparison has lost some credibility ever since the popes have taken to succeeding each other at a clip better suited to a terrible political farce—elucidated—if wearing a tie—or explained—if wearing a more casual ascot—that the uncertainty of the world we live in, you see, its incoherence, its fragility, the ever-present risk that it will fall to pieces, are such that many of our contemporaries experience the need to find refuge in the past and even, not knowing to which saint they should address their prayers, in a certain . . . yes . . . religiosity. These fine speeches—theory has its charm, but a man's got to eat—were often very quickly followed by discreet plugs for the great book written by said eminence, laying out the usual bullshit sequence on tallow, the kerosene lamp, coarse underclothes beaten on rocks at the river's edge, bees buzzing round a bowl of jam, the twenty-five layers of petticoats worn by our dear foremothers, the sense of wonder inspired by the first Charlie Chaplin movies shown by a travelling impresario and so on and so forth. Or else, in a sombre and contemplative atmosphere, we were treated to a stringy lecture on the progression that led the author from militant atheism to serving at six-thirty Mass every morning, tears in his eyes, or, struck with sudden illumination, to seeing with fresh eyes the seven-branched candelabrum he'd inherited from his idiot cousin Samuel and which until then he had only used as emergency light when those bastards at the electricity company went on strike.

No comment.

Even though it's not for a lack of desire to . . .

Could I be jealous?

. . . 'And I am certainly not about to forget that September morning when I met my grandmother Rachel for the first time in her little house in Istanbul. The flight down, my aeronautical baptism, was already an enchantment for the little nine-year-old boy I was then, not to mention the tide of wonder that washed over me in the old taxi on the way to her house. Everything, in fact, was new to me . . . I opened my eyes wide to the spectacle of the picturesque crowd, dense and colourful, that filled the streets and pavements; my ears were buzzing with the hubbub that never seemed to die down, day or night. I filled my lungs with the dusty odour, warm and pungent, that enveloped the city like powdered sugar on Turkish delight. Sitting next to me, Father concealed his emotion by taking his role as tour guide very seriously, pointing out the few buildings that he remembered and that had escaped the demolition men's wrath. "You see that, son, that was my school. A little different from yours, isn't it?" Yes, indeed, a little . . . I took a glance at the severe facade, suitable for military barracks or a prison, then I turned to face him, a little moved as well. He was smiling.

Without thinking, I put my hand on his wrist and squeezed very tight. "Come now, son," he said gruffly, freeing his wrist, "come, son, you . . ." But his eyes were bright with . . .'

Are you about finished with your bullshit stories?

The scratching on my door is so timid, so faint, that it takes me a long time to figure out what's going on. Then I go to open the door, ready for anything.

Except this.

Sebastian, smiling under an enormous cowboy hat.

Fragile little sickly mushroom.

He's pointing a plastic gun right at my chest.

'B-b-b-bang?' he stutters.

And his smile widens.

I stagger, give a loud cry, hold my stomach with my left hand and slowly sink to my knees, grimacing and swaying back and forth.

His smile freezes. He looks at me, then at the gun.

Good Lord, I have *got* to remember that this kid . . . To reassure him, I smile and wink at him.

He bursts into laughter. Some drool collects in the corners of his mouth.

'Sebastian!' a woman's voice calls down the corridor. 'Sebastian?'

'Your mommy,' I say.

He doesn't seem to hear. Staggering, I stand up and pretend to take an invisible revolver from my hip. He doesn't leave me any time. He takes aim at my right shoulder and takes two new shots.

'B-b . . . bang!' he shouts. 'Bang!'

My howl as I let my arm fall and spin around seems simultaneously to worry and delight my adversary.

'*You're overdoing it, Daddy.*'

Just as I collapse, arms crossed, onto a pile of books, dull blows shower down onto the common wall—arise, citizens, hear our call—and the voice calling 'Sebastian?' peals again, closer.

Then everything begins to happen very quickly. Still slumped on the floor, I watch my courageous little cowboy hesitate an instant, aiming his gun alternately at the wall and down the corridor. A split second later, his mother appears in the doorway carrying a bag of groceries. Open-mouthed and obviously not happy, she contemplates the scene we've created, her son and I, swallows and gets ready to say something. But she doesn't have time, because shadows loom behind her and, swaying, arms waving, she finds herself catapulted into my room. Sbritzky and his monster have taken her place on my doorstep. Behind her husband, I can make out Old Lady Sbritzky standing on tiptoe and elbowing her way to a view.

Here we are altogether.

For the finale.

Sebastian sees the dog and starts to tremble.

'What is your problem, you brute?' his mother screams at Sbritzky, 'What on earth is your prob . . . ?'

Yela growls and slowly takes three steps into the room.

The young woman falls silent.

Sebastian screams. The bitch turns its muzzle towards him. Still screaming, he backs up quickly and hides behind me. Still flat on my stomach, I'm not quite up to the mark. So I stand up, trying to avoid any sudden movements. After all, the wild beast is only a few metres away.

'Calm down, Sebastian,' his mother says. 'Calm down. Everything is fine.'

Little by little, the child's screams turn into sobs.

Sbritzky, who has been staring at us, one after the other, hands on his hips and without saying a word, finally speaks.

Thus spake Sbritzkythustra:

'What in Hell's bells are you three playing at?'

Silence.

'I asked a question, goddammit!' he continued.

In the meantime, Yela had lain down in the middle of my room. She pricks up her ears.

'Well . . .' I say.

'I wasn't playing at anything,' Sebastian's mother says. 'I just came to get my son.'

'He gave you the slip, hunh?' Sbritzky says. 'When I said that with kids like him you should . . .'

'Be quiet!' she says. 'Just be quiet!'

'Still,' Madame Sbritzky chimes in, 'we were quietly watching tele . . .'

'In fact, you'd even fallen asleep,' her husband says.

'. . . In fact, I'd even fallen asleep, that's true, when, all of a sudden, there were screams, horrible yelling . . .'

Everyone turns to look at me.

'I . . . We were playing,' I say. 'Sebastian and I, we . . .'

'There are clinics,' Sbritzky grumbles, 'there are asylums for that kind of game . . .'

'Come, Sebastian,' his mother says. 'We're leaving. We're going to do some errands.'

'The d . . . the dog,' Sebastian says.

'Yela won't move . . .' Sbritzky begins.

And then the nutcase lets loose her moans next door. We all freeze. Sebastian's mother might even be blushing slightly. For a time. Then, the dog rises majestically, goes up to the wall and sniffs at it, gives a curt bark and collapses back down in the middle of the room.

'And, so, her yelping doesn't bother you?'

'Oh, her . . .' Sbritzky answers with a shrug.

'Sebastian!' his mother says again.

Then she courageously passes not far from Yela, who follows her with her eyes, reaches her son and takes him by the hand.

'Come,' she says again, 'we're leaving.'

Eyes still glued to the animal, as if hypnotized, Sebastian shakes his head and leans backwards against his mother's grip.

A very attractive woman.

'Come, sweetheart,' she says, 'come with me. The man said that the beast won't move.'

'It's not a *beast*,' Old Lady Sbritzky says, outraged.

Holding her son's shoulders and taking care to put herself between him and Yela, Sebastian's mother pushes him towards the door. Still crying, he doesn't resist. Yela doesn't take her eyes off them. The Sbritzkys make way.

'I . . . I despise you,' she tells them. 'I despise you and your . . . monster.'

Then, the fragile little mushroom gripping his mother, they disappear down the hallway.

Time passes.

'The nerve! Well, I never—the nerve!' Mother Sbritzky says once she gets over her amazement. 'Did you hear what that . . . floozy said to us . . .'

Her husband looks at his watch and says that it's time for their game show.

'Already!' she says, taken aback. 'Fine, I'm going. Should I take the little one?'

Little one?

'If you want,' he answers.

Then, turning towards me, 'I don't think I need her.'

'Come, Yela,' she says. 'Come, my little chickie.'

Oh, the little one.

They leave.

Almost immediately afterwards, I hear a voice through the wall says, 'And now, to win a self-cleaning oven, you must tell me the current name of the ancient city of Andrinople? . . . Twenty seconds . . .'

'Edirne,' I say in a conversational tone.

'What?' Sbritzky asks.

'Nothing, nothing.'

Time passes.

'You think you're so smart, hunh?' he says. 'Really clever? Smarter and cleverer than everyone else? With your goddamn culture and your goddamn fucking books?'

'What did I do to you?' I say. 'Why don't you just leave me in peace?'

'In any case, I'd rather point out that what just happened is not going to help things . . .'

'What things?'

'Anyone else would have been easy-going. Would have tried to . . . But not his majesty, of course . . . His majesty doesn't give a shit about trying to behave like everyone else, isn't that right?'

'I . . .'

'You can't say I didn't warn you. That I didn't give you every possible chance.'

'What did I ever do to you?' I ask again.

The only answer I get is the slamming door.

As for this, I'd completely forgotten it and it only occurred to me *this instant*: my father's anger, not at all like the Swiss, his rage almost (you're overdoing it, Daddy?), his stubborn and flat refusal when, as an adolescent, I asked permission to spend time in Germany to improve my knowledge of Goebbels' language.

I'm sure I wouldn't have resented it if, instead of yelling, he'd simply explained . . . On the other hand, I'll never know if it was *by chance* that he chose Spain for my first big trip—although he didn't come with me.

For the rest of the afternoon and to Madame Sbritzky's wrath, one special news bulletin followed another. It seems that with the tacit blessing of a super . . . *activation gives your laundry a brilliant* . . . power . . . *durability and strength: our battery's main qualities* . . . in the process of . . . *you'll be there in no time* . . . extensive mobilization in a neighbouring country to my cousin's. In response, it seems, but the possible explanations are contradictory . . . *will keep your baby drier than other diapers* . . . to recent invasions of the region by foreign . . . *and strange taste* . . . troops. The commentators agree that the balance of power could be threatened . . . *for a whiter smile* . . . across the globe, to the extent that they believe the country in question already has nuclear . . . *aerosol spray kills mosquitoes and other household pests* . . . weapons and will not hesitate to use them if . . .

I also learn that the fighting in my cousin's city 'has even encroached on the cemeteries'. And why not? From the producer directly to the consumer. Eliminate the middleman. Cut delivery costs. In any case, it is, on the surface, more normal to see a corpse rotting in a cemetery than on the pavement. The journalist reporting this development seems shocked. In a 'is there no respect for anything any more?' sort of tone. You've got to be young and incredibly healthy to find anything in the slightest *respectable* about death.

Shortly after the man in the white coat's death—right about the time when the head worm turned to his companions mid-wriggle and, drooling, announced 'I did it, guys, I've cleared a way right into the coffin'—I dreamt one night that he ordered me to repatriate his dead body to his native land. 'The land of my ancestors, I want to be inhumed in the land of my ancestors . . .' For the first time in my life, for the first time in his death, I dared chew him out, telling him it was about time he thought about the land of his ancestors. And besides, *which* land? It was his fault I didn't know anything definite about the family's wanderings. 'Not a thing, you understand, you never told me a single thing about . . .'

Posthumous expostulating to settle the score.

'You seem very sombre today, my dear. What is weighing you down?'

'Mourning.'

But that's enough.

And even if the day is not more pure than the depths of my heart, the crapper still stinks less than my sentimentality. To hell with the man in the white coat, back to the thirtieth generation of his forefathers. To hell with the Jews, as well as the bastards and boneheads who hate them. I don't give a shit about the Swiss. Or about France. The Sbritzkys can piss off. Stérile, too. Stephanie can forget all about me. Sebastian can end up in a cage deep inside an asylum somewhere. And his bitch of a mother can get fucked by anyone she chooses. And my cousin with her moustache can take a bomb to the face.

The whole fucking planet can explode into little pieces. I don't give a fuck, I don't give a fuck, I don't . . .

I slam the door so hard that the lid bangs down on the seat behind me.

Bang!

Anyone in my shoes would have jumped.

Not quite as high, probably.

Once I've gathered my wits and fastened the bolt, I take a seat on my throne and grab hold of volume 'C' which I'd put on top of the first stack.

No more palinodes from now on.

Time to be a man instead of mouse, quivering deep in his hole.

Face the danger, eyes . . . eye wide open.

The Jews have been reproached enough for letting themselves be slaughtered like sheep.

I open volume 'C' energetically.

Abu Ishaq Ismail Ibn Qasim Al Anazi.

Abu Ishaq Ismail Ibn Qasim Al Anazi?

What the . . . ?

I read the first few lines mechanically as the large pipe next to me gurgles with all the excrement from the floor above:

. . . was the first Arab poet renowned for breaking with the traditional conventions of desert poetry and adopting the freer, simpler language of the cities . . .

Fine with me, but what the hell is Abu doing in volume 'C'?

Unless . . . I look at the spine. Yep, it's volume 'A'. Someone has gone to the trouble of properly alphabetizing my encyclopaedia while I was gone.

Now I've seen everything in this dump . . .

Without really buying it, I tell myself it could be a gesture of appeasement on the part of one of the Sbritzkys. Who knows? Maybe my firmness of purpose has paid off in the long run.

What firmness would that be?

I shrug and grab volume 'C'. I open it somewhere around page three hundred, where I know I'll find what I'm looking for.

Not bad: it opens to **Canaries**.

OK, let's see: **Canaries, Canaries, Can . . . Canasta, Canberra, Cancelli** . . . next page . . . hmmm . . . **Candelabra, Candia, Candler, Asa Griggs** (1851–1929), who could that be with a name like that?

. . . studied medicine and became a pharmacist. He was soon running a lucrative wholesale pharmaceutical business. In 1887, he bought the formula for Coca Cola from one of his associates— you're overdoing it, Daddy—*improved the production process and turned this drink into one of the most prosperous companies in the southern United States. In 1919, he sold his company for twenty-five million dollars . . . Founded a hospital in his hometown* . . . That's the least he could do, given the soda he was . . . Tssst.

And then I realized that I must have turned a few pages together and gone too far ahead. Because the entry I was looking for should have been between **Cancelli** and **Candelabra**.

It takes me a while to figure out that pages three hundred and thirty-three to thirty-eight are missing.

Torn out.

Very neatly, in fact.

Oh.

Ooh?

Until now, he'd only gone after the colour illustrations. Now he's after the text.

Escalation, heightened by one more degree . . .

I sit there for a moment, dumbfounded, downcast, vaguely anxious, the book still open on my lap and read without comprehending that **Augustin Pyrame de Candolle** was a renowned Swiss botanist and the author of *Prodomus systematis naturalis regni vegetabilis*.

It's cold here in this toilet. The light of the bulb at the end of the half-exposed wire is cold. The white walls are cold. I shiver slightly, at the same time something writhes in my stomach.

Since I'm here, I might as well take advantage. At least I didn't come here for nothing.

After putting volume 'C' back on the stack while unfastening my belt buckle with my left hand, I raise the toilet lid with my other hand.

Petrified. A statue of salt. Lot's husband.

At the bottom of the bowl, between two enormous turds, a few printed pages crumpled into balls float in yellowish water.

Fascinating.

Nose wrinkled and mouth twisted into a grimace, I try to unfold the stained pages with my thumbs and forefingers.

I have to know.

Long brown streaks leave no doubt as to how pages three hundred and thirty-three and thirty-four have been used.

Grimacing even more, I try to unfold the stained sheet without getting anything on my fingers.

Partial success.

Be that as it may, from what I can make out, it's not the section that interests me most.

Through selective breeding, they developed a . . . illegible . . . *in mice in which cancers of an histological or* . . . illegible . . . *regularly appeared in each generation. In man* . . . illegible . . . *genetic predispositions are generally* . . . illegible . . . *through marriage*; *in fact, two factors must be united in order for* . . . illegible . . . *cancer in man*: (*1*) *genetic background, which is not the same for . . .* illegible . . . (*2*) *one influential or causal factor that encourages the appearance of . . .* illegible . . . *in tissue predisposed to . . .*

The other side of the page, which I turn over with a thousand useless precautions, is slightly cleaner but has only numbers and statistics. I learn that in 1965, for every hundred thousand people, hundred and ninety men and hundred and thirty women women died of cancer in Austria; hundred and sixty-three and hundred and forty in Denmark; hundred and seventy-eight and hundred and thirteen in Great Britain; hundred and sixty-eight and hundred and twenty-seven in Germany; hundred and forty-three and hundred in Italy; hundred and thirty-seven and ninety-five in Japan; and hundred and thirty-eight and hundred and three in the United States.

Naturally there is nothing on France or Switzerland.

'Make a wish,' said the fairy . . .

'I want to be a Japanese woman,' he cried.

Tssst.

Fine. I drop the sheet and—*with the same pantomime*—I fish another out of the bowl and unfold it—*same game*—hoping it will be the right one.

It's the right one.

Primary symptoms and evolution of the most common types of cancer.

But he seems, alas, to have wiped off the most with this section. Under the patch of thick, brown, odorous shit, I can just make out the large titles—*Cancer of the skin, of the lip, of the tongue, of the thyroid gland, of the lung, of the brain, of the esophagus, of the stomach, of the pancreas, of the breast, of the throat*—When I finally get to the *rectum*, I can make out the following:

Illegible illegible illegible illegible illegible illegible illegible illegible illegible illegible illegible illegible illegible illegible illegib . . . *Changes in the faeces' appearance* . . . illegible.

And that's when it hits me again.

The pressure surges are faint at first, not particularly violent, as though the enemy, holding my defence in low regard, deems it unnecessary to attack at full strength. Then surprised, perhaps even enraged, by my unexpected resistance, the rate of his blows accelerates as their force increases.

To keep from falling, I brace myself with both hands against the wall.

Which doesn't prevent my knees from buckling.

Slowly, inch by inch, I slide to the ground.

On the tiles, my widespread fingers have left long brown tracks, parallel and wavering.

Sebastian is dead. Crushed to a pulp. Under a bus. Right in front of the house. According to the concierge, the bus driver said that the kid had his nose in the air under an enormous hat when he stepped off the kerb. As if he were following the flight of a pigeon or a sparrow . . .

Or a blue elephant.

Again according to the concierge, Sebastian's mother, rigid, fierce, and without shedding a single tear, has not stopped blaming herself for what happened. Not once, not for a single second, should she have let him out of her sight. And yet, lately, he had seemed to be doing so much better. Hadn't he, don't you think that he seemed to be doing much better lately?

When they knock, I'm standing with my nose glued to the pane that is my only window. The courtyard is empty except for a few eviscerated garbage bags bleeding in the rain.

Without turning round I yell that I want to be left the fuck alone.

The door opens—since the break-in, I haven't bothered getting the lock fixed—and I hear a voice I think I recognize asking well, is this any way to greet old friends?

I turn round.

That's what I thought. Asparagus. With a black tie.

'What the hell are you doing here?' I say.

'I see you've still got your quirks,' he says.

'Quirks? What quirks?'

'Plastering your face with I don't know what.'

I rub my face and look at my hands. Indeed. Strange. I don't remember having . . .

'Can we come in for a minute?' he asks. 'My buddy's coming with the box.'

The box?

Without waiting for my answer, he goes back to the doorstep and tells someone I can't see to come in for a minute.

Brick House appears, tottering in a black suit and carrying an oblong box on his shoulder.

'Hi,' he says. 'Nice of you to let us take a quick break. What've you got on your face?'

'And you, what've you got on your shoulder?'

Tit for tat.

Pivoting from the waist, with the box still on his right shoulder, he squints at the other one.

'Your other shoulder,' I say calmly. 'The box?'

'What do you think?' he says, setting the box down in the middle of the room, 'It's the coffin—for the kid.'

'The coffin? You're . . . now you work as . . . ?'

'Of course. You didn't know? My buddy didn't tell you?'

'When would I have had time to tell him?' Asparagus says. 'Hey, you wouldn't have a little something to drink by any chance, would you? Those goddamn stairs make you thirsty.'

'Just whisky. And you don't care for it, I believe?'

'Not really,' he says with a little sigh. 'But you've got to make do with what you've got. So a shot of Scotch. How about you, fat girl?

Fat girl says she's not fat and too bad if there's only whisky. But she's not going to say no to throwing back a shot.

I go rinse out my three glasses and return with them and the bottle. I'm not quite sure where to put them.

'Just put them on the coffin lid,' Asparagus says, seeing me hesitate.

'But they're wet and they might . . . leave circles, marks, I mean.'

'So what?'

So what, indeed. In the meantime, they've crouched down round the coffin.

I serve them and they drink, making awful faces.

'The English,' Asparagus says. 'The English . . .'

Then he asks me how I've been, since last time.

'So-so,' I say. 'Nothing special. But tell me instead how you . . . Why you aren't with . . .'

'Oh, it's a hell of a story . . . Just think, one day, not too long after your move, we had to take care of some guy, a real party animal, for Chrissake, with a wine cellar. That says it all . . .'

'You remember that white Moselle?' Brick House asks.

The little coffin is made of white wood. Pine?

'Do I ever. So, fine, we thought we'd play Second to Last with him—you remember that game, right?—but this guy was a tough nut, a real boozer, like I've rarely seen, even compared to the two of us, and God knows we're used to it. He even managed to make the two of us not see quite straight . . .'

'One of the best benders of my life,' Brick says, beaming. 'Plastered like you wouldn't believe.'

'Yeah . . . The problem was that the man's booze was goddamn strong in the long run and, wouldn't you know, after, I don't know, about two hours, he starts treating us like dogs, and yells that we'd had our fun, enough time wasted—get to work and make it fast! The bastard . . . Given the state we were in . . . So you can imagine that our work didn't exactly deserve a union medal. He had, among other things, a Louis XV writing desk we thought would fit in the lift, no problem, but then it didn't really—shit, remember that, Brick?—so we forced it a little. We didn't quite figure it out. The poor Louis XV was all scratched, the gilding was flying all over like shavings in a sawmill. The bronzework or whatever it was was dancing around all over the place—what a disaster, you have no idea—and to tell you the truth, the more the guy behind us was getting steamed and yelling, the more hysterically we laughed. We couldn't help it, we just couldn't stop. I can see us now, getting sick from all the laughing . . .

'Not only the laughing . . .' Brick interrupted.

'That's true . . . But anyway, taking turns pushing and pulling, we tried to get the damn desk unstuck, nothing doing.

You can imagine the scenario—the lift is blocked, all the neighbours coming by to check out what was going on . . .

'It's funny, with whisky,' Brick says, 'the first mouthful seems disgusting, and then you get used to it . . .'

Sebastian is dead.

'Right,' Asparagus continues, 'I'll keep it short. I'll leave out two or three other boneheaded moves . . .'

'Like when you fell asleep in one of his Louis-something chairs on a landing between two floors,' Brick adds.

Then, looking at me, 'But you still need the chance . . .'

'The chance . . . ?' I ask stupidly.

'To get used to it . . .'

'To get . . . ? Oh, sorry. Help yourselves.'

He pours himself some whisky, then for his friend, then for me. Puts the bottle back on the coffin. A few drops trickle down the side of the bottle and soak into the white wood.

'Better than their fucking holy water, don't you think?' Brick comments after following my glance.

'Maybe . . . I don't know . . . He . . . He was such a sweet kid, Sebastian.'

'Who's Sebastian?' Asparagus asks.

'The little boy . . . The little boy that . . . who . . .'

'That right? His name was Sebastian? By the way,' he says to Brick, 'don't get too comfortable. We just stopped in a little early to say hello to our buddy, but . . .'

'Relax, it's OK. The kid's not going to fly away . . .'

'And so,' I say, 'you've become underta—you're working for a mortician?'

'You can say "undertakers", you know,' Asparagus says. 'It doesn't bother me . . . OK, fine, to finish my story, the bastard raises hell with the office and no matter how much we tried to explain that he's the one, dammit, who made us drink, they say piss off and the customer is always right . . . To make a long story short, they fired us on the spot and, overnight, we found ourselves out of work. Fortunately we saw this ad and . . .'

'Just think of how much we laughed when saw that one of our first stiffs lived in the same building as you,' Brick says.

'A good opportunity to come shake hands with our buddy, the clown,' Asparagus adds.

'Don't call me that!'

Not only do I yell, but I almost bang my fist on the coffin.

'What's the problem?' Asparagus asks. 'I didn't mean anything by it. It's just that, what with all the colours on your . . .'

'I don't want you to call me "the clown", that's all.'

Time passes.

'OK, guys,' Brick says. 'How about we have a drink to make up?'

He takes charge and pours whisky for everyone. I make a gesture of refusal, but he doesn't see it. Or doesn't want to see it.

'It's all just to say,' Brick goes on, 'that if we didn't have to wear these shitty black suits, this job is pretty much like our last one. In fact, it's even easier . . . And like my buddy here says, at least this job won't have a dead season, if you see what I mean?'

'I see,' I say, my nose deep in my glass.

A thin bar, a light strand of barbed wire is starting to tighten round my skull.

Suddenly, the booming, lisping voice of the newscaster on the television next door cuts through the wall and announces that she must interrupt the quarter of an hour reserved for the deaf to broadcast an extraordinary communiqué from the head of the government. But first, one brief advertisement . . .

'Speaking of the deaf,' Asparagus says, raising his voice to be heard above the advantages of a particular dishwashing detergent, 'how's your neighbour, you know, the one who wouldn't stop moaning?'

It's true that I haven't yet heard anything from her today.

'Maybe she finally kicked the bucket,' I say. 'Are you sure you're not here for her?'

'Don't fuck around. Just look at the size of the coffin, a Baby Number Three, you can tell it's for a kid . . . Our first, by the way . . .'

'Your first . . .'

'Small one, of course.'

'You need small ones, too,' Brick says philosophically. 'And they're not as heavy . . . Speaking of small ones, I . . .'

'Go ahead, help yourself. You might as well take advantage—I won't be here much longer.'

'How's that?'

'They're throwing me out. It would take too long to explain, but they've given me three months to move out.'

The landlord's letter did not mention the bailiff's report. She must have swallowed her pince-nez when she came across the story of the shitter, sprinkled with improbable legal terms.

'And where are you planning on going?'

'I don't know. Maybe Spain.'

'Spain . . . That's not a move, that's an exodus. Why Spain?'

'I don't know. To close the circle, I suppose . . .'

Struck dumb, they close their mouths for a second. Then, 'If you need movers . . .' Brick begins. 'How'd it go again, Asparagus, what we were supposed to say?'

'Our-office-hopes-that-should-you-need-anything-you-will-not-hesitate-to-call-on-our-assistance-again.' Asparagus intones. 'Can you see us coming out with that to the widows and orphans?'

Their hilarity is cut short by the national anthem. Then, a serious voice announces that the deterioration of the international situation is such that the government has been driven to look into fallout shelters and deplore the fact that they are almost non-existent. Admittedly, these shelters serve no purpose whatsoever and that is why public officials, in their great wisdom and commendable concern about unnecessary expenditures, had not taken any prior action with regard to them. However, with storm clouds gathering in the skies of Peace and previous conflicts having caught us completely by surprise and totally unprepared, the authorities believe it their duty to suggest—it would be thoughtless of the officials, and shortsighted, to coerce citizens to undertake work everyone knows in advance will serve no purpose—to *suggest*, therefore, to the population that it would be thoughtless and shortsighted not to take all useful precautions to protect oneself against the risks of an eventual nuclear conflict . . .

It's my turn for a fit of hysterical laughter.

Nerves.

'If I were you, I'd stop drinking,' Brick said, looking at me with a frown. 'Because if things like that make you *laugh* . . .'

Asparagus shrugs and grumbles that it's just one of their ploys to scare people into voting for them in the next election.

'Whose votes?' Brick asks. 'Dead people's?'

'Don't be stupid . . . Besides, dead people are good for us, aren't they?'

'Yeah . . .' Brick says, unconvinced.

Time passes. A dog's life. A dog that howls at the . . .

'Aaaoouuuh-aaooouuuhhh.'

Mutely.

They stare at me, stupefied.

'I'm not kidding,' Brick says again. 'You should quit drinking. It doesn't help you . . .'

I down what's left in my glass as an answer.

He shrugs and says that, after all, it's my own business.

'OK, should we get going?' Asparagus asks.

'Whenever you want,' the other one answers.

Holding the bottle upside down, he shakes the last few drops into his glass.

'What's it like on the inside?' asks a dreamy voice that sounds like mine.

'On the inside? . . . The inside of what?'

'Of this . . . this thing.'

I force myself to place my hand on the coffin lid.

'Oh?' Asparagus says, 'The coffin? You want to see?'

'No! No . . . I . . .'

But he has already put the bottle and glasses on the floor and raised the lid.

Greyish felt and a tiny pillow in the same colour. Screws, rivets, nuts, bolts and I don't know what else. A pair of pliers. And two bottles of wine.

'It's our simplest model,' Asparagus says, very professional all of a sudden. 'But if you're interested, we also have . . .'

I interrupt him by asking what's with the two bottles.

'Guess,' he says.

I guess.

Fortunately, the cops don't do blood-alcohol tests on hearse drivers.

Asparagus is ready to close the lid. My friends are about to leave and I'll be alone.

Alone.

'Hey guys,' I say, excited, 'since we have . . . supplies, why don't we play a round of Second to Last?'

They consult each other with a look.

'It's just that we're not exactly ahead of . . .' Asparagus begins.

'And besides, it will probably be too easy,' Brick adds, 'with the state you're in . . . If you could see your face . . .'

'I'm feeling very well. In great shape. Just wait 'til you get plonked when I drink yours.'

They don't fully appreciate my wit. All the more because their plonk isn't. It's Bordeaux, Mister, and it costs twenty . . . thirty francs a bottle.

Oh please. But the pleasure of their company is priceless.

Who was it who said, 'Man loves companionship, even if his only companion is a lit candle?'

'So what's the story?' I say. 'Should we start?'

Brick gives his buddy a pointed look, which I pretend I don't see.

'If you insist,' Asparagus says. 'But it's got to be quick, we can't keep our customer waiting too long.'

Sebastian is dead.

My fingers brush against the coffin's cloth lining when I grab the first bottle. A strange shiver runs from my head to my toes. For a second I freeze, immobile, with a slight grimace before straightening up, looking for the corkscrew, and asking my table companions to take out the other bottle and close the coffin. It will be more practical for the game, won't it?

'Do you still get those . . . tremors, those shockwaves, in your arse?' Brick says to my back.

'Why do you ask?'

I turn back abruptly, the corkscrew pointed at him.

He shrugs and answers just because, to know . . . because just now it seemed like . . .

I don't answer and sit back down with them at the head of the coffin Asparagus is trying close again.

'It just occurred to me,' I say while Brick is taking the cork out of the bottle. 'I . . . You remember my great encyclopaedia?'

The two of them nod, dismayed.

'I've been trying to get rid of it for a while and I was wondering just now, seeing you with your coffin, if you couldn't slip a few books under the kid or next to him? . . . I . . . Sebastian loved the illustrations, especially the colour ones and . . .'

Why do they always look at me like that?

'I take it you're joking?' Asparagus says.

From his tone, I deem it best to laugh right away and say that of course, I was only kidding.

In the meantime, Brick has taken a swig and hands me the bottle.

'Your turn.'

'And make it *quick*,' Asparagus adds.

'Give me enough time to plan my strategy . . .'

They snicker in harmony.

'You don't have to be a Clausewitz, you know,' Asparagus says. 'Either you finish it in one go and my buddy here is second to last or you . . .'

'Who's Klaus . . . whatever you said?' Brick begins.

Then he stops and looks at me half amused, half concerned.

'Well now,' he says, 'weeelll . . .'

The mouth of the bottle glued to mine, my head thrown back, I'd already drunk more than half of the bottle in one draught.

Then I stop for a second. To take a breath.

Asparagus reaches over and grabs the neck of the bottle.

'Not bad,' he says protectively, pulling the bottle towards him, 'especially considering how much whisky you've downed already.'

I hold on tight and pull it as well.

'Not d-d-done, ' I say, 'I'm not done!'

I can't bring him into focus.

'Don't be an idiot,' he says. 'You know that you . . .'

His voice seems to be coming from very far away.

I stubbornly try to drink again. But the next gulp won't go down. Can't be helped. I feel the wine dripping down my chin onto my shirt.

'I told you it was a bad idea,' Asparagus says and takes the bottle out of my hands. 'I told you that you . . .'

This time I don't resist. I don't think I even *could*. Hiccups. Nausea. Buzzing in my ears. And that goddamn barbed wire squeezing my skull.

Asparagus drinks the rest of the wine almost negligently. Like a golfer who has missed the hole by a few millimetres and on his next turn gives the ball a casual tap with his club.

'One to nothing!' Brick announces. 'Should we attack the second one now?'

'Depends on the opponent,' Asparagus answers, looking at me doubtfully. 'Are you going to forfeit or do you feel up to . . . ? Heeyy!!!'

He suddenly falls to his knees and pushes the coffin forward with all his strength. Brick, distracted by the label on the second bottle, takes it right in his shins and jumps backwards.

'Are you out of your mind?' he says. 'You . . .'

Then he sees me and catches on.

'Oh,' he says. 'Ooohhh . . .'

'I had to, you see,' Asparagus says, 'or he might have thrown up all over the coffin . . . He's impossible, this guy, he's really impossible . . . Come on, let's go. This time we're leaving for good. I've had it with his circus!'

'And the money? What about the money he owes us?'

I don't hear the answer. I hardly hear the door slam. All I can hear, and just barely, is shouting from a game show next door.

The sound of steps.

Then a knock on my door.

A dull blow.

The Sbritzkys' dog begins to bark.

I get up as best I can, staggering, vision blurred, and I open the door.

But it's nothing. Just the coffin passing through the narrow hallway.